SKELETONS IN THE CLOSET

An absolutely addictive and heart-pounding crime thriller

BILL KITSON

DI Mike Nash Book 15

JOFFE BOOKS

Joffe Books, London
www.joffebooks.com

First published in Great Britain in 2022

ISBN: 978-1-80405-605-9

For Val
My all-round superstar

PROLOGUE

The room had once been elegantly furnished, although neglect had taken its toll. At first sight, the woman seated at the dining table appeared to be at ease, as if she was waiting for her meal to be served.

However, all was not as it seemed.

She was unable to move, her wrists and ankles secured to the carver chair by straps. Her eyes flickered — then opened wide with fear. She wanted to scream for help, but that was not an option. Her mouth was covered with a rough gag, the knots digging into the back of her neck.

She had no memory of how she had come to this place. She didn't know how long she'd been held prisoner. The outlook was worse than bleak. As the sedatives used to abduct her wore off and rational thought returned, she looked around. This was certainly not her home, although the furnishings were familiar. It took a while before she realized where she was. The location told her beyond doubt the identity of her kidnapper. Worse still, she knew their motive, and with it came the acceptance that she would not be released. Tears rolled down her cheeks as the captive realized that without help, she would die here. Barring a miracle, she would die alone. And miracles, it seemed, were in short supply.

CHAPTER ONE

'Robert Simon Pickles, on the charge of the attempted murder of Terence Franklin, how do you plead?'

The defendant straightened to attention at the sound of his name, a fact that did not escape the jury's attention. His voice was quiet but steady as he answered the charge, 'Not guilty.' Prior to the trial, he had been advised by the barrister representing him that he must enter this plea.

He had been reluctant to do so. 'But it's true, I did attack him,' Pickles pointed out. 'What's more, I'd do it again, given chance.'

'That's as may be, but if you enter a guilty plea, I won't be able to cross-examine witnesses and bring out the extenuating circumstances. Having read the statements given to the police by the prosecution witnesses, it's obvious that they're trying to portray the incident in an even worse light than the true facts show. There is one other thing you must do when you appear in court,' the barrister insisted.

'What is that?'

'You must wear your uniform, complete with medals.'

'Why? I'm no longer a serving soldier.'

'I appreciate that, but we need to convey the correct impression to the judge and jury. It's a case of using every weapon in our armoury.'

Pickles' barrister knew that his client was suffering from PTSD, his mental state fragile. His words were carefully chosen, knowing the former soldier would relate to them.

The case outlined by the prosecution was a strong one. Despite the defendant's plea of not guilty, leading counsel pointed out that Pickles had admitted the offence when questioned by the police.

'The injuries sustained in this unprovoked attack were severe enough to keep Mr Franklin in hospital for three days with suspected concussion and a broken rib. Injuries that left him unable to work for over a month.'

Counsel went on to comment, 'The victim was beaten unconscious. Thankfully, his injuries were not life-threatening. Had the defendant's vicious assault not been interrupted, the charges would not have been attempted murder. How different might that have been but for the timely intervention. For the defendant now to plead "not guilty" is a travesty. Moreover, one that is a waste of everyone's time and will cost the taxpayers a considerable amount of money — an unnecessary expense.'

The first prosecution witness was the arresting officer, who answered questions purely designed to set out the facts, time, date, place, and to obtain confirmation of the defendant's admission of guilt. His evidence went unchallenged, which was more than could be said when the alleged victim of the attack, Terence Franklin, took the stand. The prosecutor took Franklin through his factual account of the incident, without elaboration or detail such as motive.

Then defence counsel rose to cross-examine Franklin.

'The prosecution referred to this as being an unprovoked assault, but that's not exactly the case, is it?'

Franklin stared hard at the barrister, but did not answer.

'Let me put it another way. How long have you known the defendant?'

'Since we were at school.'

'I see. So, somewhere in excess of ten years?'

'That's right.'

'And you were friends, is that correct?'

'Yes.'

'Close friends?'

'I thought so.'

'I see. So you and the defendant have been close friends for a long time?'

'Yes.'

'And how many years have you been sleeping with the defendant's wife?'

Franklin looked down at the polished wooden rail of the witness stand, conscious of the jury's gaze. 'I can't remember.'

'Can you remember the date when her divorce papers were sent to Mr Pickles?'

'Not exactly. Sometime last year, I think.'

Counsel glanced down at his notes. 'It was delivered to him on August seventh of last year, to be precise. Did Mr Pickles know you were having an affair with his wife?'

'No.'

'I see. So the divorce papers would be the first he heard of your liaison?'

'I don't know.'

'Of course not. But you did know where Mr Pickles was at that time, when he received the shocking news contained in those divorce papers, didn't you?'

Franklin remained silent.

'He was overseas. Except that he wasn't *Mr* Pickles then, was he? He was *Sergeant* Pickles, and he was serving in Helmand Province in Afghanistan. Five days after he received the divorce petition, which has to be the ultimate in Dear John letters, Sergeant Pickles narrowly escaped death and sustained injuries that led to his being discharged from the army on medical grounds. In addition to his physical wounds, he was diagnosed with post-traumatic stress disorder. I'm not certain whether you're aware of the facts, or if you would be bothered in the slightest by the traumas Mr Pickles has suffered. Do you know what the initials IED stand for?'

Franklin muttered a scarcely audible, 'No.'

'Then let me explain. It stands for improvised explosive device. In other words, a roadside bomb of devastatingly destructive power, like the one that wounded Sergeant Pickles, killed two of his colleagues and destroyed the armour-plated Land Rover they were travelling in. The news contained in those divorce papers would be the emotional equivalent of an IED, don't you think? It must have been a major contributory factor to the PTSD that Sergeant Pickles is suffering from, and which my learned friend very conveniently forgot to mention in his opening argument.'

Prosecuting counsel was already on his feet, but the defence barrister held up one hand. 'It's all right; you don't have to answer. It was a purely rhetorical question.'

The barrister turned, as if about to sit down, and Franklin was preparing to move from the witness box, when the defence counsel asked, almost as an afterthought, 'The prosecution stated that had Sergeant Pickles not been interrupted, you could have suffered even worse injuries. Tell me, what was the nature of the interruption?'

'Paula hit him with a poker.'

'Paula?' Defence counsel turned to the jury in order to explain. 'That's the defendant's ex-wife.' He turned back to Franklin. 'The wife you were cavorting with whilst he was risking death, serving his country overseas?'

'Yes.' The admission was grudging.

'And you say she hit him with a poker?'

'Yes.'

'And you're certain it was a poker she used?'

'Absolutely.'

'How can you be sure? It might have been a plank of wood.'

'No, it was definitely a poker.'

'Can you describe the poker she used as a weapon?'

'It had a fancy curved shield round the handle, making it look like a sword.'

'Silver or brass?'

'Sorry?'

'The metal on the handle, was it silver or brass?'

'Oh, yes, it was brass.'

'I'm surprised a poker deterred him, if he was as angry as your injuries suggest. Can I assume she hit him more than once?'

'Yes, I think it was about three or four times.'

'Did she use her left hand or her right? Or was it with both hands?'

'It was her right hand.'

'You're certain?'

'Yes.'

'And when you said she hit him three or four times with a poker, are you certain? Could it have been more? A dozen times, say?'

'No, no, it wasn't so many.'

'And he stopped beating you as soon as she hit him, correct?'

'Yes.' Franklin was nodding in agreement, ensuring the facts were correct.

'OK, so you saw her hit him three or four times with the poker. And it was definitely in her right hand. You couldn't have been mistaken? You're absolutely certain it was her right hand.'

'I am.' Franklin didn't see the trap until far too late. 'Er, I mean . . .'

'How is that possible, Mr Franklin? We've already heard how Sergeant Pickles beat you unconscious. And if you were unconscious, you couldn't have seen his wife hitting him with the poker. You certainly wouldn't have been aware of what was going on, and able to tell the court how many times she hit him. And with what hand she was holding the weapon, and to describe the poker so accurately. Unless, of course, you're not telling the truth, and the attack was far less severe than you would lead the court to believe?'

Franklin didn't answer. There was a long silence as the barrister allowed the jury to absorb the significance of the contradiction in Franklin's last statement.

Having ensured the panel was aware that Franklin had been lying under oath, the defence barrister terminated his cross-examination with a final question, thereby destroying the defendant's last shred of credibility.

'Just one more thing, Mr Franklin.' The counsel smiled sweetly at the witness. 'My learned friend stated you were off work for over a month, because of the injuries sustained in the attack. I'm a bit puzzled, so perhaps you would be kind enough to enlighten me, by explaining exactly how you were able to ascertain the length of time those injuries prevented you from working?'

'I don't understand.'

'Let me put it to you another way, then. What exactly do you do for a living?'

'I'm not actually working at the moment.'

'At the moment? Wouldn't it be true to say you were unemployed at the time of the assault, and haven't actually held down a job of any description for the past five years?'

'Maybe.'

'There's no *maybe* about it, Mr Franklin. And the employment you had five years ago was only a short-term job, wasn't it?'

'I got made redundant.'

'I understand you were dismissed after only a few weeks for poor timekeeping. I also believe you haven't had a single day's paid employment since then. Am I correct?'

Again Franklin failed to answer, so the defence counsel continued his remorseless character assassination. 'I suppose many would consider it regrettable, and possibly become depressed by this failure, but you seemed to have seized the opportunity to fool about with another man's wife, thus destroying their marriage. You had all the time in the world at your disposal, and used it to cavort with the defendant's wife, blowing away the sanctity of those wedding vows — as effectively as an IED. You did all this without seemingly showing a crumb of remorse. He was away serving his country, exposed to mortal danger, while at the same time, you lived it up on benefits provided by the state.'

Counsel turned away from the witness box towards the jury, whose members could see the disgusted expression on his face and hear the contempt in his voice as he said, 'That will be all. I have no further questions of this . . . witness.'

The pause before his final word was slight, but sufficient for the jury to guess he had been about to utter another, far more derogatory word.

Even the judge put his hand to his mouth to conceal a smile, before he called a halt to proceedings and summoned both counsel to his chambers.

'This is a very unsatisfactory prosecution,' he told them. 'Given Sergeant Pickles' service record, the physical and mental injuries he has sustained, and the circumstances of the affray, I have grave doubts as to whether this jury will convict, despite the defendant's admission of guilt. The wholly unsatisfactory performance of the alleged victim in the witness box has weakened what was an already shaky prosecution. I suggest you get your heads together and come up with a mutually acceptable solution.'

The deal was done swiftly, a rare event in the British legal system. The judge listened to their arguments and concurred. 'The defendant changes his plea to one of guilty to the lesser charge of ABH, actual bodily harm. As he has been diagnosed with post-traumatic stress disorder, I will recommend he serve the term of his sentence in a suitable medical facility, which may be to his benefit, rather than being incarcerated in one of Her Majesty's Prisons. Agreed?'

As counsel were about to leave his chambers, the judge added a barbed comment to the prosecuting barrister. 'I trust you will inform the Crown Prosecution Service that I expect an explanation for this shoddily prepared case. And I would also ask why the ex-wife is not before me on a similar charge.'

The resulting sentence, a term of twelve weeks' detention in a psychological unit and a fine of £50, demonstrated exactly where the judge's sympathies lay.

CHAPTER TWO

Robert Pickles had been at the facility for almost four months and was now a voluntary patient, free to leave when he wished. A chance remark by his therapist decided his course of action. 'Try and remember a time and place when you were happy — perhaps when you were younger, and not all alone. Whenever things threaten to overwhelm you, focus on that memory. Believe me, it works.'

That was easy to say, but with your thought processes clouded by medication, not quite so easy to achieve. It was no easy task.

When had he been truly and completely happy? It was a long time before the answer came to him. It felt odd — odd that he had never thought of it before. And it had taken a complete stranger to prompt that memory. It centred round a cottage. An image of the building sprang to mind, sharp and detailed.

He had been four, or maybe five, years old, when he visited the cottage for the first time. It was in North Yorkshire, that much he could recall. The nearest town was a few miles away, but it took him both time and effort to recall it. Eventually, it came to him . . . Helmsdale!

They had stayed at the cottage during the long summer holidays, which he remembered being filled with sunshine, laughter, and enjoyment. Barbecues, fishing, long walks, visits to tearooms and castles. They had gone there for four successive years, until his mother told Robert that his father had died. There were no more holidays.

Robert had been saddened by the news, but his father was little more than a friendly stranger to the little boy. He only saw him during their visits to the cottage. His mother explained he worked abroad, and had a very important job, so he only got a short leave of absence every year.

Then his mother quit her job, and they moved to Nottingham. With no friends and new schoolmates, Robert remembered feeling lonely, neglected — abandoned, almost. Following their move, his mother became ill, the diagnosis terminal. By the time he was ten years old, Robert was alone. The following years consisted of several foster homes, until at the age of sixteen, with no clear idea of what he wanted from life, Robert had entered the army recruiting office on little more than a whim. He soon discovered that army life, with its disciplined, ordered existence, suited him.

As he recalled those days, Robert stopped at the time he enlisted. That line of thought would lead inevitably to Paula, and to Afghanistan. He certainly didn't need any painful reminders of those twin disasters.

Instead, Robert concentrated on the cottage. He could vaguely recall his mother explaining the property belonged to a distant relative who lived abroad, which was why the house was available whenever they wanted it. Now, having resurrected the memory, it refused to leave him. Within days, he could think of nothing else. He knew he had to go, had to return, to revisit the only place where he had been truly happy.

The therapist's final words, 'not all alone', ignited another spark in his memory.

'All Alone' was the name of the cottage. The location was remote, far off the beaten track. Then he remembered

Lulu-Belle, the little girl who lived nearby and became his playmate.

> *Ding dong bell, pussy's in the well.*
> *Who put her in? Little Johnny Flynn.*
> *Who pulled her out? Little Tommy Stout.*

From out of nowhere, or so it seemed, Robert remembered reciting that nursery rhyme as he and Lulu-Belle played in the garden, romping around the ancient well that had originally been the only source of fresh water. When the visits ceased, Robert remembered being sad, knowing he would miss the companionship of his friend.

But where was that cottage? After a lot of thought, he remembered the nearby village, a place with a strange name, Drover's Halt. Was he correct? Or had the name been conjured up by false memory?

He'd asked his therapist for help, and the man reported back. 'It wasn't your imagination, Robert. Such a place does exist, but it's a long way from Nottingham.'

'That cottage is the only place that comes to mind. I'll go there and hope I can be happy again.'

The therapist briefed the chief medical officer on his patient. 'He has responded to some of the treatment, although he still has momentary lapses which cause him to panic. And other than the cottage from his memory, which could be a wild goose chase, I don't think he's got anywhere to go. Technically, he's homeless.'

'We're not running a shelter for the homeless. If he's fit to return to normal life, he must leave. Our funding is limited, and must be conserved for those in greatest need.'

'I'd prefer to leave it a bit longer, as he's showing some small progress — but if you insist.'

* * *

Three days later, with his worldly goods stashed in a kitbag, Robert began the journey north. He had some cash in his wallet, although where it came from was a mystery. There were old bank cards too, but he couldn't use them. Such cards are no good if you can't recall the PIN number. He was fortunate to get a lift to Leeds, and using the map supplied by the therapist, scrounged another ride as far as Netherdale. He caught a bus to Helmsdale, and from there went on foot. It was a long trek towards the head of the dale, but eventually, having passed through the village of Drover's Halt, Robert reached the end of the lane leading to the cottage.

He looked around and saw the mountain to the west. Consulting the map, he saw it was named Stark Ghyll. As children, he and Lulu-Belle had been convinced there were dragons living in caves on the slopes of the mountain.

He looked sadly at the rotting sign, the letters all but indecipherable from neglect. All Alone Lane, it should have read. The house was named All Alone Cottage. And the description fitted it to perfection. Robert acknowledged that the name fitted his situation equally well.

He marched down the lane, which was little more than an overgrown track. He rounded the bend concealing the house, lowered his kitbag, and stared at the building, his expression one of dismay.

The house was unrecognizable from the picture in his memory. The windows were boarded up. Grass sprouted profusely from the sagging gutters. Slates were missing from the roof, and the garden, once a picturesque riot of colour, was now a jungle of weeds. *Derelict* was the word that came to mind. He felt a wave of depression, but fought against it, picked up his kitbag and moved forward. He hadn't come all this way to be defeated by a few plywood boards.

Questions flooded his mind. What had happened to the relative who owned the house? How had they let it get into this terrible state? Were they still alive? And if not, who owned it now? How long was it since this house had fallen into disuse? And who had boarded up the windows?

He searched for something to use as a crowbar. Among the weeds, he found a rusty iron stake that had once supported a fence. The stake was pointed at one end, and would suit his purpose.

Robert looked at the solid wooden door, decided it would be too strong, and headed for a window. He braced the end of the stake behind one of the boards and pushed it home. He felt the board move. Seconds later, he got his fingers behind it and tugged. The whole section came clear, revealing the frame, devoid of glass, making it easy to climb through, dragging his kitbag behind him.

Despite the warm evening, the house felt cold and damp. He was about to switch on the torch he'd bought, when he heard faint scuttling sounds that indicated that he was not alone. The house definitely had some occupants, though not human ones.

Robert tried to recall the layout. This had been the sitting room. Across the tiny hallway was the dining room with the kitchen behind. Upstairs were the bedrooms, one double, one single, and the bathroom. He remembered lying awake at night hearing the unmistakeable sounds of intense physical exertion coming from the room opposite his, accompanied by a series of moans and gasps that might have indicated pain. His innocent belief that someone was in distress.

But the memory disturbed him, and he inched his way towards the door. Damp had swollen the wood. It gave, eventually, and he stepped into the hall. Here, the musty smell of rot was stronger. He paused for a second, uncertain which way to turn, before opting for the dining room. He leaned his shoulder against the door and shoved. After a short struggle, it gave way. As he stepped forward, he felt something under the sole of his shoe. He stepped back and shone the torch down. The beam picked out the object clearly.

He frowned. What was *that* doing there? Without conscious thought, he picked it up, examining it closely before placing it in his pocket. He swung the torch, which illuminated the dining table he remembered from his childhood. He lifted the torch slightly and the beam picked out something at the far end of the table. He stared at it for a long time, frozen into immobility by horrified disbelief.

Robert had been wrong in assuming he was the only person inside the house. There was another human occupant. Unblinking, unmoved by the disturbance, the figure seated in the carver chair stared sightlessly back at the intruder. Sightless because the eye sockets were empty, the flesh surrounding them long since eaten away. The jaw was slack, the skull laughing at him, while the skeletal hands gripped the chair arms.

For a moment, he thought someone had died of natural causes here, in solitary isolation. But then remembered the house had been boarded up. Why hadn't the workmen who had done that noticed the body? He stared in horror as his torch picked up more of the skeleton, and he could see why the figure hadn't moved, even after years of scavenging and decay. The straps that held both wrists and ankles in place would prevent the corpse from slipping from its final resting place, whatever the attention of feasting creatures. Around the neck hung a tattered piece of fabric that had once been a gag.

Suddenly, Robert saw, and heard, something move on the periphery of the torch beam. He swung it slightly, and the light picked out two pairs of sharp, beady eyes. Rats!

Enough was enough. The soldier who had braved the terrors of Helmand Province, and witnessed death in many forms, turned tail and bolted through the hall, through the sitting room and out of the window. Not even pausing to draw breath, he half-stumbled, half-ran the length of the track to the road.

When he reached the lane leading to Drover's Halt, he paused for breath. As he looked round, desperate for help, Robert noticed a building in the distance. There might be people. He headed towards it and soon found a gateway. He set off down the drive, his pace little short of a gallop.

* * *

Louise Gough was unhappy. Her anger was down to the problems caused by her ex-business partner. Getting rid of him due to his gambling problems was bad enough. Paying for the privilege made matters worse. A reminder of how expensive the split had been came that morning, via her bank statement. The day that started badly got worse when she discovered that one of the residents of her animal sanctuary, a donkey, had gashed his leg on barbed wire.

Now she was trying to decide whether to watch TV or read a book, when she heard someone banging on the door. She was alone. Alone, and suddenly very scared. Scared because she realized how vulnerable she was. She heard a man's voice, his shout almost a scream. 'Let me in! Let me in! There's a body. It's murder, murder!'

Fear turned to terror. Some lunatic was pounding on her door, screaming murder. She needed help — and needed it fast.

She ran down the hallway to the phone and dialled treble nine. After gabbling her message, Louise slammed the handset down and hurried to the kitchen, as far from the front door as possible. She listened again, but this time couldn't make out anything but a moaning, sobbing sound. Was someone in distress, or was it a ruse to get her to open the door? Her fear intensified.

Outside, Robert sank to his knees, the disorder that plagued his every day returning in full measure. He began to weep, unable to control his emotions.

* * *

The Netherdale emergency operator put out a call for any patrol cars near to Drover's Halt. Seconds later, one reported that they were five miles from the village.

'The caller was Ms Louise Gough of Simeon House, outside Drover's Halt. She's alone, and sounded terrified,' the operator instructed the officers.

Robert had only been crouched in the doorway for ten or fifteen minutes, although it seemed longer, when he heard the siren. The noise increased, and as it reached a crescendo, he saw a blue flashing light reflected in the side pane of a bay window. Was this to do with his cry for help?

A car swung across the gateway. Inside the patrol car, the passenger pointed towards the crouching figure. 'There's the guy who was threatening Ms Gough.'

The car shuddered to a halt. Both officers leaped out and approached their target with caution. The driver spoke first. 'Who are you, and what are you doing here?'

Robert looked up. He didn't know who they were or what they were asking him. All he could think of was that skeleton. 'Don't hurt me,' he whimpered.

'Why were you pounding on this door, scaring the occupier?'

'A body. Murder, it was murder.' His eyes were wide, staring, as he sat huddled against the wall.

The driver signalled to his colleague and muttered, 'Cuff him.'

Robert felt one wrist being grabbed. Then something cold and metallic touched his wrists. In his dazed state he barely heard the officer report, 'Prisoner secure.'

'OK, let's try and raise the occupier.'

The driver rang the doorbell and called in a loud voice. 'Ms Gough? It's the police, can you please open the door?'

The door opened a fraction on the chain, and Louise looked at the distressed man. She turned to the officers, her relief apparent as she asked, 'Who is this man? Do you know?'

'Not yet, but he said something about a murder, so we've got him in handcuffs until we can find out what's going on.'

'Thank goodness for that. I was scared stiff. I'm all alone here.'

The words triggered Robert's memory. 'All Alone. All Alone. Inside — inside the cottage. There's a body. Tied to a chair,' he stammered.

Louise looked astonished. 'I don't know whether he's drunk or hallucinating, but there is an old house, half a mile or so away named All Alone Cottage.'

'Can we bring this guy inside while we try to make sense of what he's saying?' one of the officers asked.

She released the door chain. 'I suppose so. Come through to the kitchen. I'll put the kettle on.'

They entered the large kitchen, where the officers sat Robert on a chair by the table. Before they had chance to question him, Robert noticed a photo on the nearby dresser. The image was of two small children, a boy and girl, seated against a garden wall. The boy was clutching a distinctive teddy bear. 'Lulu-Belle,' Robert whispered.

There was a resounding crash as Louise dropped the mug she was holding. Ignoring the debris on the floor, she stared at Robert for a long time, before demanding, 'What did you say?'

He attempted to point to the photo, but with his hands manacled the effort was futile. 'The girl in the photo, I called her Lulu-Belle. I don't think that was her name, though.' He shook his head in bewilderment, tears still streaming down his face.

Louise ignored the officers, who were staring at Robert, then at her, clearly bemused. 'Bobby? Bobby Bear? Is it you?'

Robert frowned, clearly puzzled by the question. 'I suppose it must be,' he said, after a while. 'But I'd forgotten Lulu-Belle called me it.'

Louise crossed the kitchen. 'I'm Lulu-Belle. You called me that almost from the first time we met. And I called you "Bobby Bear" because you were always carrying a teddy bear around with you.' Louise paused, and then asked gently, 'Bobby, what did you want to tell us about the cottage?'

His eyes were wide as he stammered. 'I went there to see if I could stay. The doctor said I had to find somewhere I'd been really happy. But the cottage was boarded up. I got in and I found it.' He started to shake.

'What was it you found, Bobby?' Louise's tone was gentler still now.

'A skeleton. There were straps. It's fastened to a chair. I ran, and came to raise the alarm, to get help.'

One of the police officers interrupted. 'I take it you know this man?'

'I certainly do,' Louise replied. 'You can take the handcuffs off. Bobby would never hurt me. I knew him when we were little. His name is Robert Pickles. He stayed at the cottage every summer.' Louise was about to say more, but then changed tack abruptly. 'I think you should go and find out if he's telling the truth, which I feel sure he is.'

'We can't take the cuffs off, and we certainly can't leave you alone with him,' the officer responded. 'The fact that you knew each other years back doesn't mean he's safe now.'

Turning to his colleague, he suggested, 'I think we need backup. If this guy's story is kosher, it's a matter for CID, anyway.'

After consulting Netherdale control, one of the officers reported, 'There's no other patrol in the area, so they're sending someone from CID.' He grinned at his colleague, and added, 'Your luck's in. Detective Sergeant Mironova's on duty tonight.'

'Much good that'll do — she's a married woman now. Add to that, her husband's ex-SAS. So now I prefer to admire her from a distance.'

Louise cleared up the shattered remnants of the mug and brewed tea. The officers sipped theirs as they waited.

She took a mug to where Robert was seated, and remained crouching alongside his chair talking in a low voice. 'I missed you when you didn't come to the cottage, Bobby. I was lonely with nobody to play with. I remember getting excited every July, because I knew you'd be here soon. Why did you stop visiting?'

Robert had now calmed, regained his composure, and was feeling less tense. 'My father died. Then we moved to Nottingham. I missed coming here too. The cottage was nice, but I really wanted to be with you.'

Louise's sympathy increased as he told her of the following years. 'Things only began to improve when I joined the army. Life got better for a while, and then it went downhill.'

'Was that due to what happened in Afghanistan?'

'Not really, although I don't suppose it helped. When I was at school I made one friend, but he, and the slag I was stupid enough to marry, betrayed me, big time. When I was being treated, one of the psychiatrists told me I was suffering from PTSD and asked if I knew what the initials stood for. I think he was shocked when I replied, "Paula The Slut Disorder".' Seeing Louise's confusion, he explained, 'Paula is the bitch I married.'

Louise put her hand on his arm, a gesture of sympathy. 'That's all behind you now, Bobby. What we must hope for is that things will improve for both of us.'

Robert caught the wistful tone in her voice, and asked, 'Have things been tough for you as well?'

'They have been, but nowhere near as bad as yours. The positive side of living alone is that you don't have to answer to anyone. The negative side is that you have nobody to share your concerns with, or turn to for advice.' Louise explained about her business partner's misdemeanours, and the money it had cost her to get rid of him. 'Luckily I inherited this property after my parents died. Otherwise, I'd have had to sell it when my partner donated all our earnings to casinos and bookmakers.'

'Were you and he an item?'

Louise shuddered at the thought. 'No, thankfully that's one mistake I didn't make.'

CHAPTER THREE

After receiving the call from the control room, DS Clara Mironova contacted Steve Meadows, uniform sergeant at Helmsdale police station, who was at home. Clara asked him to go back to work to supervise proceedings. As a subdivision, the station only operated on office hours unless there was an emergency. His first task on arriving was to check out the man who had made the bizarre claim about a murder. He called Clara on her way to Simeon House.

'Robert Pickles was medically discharged from the army after being injured by an IED in Afghanistan, and now suffers with PTSD. His wife divorced him while he was serving, so when he arrived home, he went looking for his best friend, who had been having it off with her. He set about the so-called mate, but his ex-wife brained him with a poker. He was charged with attempted murder, but when the facts of the case emerged, this was reduced to ABH. He pleaded guilty to the lesser offence, so I was able to get a lot of information and read the details of the incident.

'He was convicted, but the judge ordered that his sentence should be served in a psychiatric clinic rather than a prison. That all took place in Nottingham, so what he's doing in this neck of the woods is a mystery.'

'I think the best bet would be for me to ask him,' said Clara. 'I'll go to Simeon House, and while I'm talking to Pickles, I'll ask the uniform lads to take a look at the cottage. If Pickles' story is correct, I'll have to summon Mike, and won't he be pleased?'

Detective Inspector Mike Nash, Clara's immediate superior, had just returned from honeymoon, so being disturbed was unlikely to prove popular.

'Thanks for your help, Steve. It's just like having Jack here, and that's saying a lot.' Sergeant Jack Binns, a long-serving officer and Steve's predecessor, had retired a few months ago.

It didn't take Clara long to discover the reason for Pickles' journey to North Yorkshire. She detailed the two uniformed men to visit the nearby cottage.

'The place is almost a ruin,' Louise warned them. 'I tried to rent it a few years ago. It would have been ideal for the animals. I got turned down, though. Now I'm glad I didn't get it.'

When the officers returned, they confirmed Pickles' story. 'We climbed in through the window to check, and before we left, we used the big red key to open the door for better access.'

Clara nodded at the reference to the manual battering ram, made of metal and conveniently painted red, before she called Steve Meadows and updated him. She hesitated before pressing the short code on her mobile for Nash's home.

Nash listened and told her, 'I'll join you at Simeon House, and we can go from there to the crime scene.'

* * *

When Nash arrived, Clara met him outside and apologized again, telling him that she hated having to disturb him.

Nash smiled and said, 'Alondra's had to put up with me night and day for three weeks, so she might see this as a spot of relief. I owe you one anyway, for looking after Daniel

21

during half-term and getting him back to school. And for all the dog walking while we were away.'

'David and I had great fun with them both. Although, I still can't get over how seriously Daniel took his role as best man at the wedding. He did really well — for a twelve-year-old.'

'As he brought Alondra and I back together, he insisted it should be his job. I didn't get much choice in the matter.' He shrugged and laughed. 'So, what have we got?'

It was soon apparent that Nash's summing-up of Pickles matched Louise's, for he'd only spoken to the ex-soldier for a few minutes when he asked the officers to remove the handcuffs. 'We'll need to take your statement,' he told Pickles. 'But that can wait until tomorrow. In the meantime, we must find somewhere for you to stay overnight. You must be exhausted after what you've been through.'

Louise, who had been standing alongside, interrupted. 'That won't be necessary, Inspector. Bobby can stay here.'

'Are you certain, Ms Gough? He's almost a total stranger.'

'No, he isn't. I've known him almost all my life. Admittedly, we haven't seen each other for a long time, but I'd trust Bobby with my life. In fact, I already have done.'

'What does that mean?'

'When we were seven years old, we went fishing in the stream. The usual kids' thing, just a garden cane, and some cotton with a bent safety pin on the end. I fell in. I was out of my depth, and would certainly have drowned, if Bobby hadn't pulled me out.'

'I'd forgotten all about that,' Pickles admitted. He looked at Nash and Clara and added, 'Believe me, I would never harm Lulu-Belle. Apart from my father, who I barely knew, and my mother, who died when I was a kid, Lulu-Belle is the closest to a family member I've ever had.'

* * *

It was still daylight as Clara joined Nash in his Range Rover and sat in the back to greet Teal, Nash's black Labrador, before fastening her seat belt. 'This is a new experience for me. I've never had the back of my neck licked as I'm travelling to a crime scene before.'

'Really, that does surprise me.'

When they reached the cottage, the detectives switched their torches on, and Clara pointed towards the kitbag standing, sentry-like, in the hallway. This provided further backup to Pickles' story.

Nash swung his torch right and left, the beam penetrating the gloom. The front door had not been boarded over, but despite that, the hall floor was free of litter. Nash frowned. 'That's interesting. You'd expect there to be some post, if only junk mail. After such a long time, there should be a mountain of it.'

'Maybe the Royal Mail doesn't know this place exists,' Clara pointed out.

'That wouldn't surprise me.'

The dining room door was not fully open, so Nash pushed against it. It groaned, like a horror movie sound effect, Clara thought. As their torches illuminated the interior, the scene was exactly as Pickles had described.

They stepped cautiously inside, and as Clara breathed in the musty smell of decay, her nose wrinkled in disgust. Their attention homed in on the skeletal remains secured to the chair. A few pathetic shreds of cloth still clung to the remains, somehow heightening the horror of the scene. Clara hoped the victim's death had been swift, but seeing the securing straps, she guessed that to be a vain hope.

Nash moved his torch to inspect the rest of the room. The beam picked out a small bundle in the corner. 'Look there. Those are old newspapers. I don't think we should touch them, they might disintegrate. We have to assume they've been here as long as the body, in which case, the dates on them might be a useful clue. Make a note to tell CSI about them.'

'Should we inspect the rest of the house? Once Pickles found this, he bolted. You never know what might be upstairs.' Clara didn't say there could be more bodies, but Nash caught the implication.

'Yes, and then we'll ring the professor and a CSI team. They'll have a field day in here.'

Much to their relief, their search revealed nothing untoward, and they were soon outside. They spent several minutes breathing the cool evening air, cleansing their nostrils from the smell of death and decay. Only then did they start making calls.

'I haven't heard from you for several weeks,' Professor Ramirez, the pathologist, told Nash. 'I should have known it was too good to last, and that you'd be the one to call me out at this ungodly hour. And only one skeleton, you say? My word, Nash, you really are slipping. Mind you, I suppose there's time for you to find more corpses before I arrive.'

Clara saw Nash smile as he ended the call. 'Mexican Pete on good form?' she asked.

'He certainly is, if sarcasm is anything to go by. We'd better examine the outbuildings. Mexican Pete said there was chance for me to come up with more bodies before he gets here. He made it sound like a challenge. Phone Steve again, will you, Clara? Ask him to notify CSI that we'll need a generator and lighting for the interior. It looks as if we're in for a long night. I'm going to phone Alondra, and I suggest you make grovelling apologies to David.'

Nash phoned Smelt Mill Cottage, and after a brief chat, waited for Clara to finish her call. The detectives made their way through a morass of weeds and long grass, skirting a circular brick wall topped by a pitched roof that had obviously once been a well, and walked towards the outbuildings, picking their way carefully. At one point, Clara looked back at the cottage. 'What a crying shame to let such a beautiful property go to rack and ruin.'

'I agree, but it's hardly the worst crime that's been committed here. Perhaps the state of the place is connected to the murder. You'd hardly want to live in the place with the body of someone you've murdered *in situ*. And I can't imagine anyone showing potential tenants round and telling them, *Ignore Fred, he's been there long enough now for the smell to have gone.*'

Mironova stared at him. 'Have I ever told you what a sick sense of humour you have?'

'I believe you may have mentioned it somewhere along the line.'

The stables were unlocked, and the detectives found nothing until they reached the last loose box. Nash opened the door, and for a second, it seemed that this, too, would yield nothing. Then his torch beam picked out something in the farthest corner. 'Ugh!' he exclaimed. 'What's that? It certainly doesn't look human.'

They moved inside and examined their find. The remains were as skeletal as those in the house, although far smaller. 'At a guess, I'd say it was a dog,' Clara stated.

'I agree, given the size and shape, plus that highly distinctive collar. The other difference from the human skeleton is that we can tell the cause of this poor creature's death — and a fairly unpleasant one it must have been.'

Nash's torch beam played along the iron bar that had impaled the unfortunate animal to the floor. The stake had penetrated the rib cage, and the darker stain on the earth surrounding the corpse seemed to confirm Nash's theory that the wound had been inflicted while the animal was alive. After a few seconds, he turned to Clara. 'I want CSI to conduct a detailed examination, not only of the cottage and the outbuildings, but also the area surrounding them.'

Clara looked aghast. 'You surely don't think there are more bodies?'

'I have no idea, but I'm not discounting the possibility. What I do know is that it's up to us to make certain, one way or another.'

Although Nash expected a further degree of sarcasm from Ramirez, the pathologist surprised him by sticking strictly to business. He watched the photographer at work and said, 'We'll need a post-mortem to determine when this unfortunate woman died. The result will only be an estimate, and cause of death might be difficult to determine. However, I think it's safe to assume we're looking at a murder victim here. Post-mortem, 9.30 a.m. tomorrow.'

Clara watched as the mortuary attendants loaded the victim, chair and all, into their van, and commented, 'Mexican Pete seemed very affable tonight. I wonder why he's so cheerful.'

'No idea, Clara. Just don't question it, because knowing him, it won't last.'

By the time they handed the crime scene over to the forensic officers, it was dark. The detectives returned to Simeon House to collect Clara's car, and deliver Pickles' kitbag.

They were surprised to find Louise alone. 'I insisted Robert get some rest. He's exhausted and distressed. I put him in the spare room, and last time I peeked in, he was asleep.'

'Strictly speaking, his kitbag should remain *in situ* as part of the evidence, but in this instance, it won't be necessary,' Nash told her. 'Would you remind him we need his statement?'

'Of course, and I'll see what I can do to help him while he's here.'

Clara seized the opportunity to ask, 'Are you certain you're OK having Pickles to stay, given his recent problems?'

Louise snorted with anger at the implication that Robert could pose a threat. 'If you're referring to that cow he married, I reckon she's the one with problems. Put it this way, I feel totally safe with Bobby in the house — safer in fact, because I know that if there was any danger, he would protect me.'

* * *

Despite the traumas of the day, Robert slept well, better than he had done for a long time. He opened the bedroom door and found his kitbag on the landing. He went downstairs and headed for the kitchen. Louise was already there, sitting at the table staring moodily into a mug of coffee. She looked up and gave him a weak smile in response to his greeting.

'I'd better collect my things and move on,' he told her. 'I appreciate your putting me up last night, but I don't want to get in your way.'

'You need to give the police a statement before you leave. Where will you go?'

'I have no idea yet.'

'You could stay here, if you like.'

'You didn't seem very happy when I came in. I thought you'd want rid of me.'

'That wasn't because of you, Bobby.' She shook her head. 'My assistant has just handed his notice in. That means an extra workload for me, and as things stand financially, I can't afford to hire a replacement.'

'Is there anything I can do to help? I'll happily do what I can. I'm a quick learner.'

Louise smiled. 'Really? If you're prepared to work for board and lodging, I'll gladly accept. You wouldn't have the worry of finding somewhere to live, and I'll have someone alongside me I can rely on.'

They shook hands to seal the bargain, then Louise suggested they eat. 'You must be famished. I should have offered you something last night.'

'I am a bit peckish, but I don't think I could have faced food last night, not after what I'd seen. I assume the police came back. I found my kitbag.'

'Yes, that's when the detective said he'd want another word with you.'

After breakfast, Louise took Robert to visit the stables so she could introduce him to the animals in her care. As Robert put his coat on, he felt something move under one of the pockets. It was then he remembered the item he'd picked up off the cottage floor. He rummaged inside the pocket and realized it must have dropped through a hole into the lining.

As he tried to retrieve the object, Louise asked what he was doing. 'It looks as if you're rehearsing a contortionist act.'

He explained, and Louise suggested she should help. 'My hands are much smaller.' She slipped her hand in, and delved through the hole in the lining. 'If you remind me tonight, I'll stitch this up for you. It's too good a coat to throw away.'

A few seconds later, she removed the foreign object. They stared at the ornate brooch in her hand, twinkling in the daylight. 'Gosh, this is absolutely beautiful,' Louise exclaimed. 'I wish I had something half as pretty as . . .' She stopped suddenly, her expression changing to one of dismay. 'Bobby, do you think this might be connected to the murder?'

'I suppose it could be.' He took the brooch from her and turned it over, peering at the back. 'The pin is broken. That might have happened during a struggle.' He looked closer. 'I reckon this might be quite valuable. There are hallmarks on it.'

'I think we should phone Inspector Nash, or Sergeant Mironova, and tell them about this. It could be an important piece of evidence.'

CHAPTER FOUR

Despite the late night, Nash was in the CID suite early next morning. He updated his two detective constables.

Viv Pearce, the tall male Antiguan, named after Isaac *Vivian* Alexander *Richards* by his cricket-mad family, had continued the tradition with his son, Brian, after Brian Charles Lara. Now, Pearce looked aghast. 'I'm glad I wasn't on call.'

'Me too,' Lisa Andrews agreed. 'Yuk!'

'Viv, I want you to use your internet skills and find out who owns All Alone Cottage. We need to know why it's been derelict for so long, and who had access to the building. Lisa, you can give him a hand. Get on to the local council. Find what you can.'

Nash then asked Clara to write up the report on the incident.

'Why me?' Clara asked.

'Because you were first call. When you've done that, send a copy over to Netherdale HQ, and ask Tom Pratt to set up a case file. After the PM, I'll go and see Jackie and welcome her back.'

'Is Superintendent Fleming back at work?' Lisa asked. 'She's been off an awfully long time.'

'Yes, the medics have given her the all-clear at last. Although she'll be at HQ most of the time, her role will be more admin than before, supporting the chief.'

'Well, going to HQ sounds like a very convenient excuse for you to get out of doing some work,' Clara stated.

Nash smiled sweetly at her. 'It does rather, doesn't it? Alternatively, you can attend the PM, if you prefer?'

With that, he headed for Netherdale mortuary.

* * *

Following the post-mortem, Nash called at headquarters. There, he updated Chief Constable Ruth Edwards and Detective Superintendent Jackie Fleming with the findings, and what little they had discovered at the cottage. 'We were convinced by the derelict condition of the building, and the decomposition of the body, that the victim had been dead for many years. However, Ramirez says her death occurred more recently, no more than five years ago, possibly even less. The skeleton is that of a woman, who he reckons was somewhere in the region of thirty to forty years of age. There were no signs of violence, and he concludes she died of malnutrition combined with dehydration. The only other significant fact is that she had given birth to at least one child.'

'How was our worthy pathologist able to pinpoint her time of death, Mike, or shouldn't I ask?'

'It's due to the rate of decomposition, plus the amount of insect and rodent scavenging.'

'I knew it was a mistake to ask,' Ruth muttered.

'We might get a more precise date, but if Ramirez is correct, that leaves us with another puzzle.'

'Care to explain, Mike?' the superintendent asked. 'Sometimes listening to you is like trying to solve a cryptic crossword.'

'Is that how you spent your convalescence, Jackie?' Nash grinned at the rude gesture from his immediate superior.

'There's a pile of old newspapers near the body. The publication date might give us a guideline. Alternatively, they could be from 1945 and were there to use as firelighters. In addition, we found another item at the crime scene that could help identify the victim and establish when she went missing. It's a distinctive, and probably expensive, dog collar worn by the second victim.' Nash explained about the canine remains in the outhouse.

'We assumed the cottage was abandoned after the body was placed there, but that can't be so. I'd say the building has been derelict for much longer. My guess is it's been deteriorating for at least ten years, if not more. I've asked CSI to treat the body of the dog as if it was human, so with all their other work, I reckon they're going to be on site for a while yet.'

He had barely finished speaking, when the chief constable's phone rang. She answered the call and then held the receiver out. 'It's Clara for you, Mike. She says your mobile's switched off.'

'Sorry, I did it for the post-mortem and forgot to switch it back on.' He took the receiver. 'Yes, Clara, what's the problem?'

He listened and then said, 'OK, I'll collect you from Helmsdale and we'll go straight there.'

Having ended the call he told Fleming and Edwards, 'Clara's just learned of another piece of evidence from the crime scene that might be important, so we're off to take a look.'

* * *

When Nash collected Clara at Helmsdale, she reported, 'We don't have any civilian support. Tom Pratt's on holiday, and Maureen Riley's also off work. Her son's ill and she's his carer. That might restrict us when it comes to reporting and getting info.'

'Who's handling the paperwork?'

31

'Bob Greenwood. He used to work at Bishopton station before they closed it. He usually concentrates on uniform branch's stuff, RTAs, and the like, but he's been seconded to deal with our work as well.'

'We'll have to manage as best we can.'

Before they reached Drover's Halt, Clara explained, 'It was Louise Gough that phoned. Robert Pickles was so upset last night he completely forgot he'd picked up a brooch from the cottage floor, just before he found the body. He'd put it into his pocket, but after seeing the corpse it slipped his mind.'

'That's hardly surprising.'

'It sounds as if it might be quite valuable, because it's hallmarked. They also thought it could be important, so I told them to hang on to it until we can collect it. We can take their statements while we're there.'

It was late afternoon when the detectives reached Simeon House. After inspecting the brooch, they agreed with Louise's estimation of its value. While they were talking, she also informed them that if they needed to contact Robert, they could always do so there. 'Bobby and I have come to an arrangement. He's going to work for me. In exchange I'll give him board and lodging. That way, we both benefit.'

Having taken statements, they drove back to the station. Clara asked Nash what he thought about Louise's news.

'I think it will be like she said, beneficial to both of them.'

'I wonder if perhaps it might end up being more than that,' Clara speculated.

'What leads you to say that?'

'Louise is obviously fond of Robert, has been since they were children. Why else would she have kept that photo for so many years? What's more, the photo has pride of place on the Welsh dresser in the kitchen.'

Nash shook his head. 'You're an incurable romantic.'

* * *

It isn't only police officers who rely on informants. Obtaining news from inside sources can be useful to many other professionals. As a practising solicitor, Gavin Mitchell needed to be *au fait* with all local events in order to be proactive. Mitchell was about to leave his office late in the afternoon, when his mobile rang. He glanced at the screen and then answered the call. 'Bob, long time no speak. Have you got news for me?'

'Yes, sort of. Although it's a bit old hat. You once asked me to let you know if anything interesting happened in or around Drover's Halt. Is that still relevant?'

'It all depends what you're referring to. Not if somebody's been nicking beer mats from the local boozer.'

'It's a bit more than that. There's a report come in I had to type up for Helmsdale. It's only very basic information to be used in creating a file, and allocating an incident number, but it concerns a skeleton, and a dead dog, found in an abandoned property.'

'Really? That does sound interesting. Where was this?'

Mitchell almost dropped his phone when he heard Greenwood's reply. 'It's called All Alone Cottage. According to the report, the place is in ruin, and the bodies were skeletons, so they must have been there a while.'

Mitchell hesitated, before he said, 'Makes you wonder how someone stumbled across a corpse in such a remote, rundown place. I mean, with a name like All Alone it must be in the back of beyond.'

'That's where it gets a bit weird. The bloke who found it is a homeless ex-soldier who broke into the derelict building, looking for somewhere to stay. If he hadn't done that, who knows how long they'd have remained undiscovered?'

Mitchell discarded Greenwood's last statement as being immaterial. 'Is that everything, or is there more?'

'No, that's all I've got. Like I said, it's only a preliminary report. Do you want me to update you with any developments?'

'I don't think that will be necessary, but don't worry, I'll ensure you have the usual, via bank transfer.'

Having ended the call, Mitchell removed his coat and jacket. The room felt suddenly hot and stuffy. Any plans for returning home had now to be put in abeyance. He consulted his telephone index before picking up the handset and dialling.

When the call was answered, he said, 'Hi, it's Gavin Mitchell again, can you talk?' Given the go-ahead, he continued, 'Remember I told you earlier that a police officer had been fishing for information about All Alone Cottage? Well, there has been a very disturbing development.' Mitchell explained, and when he'd ended the call, knew he'd done all he could. The rest was up to his client.

The person Mitchell had called pondered the new information for a few minutes, before deciding on an action plan. Everything they had worked for was now under threat. It was time to start cleaning house. The only question to be resolved was where to start.

CHAPTER FIVE

Next morning, Nash was watching Alondra feed the dog. 'Have you anything special planned for today?' he asked.

'I'm going to start work on a new series of landscapes, so I'm taking Miss Greedy here to the first site I've chosen, where I can make a couple of sketches.' She explained her intended destination, and added, 'It's ideal, because the hills plunge so steeply, it will make a dramatic painting if I choose the best angle. I'll do the sketches using different vantage points, and return later to commence work on the painting, weather permitting.' Alondra smiled as she added, 'North Yorkshire has some terrific scenery that presents a lot of opportunities for an artist, but the climate can be a bit of a drawback. It's rare to get wall-to-wall sunshine like I had in Spain.'

Nash grimaced at her mention of the site she had chosen. The memories it brought back still saddened him. Added to that, the drive there was not without peril. 'Be extremely careful,' he warned her. 'That road is notoriously tricky. Our Traffic lads have to attend quite a number of serious fender benders there every year.'

'Don't worry, Mike, I'll be extra careful. I'm used to driving on the left now. Besides which, on that road everyone has to drive in the middle, because there are only a few places where it's wide enough for two cars. It's quite a surprise driving on a lane with grass growing in the middle. What about you? Have you anything lined up?'

'Just this new case.'

'Don't fret, Mike, if anyone can solve the mystery, you're the man.'

After breakfast, Nash kissed Alondra, stroked Teal, reminded the dog to take care of her mistress, and left. His final sight as he drove away was Alondra waving goodbye from the doorway while, with the use of her right leg, preventing Teal from following him. He was still smiling as he glanced back in his rear-view mirror, but could only see the bodywork of her new car.

* * *

When he reached Helmsdale, Nash was called over by Viv Pearce. 'Mike, you asked me to look into the ownership of All Alone Cottage. I did so yesterday, but I've hit a snag.'

'What sort of snag? Is it a big one or a small one?'

'I'd actually describe it as a showstopper. I did a Land Registry search, and that threw up the name of Mitchell & Co., Solicitors, in Netherdale, as the owners. I assumed the property is in trust for one of their clients. That might well be so, but when I asked them, they refused to divulge any information, citing client confidentiality.'

'Did you explain why we were enquiring?'

'No, I remembered what you said about not releasing any info at this stage. However, I did speak to their senior partner, but even he refused to reveal anything. I went so far as to ask him to consult his client.'

Nash saw the grimace on Pearce's face. 'What reply did you get?'

'I got the disconnect tone.'

The problem seemed insoluble, but that evening, as Nash and Alondra were watching TV, an idea came to him.

They were curled up on the sofa, their favourite viewing position. The programme being shown was a documentary about British couples seeking properties abroad. One of the clients of an estate agent based in Almeria, in southern Spain, was talking on camera about the happy times she'd spent in that area as a child. 'My parents used to rent a *casita* here, and we visited it every summer during the school holidays.'

'*Casita* is Spanish for cottage,' Alondra explained. 'The literal translation would be "little house".'

Nash sat bolt upright, almost dislodging Alondra in the process. She protested, asking him what was wrong.

From her position on the dog bed, Teal looked up, startled by her pack leaders' sudden movements, but when they settled down, she returned to dreaming of chasing rabbits.

'Sorry, darling, but what the lady on TV said, plus your translation, has just given me a possible solution to a problem that's been bugging me all day.'

* * *

Rather than setting off for Helmsdale next morning, Nash rang Clara and asked her to come to Smelt Mill Cottage. He explained why, and then rang the station. His conversation with Steve Meadows was short and to the point. 'Clara and I won't be in until late.' He then said goodbye to Alondra and Teal, reiterating his words of caution from the previous day, regarding the road they were to travel on.

When Clara arrived, the detectives set off for Drover's Halt. On the way, Clara updated Nash. 'I took that brooch to the jeweller yesterday, and he's agreed to supply us with a written report. However, here's the gist of what he told me.' Clara opened her pocketbook and continued, 'The brooch was hallmarked as sterling silver by the London Assay Office with a date letter showing the year of manufacture as 2014. The setting is encrusted with cushion-cut diamonds, and the centrepiece is a large sapphire. His opinion is that the stones are of particularly good quality. He talked about carats, but that went way over my head. When I got him to drop the techno-speak, he reckoned the brooch is worth somewhere between five and a half to six thousand pounds.'

Clara paused to let Nash absorb this, and then added, 'The jeweller told me something else that might be relevant. He said that with a piece of this quality, the owner might have matching accessories, such as a bracelet, a necklace, or a pair of earrings. Apparently that's the sort of thing people with money to burn go in for.' She grinned. 'Not something I've much experience of on a detective sergeant's salary.'

When they rang the doorbell at Simeon House there was no reply. They found Louise and Robert in one of the loose boxes grooming a Shetland pony.

Nash explained the reason for their visit. 'Robert, if you can, I want you to cast your mind back to the times you visited the cottage as a boy. Do you recall who owned the property then?'

Pickles shook his head. 'If I was told their name, it certainly didn't register. I always assumed it was something to do with my father, or his family. I never knew much about him or met them. That sounds strange, but the only time I saw him was during those holidays. Mother told me he worked abroad all year, and only had that one period of leave. She never mentioned what his work was, or where he went to carry it out. In fact, she didn't tell me much about him.'

'Didn't you think that was a bit odd?'

'I suppose so, looking back. But I was only young. Then, mother told me he'd died suddenly, and before I knew what was happening, we'd moved to Nottingham and life went downhill from that point. I lost interest. I haven't thought about him for almost twenty years, I guess.'

'I remember Bobby . . . er . . . Robert's father,' Louise interrupted. 'He was a tall man with grey hair and a beard. He looked distinguished, almost like a military man.'

'Is there anything else you can tell us about your parents, Robert?'

'Not really, apart from my father's unusual Christian name. He was called Bartholomew. The only reason I know is from my birth certificate. He's listed as Bartholomew Pickles, and my mother as Iris Cameron.'

'You said your father worked away all year, but what did your mother do while he was absent? Did she have a job?'

'Is this relevant to the body I found?'

'Only that we're trying to establish who owned the cottage then, and we're not having much success.'

Louise interrupted. 'Perhaps that solicitor might be able to help?'

'Solicitor?' Nash asked.

'Yes, I told Sergeant Mironova I tried to rent the land some time ago. He was downright rude, most obstructive.'

'And who was this?'

'Mitchell's in Netherdale.'

Clara caught the glance from Nash as he said, 'Thank you, Ms Gough. That might be helpful.' He turned back to Robert. 'I was asking about your mother.'

'She was a secretary, and worked for a firm based in Netherdale. I think they were quite a big concern. But I could be totally wrong. I *do* know she was furious about the callous way they treated her.'

'Why was she so angry?'

'She was made redundant only a few weeks after my father's death.'

'Did you go to his funeral, or memorial service?'

Robert looked surprised by the question. 'No, I don't remember there being one. If there was, I assume it must have been abroad, because I'm sure Mother would have gone, even if she didn't take me along.'

Clara noticed that Louise, seeing how upset he was, took his hand in a sympathetic gesture.

As they drove away Clara said, 'I told you so.'

'Told me what?'

'I reckon Robert might end up living at Simeon House permanently. What's more, I wouldn't be in the least surprised if he and Louise end up sharing the same duvet.'

'Just because they were pals as kids doesn't mean they'll become lovers. I had a best friend when I was little, but we certainly didn't fall in love.'

'What was her name?'

'George!'

When Clara stopped laughing, she told him, 'I noticed the way they looked at one another, and when Robert was upset, she took his hand. That, plus the fact that she calls him Bobby, not Robert, is what convinces me that they'll become more than just friends.'

'She's always called him Bobby, and I think that's all purely reassurance. You've been reading too many Barbara Cartland novels,' Nash teased her. 'I also reckon that Iris wasn't married to Robert's father. In fact, if I had to guess, I'd say Bartholomew Pickles was married to someone else, and that Iris Cameron was his mistress.'

'If you think I'm being overly romantic, then I reckon you've got a dirty mind. What gives you cause to make that slanderous allegation?'

'Point one, the couple only got together once a year. Point two, when Bartholomew died, neither Iris nor Robert attended the funeral. Admittedly, he might have been buried or cremated overseas, but even then, there would probably have been a memorial service. I also reckon he might have been connected to the place where Iris worked. The fact that she got sacked only weeks after his death suggests someone putting the boot in.'

* * *

Nash asked Viv Pearce to check out Robert Pickles' parents. 'When you've done that, you and Lisa can join Steve's men in Drover's Halt village, and give them a hand with the door-to-door. They're trying to find out who owns the cottage — in fact, anything anyone can say about it.'

He and Clara went into his office. As they were studying a report from Lisa Andrews into a burglary the previous day in Netherdale, Viv interrupted with news — or rather, the lack of it. 'I've found Robert Pickles' birth registration. Like you said, Mike, his mother is listed as Iris Cameron and his father as Bartholomew Pickles. However, there's a problem.'

'What sort of problem, Viv?'

'He doesn't exist.'

'Sorry, who doesn't exist?'

'Bartholomew Pickles — there is nobody of that name recorded in the Births, Marriages, and Deaths registry.'

'Oh good,' Clara interjected. 'Just what we need, another mystery.'

CHAPTER SIX

With budgetary constraints a priority, Helmsdale was classed as a rural unit and therefore had limited resources available. This applied to all aspects of police work in the area. One of those affected by the cutbacks was the Forensics division, based in Netherdale, which had only two units to cover all incidents. Extra backup from outside areas was available to be drafted in for major crimes.

One team had been obliged to suspend their operation at All Alone Cottage for a day. They had attended the burglary in Netherdale which Lisa Andrews was investigating. When they returned to Drover's Halt and joined their colleagues, their next task, following Nash's insistence, was to continue to check the areas immediately surrounding the cottage and outbuildings. Their leader had objected, pointing out that anything material would have been compromised during the period since the crime took place. As he had spoken, the look on Nash's face told him he was wasting his breath. Reluctantly, he'd accepted the inevitable.

It was a warm, sunny day, ideal for the work, but they failed to discover anything significant during the morning. The leader called a halt, and declared that it was time for lunch. One of the officers collected his flask and sandwiches from the van, and looked for a convenient place to dine. He headed for the ancient wishing well in the garden. The wall would be ideal for him to perch on.

The position was all he'd hoped for, with the warm sun directly in his face, and the overhanging branches of trees on either side forming an effective windbreak. Admittedly, the brick was a little too narrow for his posterior, but the wooden cover that stretched across the circular top would add extra support. Or so he thought — until he tried to sit on it. There was an alarming creaking sound. He could feel the cover beneath his backside moving. Hastily, he leaped away, turned, and stared.

The wooden panels were in two halves, and where they met in the middle, two iron lifting handles had been secured with a chain and padlock. It was only these latter items that had staved off disaster. Years of neglect had caused the timber to rot. This decay had spread, resulting in the screws that should have secured the lifting handles working loose. Had it not been for the chain and padlock, he might have plunged into the depths. Now, one of the handles was completely free of the timber.

Out of pure curiosity, to see how far he would have fallen, the officer prised the cover open. Two slats of wood came loose, dropping into the void and splashing noisily as they hit the water. He deployed his torch to assist as he peered into the gloom. The well wasn't deep, no more than eight or nine feet, he reckoned, but despite that he could have sustained a nasty injury had he fallen in.

He moved the torch slightly. The beam picked up something that definitely didn't belong in the well. Hardened though he was, the sight caused him to recoil in horror.

* * *

Nash had just taken a bite of his sandwich when his mobile rang. Muttering something impolite about people who don't realize when lunchtime happens, he answered the call, his displeasure masked by ham, cheese, tomato, and bread.

Seconds later, all thoughts of food were forgotten. 'We'll be straight there.' He swept the bag with the remains of his sandwich into the waste bin, and strode out into the main office. 'Are Viv and Lisa still door knocking?'

Clara ceased chewing. 'Yes, Viv's just phoned to say they're not getting anywhere. They've been to the nearest properties to the cottage, but no one knows anything about the possible owner. He said the uniform boys are having the same result. They're nearly finished.'

'We can't wait for them — come on, you're with me. We'll brief them later.'

'Where are we going, and what's the panic?'

'Back to Drover's Halt. I don't know any details, but their team leader just phoned to say they've found another body. You can have the dubious pleasure of telling Mexican Pete once we're en route.'

'Thanks a bunch, Mike. I'm really looking forward to that.'

Pausing only to give Steve Meadows a heads-up, they hurried to Nash's car. With little traffic on the road, they made good headway, and were soon bouncing along the rutted track leading to the derelict cottage. The forensic team leader was obviously on the lookout for them, because he signalled them to accompany him. As they passed the CSI vans, Clara noticed the other officers lounging about, eating their lunch or reading. Obviously, all investigative activity had been halted, in light of their recent discovery.

As the officer led them through the gate towards the garden, he explained what had happened, adding, 'We've stopped work until we get instructions from El Cid.'

Clara was puzzled momentarily, until she realized he was referring to the pathologist. Obviously, Mexican Pete had acquired another nickname.

They inspected the site, and Clara was puzzled by one item. 'Why was the cover padlocked? Surely there would have been very little likelihood of anyone lifting it up, not in so remote a place as this?'

She glanced at Nash as she spoke, and saw the grim expression on his face as he asked, 'Why do you think, Clara?' Nash bent down and inverted the cover. He turned it to face her and pointed to a series of scratches on the underside of the timber.

'Oh no, not buried alive, surely? That's absolutely revolting.'

'I agree, and I reckon whoever did this must have felt extreme hatred for the victim. Either that or they were down-right sadistic — or possibly both. This is pure, malicious evil.'

Clara was still dwelling on this appalling revelation when they were joined by the pathologist, accompanied by his two mortuary assistants. Although both detectives anticipated a bout of sarcasm, they were surprised when Ramirez, having taken one long, searching look at the wooden cover Nash was still holding, muttered, '*Madre de Dios*,' before crossing himself.

Although Clara had seen the pathologist attend some horrific sights, she had never witnessed him doing such a thing before. Obviously the implications of what he could see had affected him deeply. He looked at Clara, then across to Nash. 'This is truly evil, Mike. I assume from what you're clutching that you've reached the same conclusion as me?'

'We certainly have, and I don't think anyone would accuse you of exaggeration. I don't care who the victim was, or what they did wrong, nobody merits such appallingly cruel treatment. I thought what was done to the woman inside the cottage was bad enough, but this defies belief.'

Ramirez walked over to the well, signalling his assistants to accompany him. As they peered into the murky interior, Clara heard him ask, 'I hope one of you has brought his waders. Otherwise, you're going to get your feet wet.'

He looked over at the detectives and suggested, 'I think there's little to be gained from you remaining here, unless you feel it necessary. The boffins can assist with retrieval. I'll let you know when I've set the time for the post-mortem.'

Before driving back to Helmsdale, Nash phoned Netherdale, and updated Superintendent Fleming with developments. Having explained the location of the second skeleton, he paused before telling her, 'We believe that the victim was placed inside while still alive. We examined the well cover and discovered scratches gouged into the wood, which suggests they were trying to free themselves.'

Jackie Fleming's reaction was as strong as theirs. 'I don't care what it takes, Mike. We must put the evil swine that did this behind bars — preferably for life, either in a prison or a padded cell.'

* * *

It was late afternoon when DCs Andrews and Pearce returned to CID, telling Nash they had gained nothing helpful for their endeavours. In return, they were told of Nash and Clara's return visit to the cottage, and what had been found.

'I can't understand how anyone could do such a terrible thing. What on earth was their motive?' Lisa exclaimed.

'The explanations that spring to mind are that the killer was consumed by a deep hatred of the victims. Or they had committed some dreadful act against the murderer, sparking a cruel and evil revenge. The third possibility is the killer could be a complete psychopath. Take your pick,' Nash said.

'He must have had some reason for choosing that particular place to dispose of the victims, apart from its remote location,' Clara pointed out. 'If we could establish why he selected the cottage, it would be a giant leap forward.'

'Good point, Clara, but so far we've hit a brick wall regarding the cottage, thanks to the unhelpful attitude of the solicitor Viv spoke to. It's getting late. Let's pack it in for today, and start again tomorrow. See if you can find anything on this Bartholomew Pickles.'

'Do you think it's worth the effort? Viv asked.

'Got anything else worth looking at?'

'OK, boss.'

At that moment, Nash was interrupted when his mobile signalled an incoming text. He read it and grimaced. 'It's from Mexican Pete giving details of the post-mortem in his own inimitable style.'

'Why, what does he say?'

'His exact words are "Report at 8.30 sharp, skeleton staff on duty". That's sick, even for him.'

* * *

The post-mortem revealed the victim was male, about the same age as the female victim inside the cottage, and had been dead for approximately the same length of time. 'As with the other skeleton, I will attempt to retrieve DNA, but I should warn you that this is by no means certain.'

The mortuary, located at the rear of Netherdale General Hospital was only a short distance from HQ. Nash called in and updated Superintendent Fleming before returning to Helmsdale, where he briefed the team.

'Mexican Pete told me he might be able to obtain DNA if he can extract sufficient bone marrow to provide a viable sample. But as with the female, he reckons that's not certain because of insect scavenging. Bone marrow is their equivalent of Beef Wellington — his words, not mine, I hasten to add. Even if he can retrieve enough, it will be a while before the results are in. He said, "The remains of both victims might have degenerated beyond recovery, without the aid of a forensic anthropologist. And they're as rare as hen's teeth in this neck of the woods."'

'What exactly is a forensic anthropologist? I've never been sure.' Pearce asked.

'It's a specialized form of pathology, a bit similar to comparing a cardiac surgeon with a general practitioner. Anyway, even if we are successful in obtaining DNA from either victim, it might not be of much use to us, unless they've committed offences warranting them being in the national database. Failing that, our only hope is by obtaining a familial match.'

Clara was curious. 'Did Mexican Pete really say "as rare as hen's teeth in this neck of the woods"? It seems so unlike him.'

Nash smiled. 'Not really. That was my interpretation. Apart from that, he's had more success with the dog hair, and has already sent that off for experts to determine the breed. However, it will be a while before we hear more.'

Having given them the news, Nash went into his office with Clara, and told her, 'That burglary report of Lisa's. The MO sounds very similar to another one we had a few weeks ago, also in Netherdale. Correct me if I'm wrong, but I feel sure I read a report about it when I came back from honeymoon.'

Clara thought for a moment. 'You might be right. I'll get Lisa.'

Lisa came in a few minutes later with a folder. Nash took it from her and placed it inside his briefcase. 'I'll look through them this evening. I'm not on cooking duty tonight. With luck, I might have more idea how to crack the burglaries than I do with the murders. Let's face it, I couldn't have less.'

* * *

Next morning, with the full team assembled, Nash said, 'I was going to refer to this as a progress report, except that's wildly inaccurate. Let's start with the killings. I don't see how we're going to be able to make any headway on the cottage murders until such time as we get DNA results back — and even then, there's no certainty they'll yield anything useful if the victims aren't in our system.'

Clara sighed. 'It would be handy if there was a national database containing everyone's DNA, not simply that of people who have committed crimes.'

Nash shook his head sorrowfully. 'Don't even think that, let alone say it. You'll have all sorts of people screaming about infringement of civil liberty, and invasion of privacy.

Nobody will be interested in making our job easier. As we're up a gum tree with the murders, I suggest we concentrate our time and energy on other cases where we stand a chance of achieving a result, unless someone can think of another way of identifying those skeletons.'

'I did have one idea, Mike.'

'Go on, Clara, let's hear it.'

'It's a bit of a long shot, but if we work on the assumption that the two bodies and the dog are connected, might it be worthwhile checking the missing persons database? There can't be many instances where Mr and Mrs Jones and their dog Fido all vanished at the same time.'

'That's little short of brilliant, Clara. Even if it doesn't achieve a result, we have at least one avenue to explore, and that's one more than we had a couple of minutes ago. Viv, any luck with Pickles' father, Bartholomew?'

'Still digging.'

'In that case, will you follow up on missing persons as soon as this meeting's over, please? Now, let's turn our attention to those burglaries. As you were called to both crime scenes, Lisa, would you please brief us on what you found?' He handed her the files. 'I looked them over last night, but I think we should all give them some thought.'

'The MO is identical in both instances,' Lisa began. 'The burglar went to the rear of the property, smashed a pane of glass close to the door handle, and reached inside. The householders had obligingly left a key in the lock, which he turned to let himself in. I'm only surprised they didn't take out a full-page advertisement in the *Netherdale Gazette* telling everyone they were going to be away, and that the house had no alarm system. Forensics discovered some fibres clinging to the broken glass, which suggests the burglar used fabric of sorts to muffle the sound when he struck the pane. They also found a small chip from a brick on the floor inside, which we assume was his tool of choice.'

Lisa paused and glanced down at her incident report. 'The first robbery was in Daleside Avenue. The householders were on holiday, and only discovered the break-in when they returned. We're unable to pinpoint exactly when the crime was committed, except that it was within a two-week span. I'm still awaiting some details from the owners as to the make, model, and date of a couple of items that were taken, so I've not yet got a precise estimate of the proceeds. However, the thief took two TV sets, two laptops, one mobile phone, a microwave, plus an Omega watch and various items of jewellery. Ironically, the victim had left his expensive watch at home and wore a cheap one abroad. He thought it would be safer at home, and didn't want the Omega smeared with suntan lotion.'

Lisa closed that file and opened the second one. 'The other burglary was also in Netherdale, this time in Kirk Bolton Lane. Once again, the means of entry was identical to Daleside Avenue. The householders were on a Mediterranean cruise, so, like the first offence, we don't have an exact date. The items taken were also pretty similar, mainly electronic goods, plus jewellery. And in this instance, around three hundred and fifty pounds in cash. This is only a very rough estimate, but in total, I think the villain got away with around twenty-five thousand pounds' worth of goods. I'm talking retail replacement values, so I don't think he'll be able to retire on the proceeds, given that he'd probably be flogging the stuff in pubs, or at a car boot sale. That also means it's highly likely he'll strike again. He's been careful enough to avoid leaving any trace evidence behind. Forensics failed to find fingerprints, DNA, or anything that might prove useful.' Lisa closed the file and looked at Nash, signalling the end of her report.

Having thanked her, he asked for comments. 'If he's only targeting unoccupied houses, he might well have already committed another burglary — if not more,' Clara suggested. 'And how did the thief know which houses to select? Unless he's been incredibly lucky, he must somehow have gained inside knowledge that the occupiers would be away.'

'Those are both very good points,' Nash agreed, 'and frustrating as it might be, we'll have to wait for someone to return from holiday before we know. One other idea that struck me is, how did he know there were no alarms on either house? Or did he?'

'I think the last point might be down to observation, Mike.' It was Viv's first contribution to the discussion. 'When somebody has an alarm system fitted, the company installing it usually puts an external sounder somewhere under the eaves. That's fine for the occupier of those houses, but the absence of such a device might give the burglar confidence that the property is unprotected.'

'Thank you, Viv, another good point. But we're still no further forward, I'm afraid.'

On that slightly downbeat note, the meeting broke up. Sometimes, as Nash told Alondra that evening, a detective's work can be extremely satisfying, having brought a wrongdoer to justice, but at other times, such as they were currently experiencing, it could be highly frustrating.

CHAPTER SEVEN

Terry and Mary had been married for over twenty-five years. They had one child, a son, and having seen him off for his summer job as a holiday rep based on the Greek island of Kos, the couple embarked on one of their favourite annual pastimes, a walking tour of the Scottish Highlands.

Five days into their planned two-week vacation, their hiking came to an abrupt end when Mary suffered a broken arm in a fall. The humiliation of sustaining the injury by tripping over a rug in their hotel was nothing compared to the pain it generated. With all thoughts of hiking abandoned, they returned to their home in Netherdale.

Aware his wife was fretting over her inability to carry out many everyday tasks, Terry attempted to reassure her. 'One good thing is that I'll be on hand to help you over for the rest of the fortnight. Longer, if necessary.'

'That's comforting to know, and luckily it isn't my writing hand that's injured, so I'll be able to draw you a map.'

'A map? Why would I need a map?'

'So you can find your way to the kitchen — I'll draw another one so you can find the indigestion tablets.'

It was well past midnight when they reached their home, a large detached house on the outskirts of town. Terry pulled the car onto the drive, and said, 'I'll go in and switch the lights on. You wait here, until you can see where you're going.'

She didn't argue. Sometimes it was nice to be pampered. She watched her husband groping for the front door lock in the semi-darkness, the only illumination being from the streetlamp. They really should have got one of those PIR lights, she thought, but they rarely went out at night so it didn't seem worth the expense. That same reasoning had led to them dismissing the idea of an alarm system.

A split second later, the bright gleam from the chandelier in the hall dispelled the gloom. As Mary waited, lights went on in the lounge, and a few seconds later, the first floor landing was illuminated.

Time dragged by. Surely Terry should have come for her by now? After what seemed an age, her patience wore out, and she opted to follow him inside. 'Terry, where are you?' There was no reply so she tried again. 'Terry, love, are you upstairs? Is something wrong?'

Still no reply, but as she listened Mary thought she heard groaning. It seemed to be coming from their bedroom. She dashed upstairs, ignoring the pain in her arm. 'Terry, are you up here? Are you OK?'

She moved rapidly, darting across the landing. The room was in darkness, so Mary, suddenly fearful, groped round the doorframe and located the light switch.

Terry was lying on his side, blood running down his face. Surrounding his head and shoulders were the broken remnants of a large, ornate, heavy, and extremely expensive vase.

Fearful he had fallen, or worse still, suffered a stroke or heart attack, Mary reached down and touched his shoulder. 'Terry, speak to me, what happened?'

'Somebody was here. I saw them move, and they hit me.'

Mary glanced round. The room had been ransacked. Contents of the dressing table drawers and bedside cabinets were strewn in an untidy heap on the bed. 'Wait there

— don't try to move. I'm going to call an ambulance — and the police.'

Back in the hall, she realized the intruder might still be in the house. She cast a nervous glance up the staircase, before moving so her back was against the wall, and picked up the phone. Seconds later, she told the operator what had happened, slammed the receiver down and dashed back to the bedroom.

Mary knelt alongside Terry, applying pressure to his wound with a hand towel she'd retrieved from the en-suite bathroom. 'Police and paramedics are on their way,' she reassured him. 'You haven't to move, and we have to wait in this room until they've checked the house over.'

After what seemed an age, they heard the sound of approaching sirens. The wail died away, and moments later, a voice called out, the tone loud and authoritative, 'Mr and Mrs Firth, it's the police. The house is safe. We're coming up.'

Having been checked over by paramedics, who seemed satisfied that it was purely a superficial wound, and that Terry didn't need to go to hospital, the couple waited, expecting the police to begin questioning them. They had moved to the sitting room, where one of the uniformed officers told them a detective had been summoned, and they should wait until that officer arrived. 'In the meantime, would you like me to make you a nice cup of tea?'

'Oh, we've just driven home from Scotland. We didn't think to buy any milk.'

'Let's see what I can organize.' He walked outside and used his radio to contact the control room and asked if they'd spoken to someone from CID yet.

'I was about to ring DC Andrews.'

'Ask her to bring a pint of milk with her if she can, will you? Mr and Mrs Firth are in shock, and there isn't a drop in the house, I can't even make them a cuppa.'

* * *

At some point in the early hours, Alan Marshall had rolled onto his back and was snoring loudly. His long-term partner, Lisa Andrews, had dug him in the ribs several times with increasing ferocity, but to no avail. When the phone rang, Lisa answered it immediately. Seconds later, Marshall blinked sleepily as the bedroom light went on. 'What's happening?' he mumbled.

'I've got a call-out.'

'Oh, OK. Er, take care. See you in the morning.'

'Yes, and with a bit of luck, by the time I return you'll have ceased your Saddleback pig impersonation.'

'What?'

'You've been snoring like a pig for the past hour and a half.'

'Oh, er, hmmm . . .' With that, he continued to snore.

Lisa went into the kitchen and made a fuss of Nell, their black Labrador, and collected a carton of milk from the fridge. She was unlocking her car when she remembered her conversation with Nash and the team, about how the burglar knew his targeted houses would be empty. Could it be that the local milkman was supplementing his regular income? Milk deliveries take place during the hours of darkness. An extra visit on his regular round would be an ideal opportunity. More to the point, the presence of a milk float would be unlikely to arouse suspicion. Lisa smiled at the thought of the question she would ask the couple who had been robbed. It was certainly not one they would be expecting.

Having handed the milk to her uniformed colleague and instructed him how she liked her tea, Lisa began chatting to Mr and Mrs Firth. Her interview with them provided little information she didn't already know.

'It was dark inside the bedroom. The landing light was on, but all I saw was a blur of movement as I was reaching for the light switch,' Terry told her. 'Then it all went dark,' he added with a wry smile.

'I don't suppose you've had chance to see what the burglar took, have you?'

'No, but with a bit of luck it won't be much, because I disturbed him. Sadly though, I think that vase he broke over my head will be well-nigh impossible to replace now that Woolworth's has closed down.'

Mary was secretly delighted. If Terry's sense of humour was returning, everything was going to be OK.

'When you've had chance to look through the house, can you compile a list of what you think is missing, and bring it into Netherdale police station? We'll need an official statement from you anyway, so perhaps we can combine the two and save duplicate visits.'

At this point, Lisa was interrupted by the constable, who entered bearing a tray with mugs of tea on it.

'Where did you get the milk?' Mary asked.

'Actually, I brought it, at the request of these guys.' Lisa gestured towards the officer, adding, 'They can't survive for long without tea — or beer.' She paused before saying, 'I'll leave the rest for you, then you have some for later. Will you be able to get to the shops to replenish?' She indicated Mary's sling, and the dressing on Terry's head.

'We'll be OK, we have milk delivered,' Terry said. 'I'll ring the milkman and let him know we're back.'

Lisa had disguised the reason for her question well enough for Terry and Mary not to catch on.

Mary added, 'Yes, we get milk every other day. It comes from Helm Dairies. We like to support local businesses where we can. Our regular delivery man retired last year, but the young man who replaced him is just as reliable.'

Lisa made a note on her pocketbook, before asking, 'Apart from the milkman, who else knew you were going to be away?'

The couple thought for a moment before Terry replied. 'The newsagent certainly, because we cancelled the papers, so I suppose that includes the paperboy. We also told our regular postman.'

'Anyone else?'

'I don't think so,' Terry was in the middle of saying when Mary interrupted him.

'Yes, there was one other person. I told the chap from Good Buys supermarket. We use their delivery service. The one they advertise as "Good Delivery from Good Buys". He knew, because I told him why our last order was so much smaller than the previous ones.'

'What Mary means is, we only ordered half the usual number of bottles of her favourite wine.'

Yes, Terry's sense of humour had definitely returned.

* * *

Lisa was in Helmsdale CID suite early the following morning, and by the time the rest of the team arrived, she had compiled her report. She called Nash over to her desk as soon as he walked through the door. 'There was another burglary in Netherdale last night, but this time the householders returned from holiday unexpectedly, and disturbed the intruder.'

She described the incident as Nash scanned her account, noting she had asked them who was aware of their absence. 'Have you checked with the other people who were burgled to see if there's a common factor?'

'Not yet, Mike. I thought it was a bit too soon to be disturbing them. That's going to be my next job.'

Later that morning, she reported her findings. 'I've only managed to raise one of the other victims so far. I think we can rule out the potential suspects I gleaned from last night's event. The couple who live in Kirk Bolton Lane don't use Good Buys home delivery service, they don't have a daily paper delivered, and they buy their milk when they visit the supermarket.'

'They were the couple who had been away on a cruise, weren't they?'

'That's right, and what they told me seems to rule out the common-factor theory, which brings us to another dead end.'

'Just to be on the safe side, I think you should check with the people from Daleside Avenue who were burgled. There might be something we've missed.'

Two hours later, Lisa was able to update the team. 'The Daleside Avenue victims get their milk delivered, and they also take a daily newspaper, but from a different shop. Both were cancelled while they were away. However, they don't use Good Buys home delivery, which rules them out, I think. I also checked with the Royal Mail, but hit another dead end, because all three properties are on different rounds, so we can rule out a purloining postman.' She shook her head and sighed.

* * *

Over the weekend, it was Clara's turn to be on call. Her husband, David Sutton, was preparing their evening meal, when her mobile rang. She grimaced, knowing the call would probably disrupt their evening, and reached for her pen and pad. David, who was watching from the kitchen, automatically turned the pans on the hob down to simmer.

Clara tore her note from the pad as she ended the call. 'Sorry, darling, duty calls. It's another of these wretched burglaries. Hopefully I won't be too late.'

'Not to worry, Clara — part and parcel of the job.'

'True, and unlike you, at least I don't get shot at. Well, not often, anyway.'

The last sound Clara heard as she closed the flat door was David's laughter.

There was little amusement on Monday morning, however, when she reported the incident to the team. 'This bloke's getting to be a bloody nuisance,' Pearce commented.

'What's the tale this time?' Nash asked.

'Pretty similar to the others. The couple live in Ryedale Crescent here in Helmsdale. It's a large, detached pre-war house. They'd been away on one of those luxury villa holidays in Tenerife. I've attached a list of stolen items to my report — and before you ask, they don't have milk or newspapers delivered, and they don't shop at Good Buys. They shop in-store at one of the national supermarkets.'

'I said we were back to square one, but this seems to me more like being behind the eight ball. Whoever this guy is, he's running rings around us. What annoys me is that his activities are distracting us from trying to investigate the far more serious crimes we have on our books.'

'I have news on that front, Mike,' Pearce told him, 'but I'm afraid it isn't good. I've trawled the database of missing persons and haven't come up with any reports of a man, woman and dog vanishing at the same time.'

'Luckily it's Monday morning, so the week can only improve from here.'

'I still can't fathom how he knows all these people will be on holiday,' Lisa commented. 'It's almost as if they've handed him their itinerary along with the instruction, "Please burgle the house between these two dates." It's got me baffled.'

'Join the club,' Pearce responded. 'There's absolutely no connection.'

'What you mean is there's no connection we can see at present,' Nash corrected him. 'That doesn't mean there isn't one. We just have to keep looking.'

* * *

The spate of break-ins, and the conundrum posed by the burglar's apparent inside knowledge of the householders' absence, was occupying the thoughts of the detectives to the exclusion of all other incidents. Elsewhere, the forensic team was nearing the end of their search of All Alone Cottage and its surrounds. Their work had been delayed several times by the need to attend the burglary crime scenes. It was only when the entire team resumed their examination of the property, after the latest incident, that one of their officers discovered an object that puzzled him briefly.

He had been given the final task of going through the bedrooms at the cottage. The beds had been stripped long ago, and retrieval of DNA would no longer be possible. Nevertheless, he removed the mattresses, turned them over, and inspected both sides. This diligence had its reward when he reached the single room. After lifting the mattress clear of the base, he noticed a small item on the floor, wedged against the back wall.

His view was partly obscured by the slats forming the bed base. He shifted the unit to one side and reached down. He stared in surprise at the object he had retrieved. Whatever he might have expected to recover from the house, he would never have guessed at anything like this.

Closer examination gave him a clue as to the age of the small, die-cast model toy in his hand. It was a miniature vehicle, part of a range much beloved by children fifty or so years earlier. The manufacturers had replicated the life-size version with great precision. The shape of the bodywork and the design of the radiator grille marked it out as being a faithful representation of a 1960s Dennis fire engine. Although the officer placed the toy in an evidence bag, he mentally discounted it as having any relevance to the case under investigation. Obviously, to his mind, the toy had been either misplaced or discarded by a child, many years before the tragic events that had brought them to this building.

It was Tuesday afternoon when their work was complete, and that meant it would be later in the week before they were in a position to submit their report to the detectives — not that they had anything significant to add to what was already known. Even that timescale was dependent on their not having further demands on their time, the team leader thought as he drove back to Netherdale. There were occasions, and this was one of them, when he wished he were part of a larger task force, such as those in cities like Leeds, Manchester, and Sheffield. However, as he glanced at the magnificent scenery visible from his car window, he changed his mind. Second thoughts are often the best.

CHAPTER EIGHT

Prior to Nash leaving home on Wednesday morning, Alondra asked him to inspect the sketches she had drawn of the view from Riven Scar. 'I used three different vantage points, and I'd like to know which you believe I should use to achieve the best painting,' she explained. 'I'm going back there this morning, and hopefully I'll be able to make a great deal of headway, as long as Madam there doesn't interrupt me too often to participate in her rabbit hunt, or to act as her ball thrower.'

Nash looked at the sketches, taking a few moments over each of them. 'They all look good to me, so why not paint each of them, making it a themed series? I think they'll look terrific as a set.'

'Is that your excuse for not making a decision?'

Nash realized that Alondra was teasing him. 'Not at all. I have reason enough to dislike that place, but I love everything you paint. Unfortunately, I don't have the imagination to envisage the end result from sketches.'

'Why do you dislike it? The scenery is magnificent.'

Nash explained, before asking, 'Would it help if I take the rabbit hunter with me today?'

'No, I enjoy her company, and despite what I said earlier, the break from painting seems to help my creativity.

When she allows me to return to the easel, I often get better ideas, having walked away for a while.'

'OK, I must be off.' He kissed her goodbye, and turned towards Teal, who was standing nearby, a hopeful expression on her face. Nash commanded the Labrador to take care of her mistress, and, after stroking the dog, left the house.

The weather forecast for that day was for sunny periods, interspersed with patchy clouds driven by a fresh north-westerly breeze. This made ideal conditions for Alondra's work. One of the bonuses of the North Yorkshire climate was the ever-changing light value. To capture this on canvas, something she had rarely encountered at her home in Spain, represented a new challenge for the artist, but it was one she enjoyed immensely. The end product pleased her, and judging by the sale of her latest works, pleased art lovers even more. As a test of her skill, it taxed her expertise and concentration to the limit, but the reward when she succeeded was immensely satisfying. With her expectations high, Alondra loaded her materials into her SUV and opened the tailgate. She had barely got it wide enough to accommodate the Labrador, when Teal's impatience got the better of her and she leaped into the rear compartment. Alondra stroked the dog, by now seated comfortably on her bed, as she chided her gently. 'One of these days you'll bump your head on the tailgate, you silly girl.'

Seconds later, she left Wintersett, en route for Riven Scar.

* * *

At approximately the same time as Nash pulled into the car park at Helmsdale police station, a few miles down the road, Gavin Mitchell was briefing his secretary. 'I'm in court until after lunch. I anticipate the cases I'm representing will be finished by mid-afternoon, no earlier. So, as I've no idea exactly when I'll be free, I'll go straight home from there. If there's a crisis, you can text me. Otherwise, it can wait until tomorrow.'

In Helmsdale, there was mild relief that the night had passed without further reports of burglaries. However, there was no euphoria at the lack of news. 'That might only mean the victims are still sunning themselves on the Costa del Fortune or admiring the views of Fool's Paradise,' Clara commented.

'That's what I admire about you, Clara, your uncanny ability to look on the bright side,' Nash responded. 'Anyway, I'm assuming there's nothing spectacular to report from overnight and it was a quiet shift?'

Clara looked up from her computer screen. 'There were a couple of punch-ups, but none of those involved was injured, neither did they want to press charges. The landlords of the pubs where the disorders occurred were just glad it wasn't worse.'

'That sounds typically dodgy to me. Where were these delightful taverns? Let me guess. Was it on Westlea estate, by any chance?' Lisa asked.

'Certainly not, Lisa. I'll have you know that the Westlea estate is a highly respectable neighbourhood nowadays. One of the pubs hosting a prize fight was in Netherdale town centre. The other venue for Saturday night fever was on the Carthill estate.'

'I might have known that if it hadn't happened on Westlea, it must have taken place on Carthill.'

'That might be true, Lisa, but only to an extent,' Nash pointed out. 'Cast your mind back over the years and think about all the serious crimes we've been called in to investigate. Of those, very few have either been committed on, or had their origins in, either of those social housing complexes. I believe their dubious local reputation is unfounded, or at best, a distortion of reality based partly on prejudice.'

As the others digested this comment, Clara retorted, 'That lecture on modern-day society values was delivered by Professor Nash.'

'Thank you for that summary, Clara. Have you anything further to contribute?'

'Not really.' She stared at the screen. 'Although there was one rather unusual domestic, but again, the victim refused to press charges.'

'Unusual? In what way?'

'The victim lives in Bishopton, a former amateur rugby league player. A prop forward, I'd guess, judging by his build. The report says he's about six feet three inches and built like a brick shithouse.'

Nash grinned at Clara. 'Who assaulted him, the Incredible Hulk?'

She laughed. 'No, his wife set about him, using their son's cricket bat as her weapon of choice. Apparently, she'd spotted him getting rather too friendly with one of the barmaids at their local pub.'

Nash asked, 'Why didn't our rugby player press charges?'

'I guess he thought it would damage his macho image. When the officers left, he'd promised not to go near that woman again, as long as his wife promised not to use him for batting practice.'

'If that's the worst outcome, I'd say we've got off extremely lightly. How long that will last is anybody's guess.'

* * *

That afternoon, Nash was in the middle of reading a report from a multi-force operation to crack a drugs network. He and the Helmsdale team had been instrumental in that nationwide inquiry, which made the outcome of special interest. He was so immersed in the report that the sound of sirens didn't penetrate for a couple of seconds, but when it did, he recognized the differing tones of several vehicles leaving the premises they shared with the other emergency services.

Nash glanced out of the window, in time to see an ambulance, a fire engine, and two police cars heading at speed down Helmsdale high street. This was such an unusual event that he picked the phone up to ask Steve Meadows what the panic was about. Clara walked into Nash's office in time to hear one side of their conversation.

'Where did you say, Steve?'

As Nash listened, Clara saw his expression change.

'Are you sure? Do you know what sort of vehicle it was? What colour?'

Nash slammed the phone down, muttered, 'Oh God, no, please, no, no, no.' He snatched up his mobile and pressed a short code.

Clara had never seen such a look on Mike's face. He was as white as a sheet, his expression haunted. She noticed the hand holding the phone was trembling.

'What's wrong, Mike?'

He looked up and Clara was shocked to see tears in his eyes. 'There's been an accident. Car went off the road beyond Cauldmoor, up on Riven Scar. Alondra was going there today.' Nash paused and gulped for breath. 'Steve said the vehicle is a maroon SUV — just like hers.'

The wait before the call was answered was only seconds, but it seemed like hours. Suddenly, Clara heard a voice, indistinct and shaky. Then Nash said, 'Alondra, are you OK? What happened?'

He listened, and although Clara couldn't make out what was being said, it was clear that Alondra sounded deeply distressed. 'Steady on, take a couple of long, deep breaths. Then start again. Most important, are you injured?'

Clara saw the stress begin to leave his face, and as the colour returned, he said, in a far calmer tone of voice, 'That's good, as long as you're not hurt. Wait there. I'll be with you as soon as possible.'

He ended the call and looked at Clara. 'Come on. It wasn't Alondra's car that went over the cliff, but it damned near hit her and Teal as it passed. Alondra's the only witness. She rang the accident in. She thinks the driver must be dead.'

By the time he'd told her, they'd reached the car park. Nash had ignored the puzzled stare of his colleagues, and waved Meadows aside as they dashed through the reception area.

They accelerated away, and Nash glanced sideways. Clara was on her mobile. 'I'm telling Steve where we're going, and why. I'll ask him to relay the message to Viv and Lisa.'

They drove up the narrow, twisting road that led past the twin lakes of Lamentation Tarn and Desolation Tarn. Clara shivered, an involuntary reaction to the evil they had discovered there years earlier. Although much had happened since then, the memory still haunted her. 'I hate this place,' she said.

'I know, Clara, I feel the same. I tried to persuade Alondra not to come up here, but she insisted. Perhaps she'll change her mind after today's events.'

When they approached the upper slopes of Riven Scar, the road was blocked by a patrol car. The constable manning the roadblock recognized Nash and Mironova, and moved to allow them through. Nash pulled to a halt behind Alondra's car. As they walked past, Clara noticed Teal was seated in the rear compartment. She thought the Labrador looked distressed, but wondered if that was her imagination working overtime.

Further along the road were several police cars, an ambulance, and a fire engine. There was considerable activity, principally from the fire officers, who were lowering one of their colleagues over the cliff edge. Nearby, the crash barrier had been ripped apart.

Clara followed Nash to the nearest police car. He stopped and yanked open the rear door. What followed was a terse, highly charged conversation. It began as Nash took Alondra's arm, and gently pulled her out of the car. She clung to him, as the other rear door opened and a uniformed officer emerged. Clara recognized him, and knew the man to be the inspector in charge of Traffic division based in Netherdale. Rumour was the man was both pompous and arrogant. Rumour soon became fact.

'Nash, what the hell are you doing here? This is an RTA, and I'm about to interview the only witness. I don't need you interfering. Clear off and leave this to the experts.'

'You're not talking to her now. You can interview her later, when she's got over the shock — if I allow it.'

'You have no authority here. Leave that woman alone and get out of my way. I don't need you sticking your nose in where it's not wanted. I cannot permit that woman to leave here until I've got her story.'

Nash ignored him. He turned Alondra away from the officer, put his arm supportively around her waist, and led her back towards her car. The traffic officer dashed round the police car and stopped in front of them. As she saw what he was doing, Clara came up on Alondra's other side and added her support.

'Nash, I demand you leave that woman here.'

Nash walked straight past the inspector. He ushered Alondra gently into the Honda's passenger seat, then handed his Range Rover keys to Clara. 'Take my car and follow us home, will you?'

The traffic officer positioned himself against the driver's door. Nash pushed him out of the way. 'That woman, as you persist in calling her, *is my wife*. I am taking her home. When she has recovered from the shock, I might be prepared to allow you to interview her, but not before. Now get out of my way!'

Clara waited until the Honda was heading away from the crash site. She glanced at the traffic officer and told him, 'You don't realize what a lucky escape you've just had. I reckon it was touch and go whether the fire brigade would have to rescue another body from over that cliff.'

Clara watched the man stalk angrily back towards his vehicle, then she gathered up Alondra's easel, handling the canvas with care, conscious that in parts the paint was still wet. She collected the other materials, together with Teal's lead, and placed them in the back of Nash's Range Rover, before setting off after the Honda.

* * *

When they reached Smelt Mill Cottage, Clara was intrigued by the actions of the Labrador. Teal circled Nash and

Alondra until they were inside the house. When they went through to the lounge, Alondra sat on the settee, and the dog immediately took up position alongside her. Teal leaned against Alondra's leg, her head on the knee of her mistress. Everything the dog had done was protective and comforting.

'Shall I make coffee?' Clara winced slightly as she asked the question, confidently expecting a sarcastic response. Nash merely looked up and said, 'Thanks, Clara, there should be some left in the machine from this morning. It'll just need popping into the microwave to reheat.'

Once Clara had supplied their drinks, Nash asked her to sit down.

Alondra began to tell her story, with Nash holding her hand and Teal mounting guard on the other side. 'I was concentrating on the sky, trying to get the cloud formation down on canvas. There was a stiff breeze, so if I hadn't captured it immediately the whole scene would have changed dramatically. I didn't see the car at first, because I was facing the opposite direction. I heard the sound of the engine, of course, but I didn't look up. It was only when the noise got really loud that it distracted me.'

'What happened next?'

'I looked round. That was when I saw the car hurtling towards me. It was travelling very fast, and it was only a few metres away. I thought it was going to hit us.' Alondra put one hand on Teal's head as she spoke. Clara could see tears rolling down her cheeks.

Nash put his arm around her shoulder. 'Take your time. If you don't feel up to it, we can leave it for now.'

Encouraged by support from both sides, Alondra sat up straighter, shook her head, and wiped her face with the back of her hand. 'No, I'd rather tell you now. I realized we weren't directly in the path of the car, then it was past us in a flash. It was going too fast with that big bend coming up.'

'Did you see the driver?'

'No, I couldn't . . . for one thing, it was gone too quickly . . . and it looked as if the driver's seat was empty. For a second, I thought it was a left-hand drive, but there was no one in that side either.'

'So you think there was nobody in the car?'

Alondra frowned, concentrating on the question. 'I did at first, definitely. But it changed course just before the bend. I suppose somebody must have been inside.'

'So you're telling us the car was occupied when it went over the cliff?'

'Definitely. It hit the barrier with an enormous bang, went bursting through, and plunged out of sight. There was a huge explosion, and I saw smoke and flames leaping into the sky. That was when I called the emergency services. I was in shock. I should have phoned you.'

'That's not important, Alondra. You did exactly the right thing. Getting the trained professionals there was the priority. I don't suppose you had chance to see what type of car it was? The report we got simply said it was a maroon SUV. That scared me to death. I was petrified it was your car.'

'No, I took great care driving, because of your warning. The car was the same shape as yours, I think.'

'One other question: did the driver attempt to slow down? If they'd put their brakes on, you'd have seen the lights at the back of the car.'

Alondra shook her head. 'No, Mike, the brake lights didn't come on.'

'OK, that's enough for now. I think you should go upstairs, have a lie down and rest.'

'No, I don't want to rest. When I'm upset I like to paint. That relaxes me better than anything. Oh, no! I left my easel and paints at Riven Scar.'

'It's OK, Alondra,' Clara reassured her. 'I collected everything, including Her Ladyship's lead, and stored them in the back of Mike's car.'

Alondra sighed with relief and thanked her.

'I ought to be going,' Clara told them, 'but I have no transport.'

'Take my car,' Nash replied. 'You can pick me up tomorrow morning.'

As he was speaking, his mobile rang. He glanced at the screen and held up a warning hand, signalling Clara not to leave. 'It's Ruth Edwards,' he explained. 'No doubt the chief's ringing about my spat with that dickhead from Traffic. This should be fun.'

Against all his expectations, the chief constable's attitude was supportive, and far from confrontational. 'Mike, I've just heard about the accident on Riven Scar. How's Alondra?'

'She's pretty shaken up, as you can imagine. However, she has managed to tell me what she saw and heard. Clara's here too, so she'll give details, if you prefer.'

'No, that's OK. I've just had that idiot from Traffic on the phone, whining about you. How that man ever made inspector, I'll never know. Anyway, I told him you did exactly the right thing. What did Alondra tell you? All I've heard so far is third-hand.'

Nash explained, keeping his voice calm and watching Alondra all the time. 'If she's correct,' he added, 'and I feel certain she is, this doesn't sound like an accident. The fact that the driver made no attempt to avert the crash suggests something suspicious, unless they'd suffered some sort of medical episode. I assume the driver didn't survive. Have you been able to identify him — or her — yet?'

Clara couldn't hear Ruth's reply, but saw Nash's eyes widen with surprise. 'That's extremely interesting,' he said.

Ending the call, Nash looked across the room, seemingly staring at Clara, but she realized his thoughts were elsewhere. After a few seconds' silence, he said, 'The car is a Range Rover Sport, only a year old, and the registered keeper is listed as Mitchell & Co., Solicitors.'

'Mitchell? Isn't that the firm Viv had so much trouble trying to get information from?'

'It is indeed. Now, that might be a coincidence, but I—'

'Don't believe in coincidences,' Clara and Alondra chorused.

They burst out laughing. The mood became serious once again when Nash added, 'The driver was pronounced dead at the scene, and hasn't yet been identified. I was convinced it had to be Gavin Mitchell, but that can't be so. The driver was a woman.'

Nash paused, and then continued, 'There could be many reasons for this crash, whether it was accidental or deliberate. By all accounts, Mitchell attracted a lot of enemies, so there could be a queue of people seeking retribution.' Nash shrugged. 'Alternatively, the target might have been the driver, not Mitchell, or then again it might simple be a DODI.'

'What is a DODI?' Alondra asked.

'It's slang used by traffic police. The acronym stands for Dead One Did It, and the more polite version is a SOFA. That is short for Single Occupant Fatal Accident, but it argues a vehicle fault, and I don't think a twelve-month-old Range Rover Sport is prone to such defects.'

'This is very speculative,' Clara suggested. 'I'd have it down as one of your wilder theories, but I know how often those are proved correct.'

'The beauty of this one is we have an impeccable witness, who relies purely on what she sees, rather than using her imagination. However, we'll have to wait until Forensics report their findings.' Nash smiled. 'Those guys are going to be able to retire soon, the amount of overtime we're paying them.'

'Right, I'll get on my way. Mike, do you want to collect Alondra's stuff from the Range Rover?'

Outside, she put her hand on Nash's arm, and warned him, 'Keep an eye on Alondra for a day or two. She seems OK at present, but you know as well as I do how delayed shock can cause problems later.'

CHAPTER NINE

The following morning, Nash phoned Clara and informed her he was taking the day off. 'I'll speak to the chief and make her aware. You can always get me on my mobile, if needs be. I've tried to insist Alondra takes it easy, but I might as well have saved my breath. Her idea of relaxation is to set up her easel in the room commandeered as Mrs Rembrandt's atelier, the conservatory. Anything I should know?'

'Yes, that traffic officer's been on the phone, jumping up and down, demanding to speak to you. He's insisting you make Alondra available so he can interview her. He was even talking about driving to your house. I said I'd get back to him, once I'd spoken to you. What do you want me tell him?'

'Tell him not to waste his petrol, because I'm not going to allow him across my threshold. Alondra will come into Helmsdale and give her statement to you, or Viv, or Lisa. You can also inform him that if he turns up on my doorstep, I'll set the dogs on him.'

'You only have one dog, and she's a softie,' Clara pointed out.

'I know that, and so do you — but he doesn't.'

Nash's conversation with Chief Constable Ruth Edwards provided only one relevant snippet of information about the

Riven Scar tragedy. 'Forensics is going over what's left of the Range Rover, but so far we've no indication of whether the vehicle, or the driver, was at fault. We're still awaiting the post-mortem findings, which might give us some clue.'

'Has the driver been identified?'

'She has. Her name is Petra Stevens, and she is, or rather was, a partner in Mitchell & Co. Officers have gone to their offices to inform Gavin Mitchell.'

'I spoke to Clara a couple of minutes ago, and she told me that guy from Traffic division is threatening to drive out here and force Alondra to give her statement to him. I warned Clara to tell him if he turns up on my doorstep, I'll set the dogs on him.'

Ruth chuckled. 'It's almost worth encouraging him, just to see that happen. OK, I'll tell him Alondra is out of bounds, and to stop bothering you.'

'One thing I can tell you, according to what Alondra said, the driver might have been unable to control the vehicle, because she said there was no attempt made to either steer round that bend, or to apply the brakes.'

'OK, I'll pass that on. You concentrate on taking care of your wife.'

With little to occupy his time when not keeping Alondra company, Nash picked up a recent copy of the *Netherdale Gazette* and began reading it. In the back of his mind, he was conscious of the team's total lack of progress in solving either the cottage murders or the burglary spree. It was as he was pondering the latter case that an advert in the paper caught his attention.

The company offering its services was a novelty these days, he thought, as most people tend to book their holidays online. HTS, whose acronym stood for Helmsdale Travel Services, was an exception in that although they had an online facility, they also had a high street presence, with branches in Helmsdale, Netherdale, and Bishopton. The advertisement claimed they offered a wide range of vacations, from package tours to what they claimed were 'luxury holidays for discerning traveller'. These included private villas, cruises to the Caribbean, the Mediterranean, and their most recent addition, a 'Greek Islands Odyssey: A Voyage of Discovery'.

Nash stopped reading, his thoughts on the content. What if there was a common denominator to all the robberies they had failed to identify? Could it be that the victims had all booked their holidays via HTS?

When he returned to work, Nash would make this potential lead his number-one priority. In the meantime, he must ensure that Alondra was OK. She might need companionship, or a coffee. The fact that he needed both was a secondary consideration — or so he told himself.

* * *

Jonas Turner, a sprightly OAP, was angry — extremely angry. He'd driven from his home in Wintersett, in the van he'd recently acquired, to his allotment on the outskirts of Helmsdale. Jonas had set off early, knowing he had a busy day ahead of him. Alongside him was his faithful companion, Pip, a venerable Jack Russell terrier. He intended to spend the morning working on his new season's crop of vegetables. Later that day, he planned to travel to his friend Mike Nash's house, to cut his large lawns and hoe the flower beds.

When he opened the allotment gate, Jonas expected to be greeted by his pet goose, but there was no sign of Esmeralda. Almost as distressing, the hut door was wide open, and he could see all his equipment had been stolen. His mower, strimmer, chainsaw, and hedge trimmer were all missing.

Pip gave a single bark that seemed to echo his master's distress. As Jonas let loose a stream of invective, Pip issued a further series of barks. Clearly, the dog was also swearing. Jonas checked the surrounding allotments, and each told a similar story. Thieves had broken into them all — plundering anything they considered might be of value. Only one hut door remained closed, and this intrigued Jonas enough to investigate. The result offered some relief, if only marginally.

He seized Pip, bundled the dog into the van and set off for the police station in Helmsdale town centre.

* * *

As the morning wore on, Nash became confident that Alondra had recovered from the traumatic event of the previous day. He glanced out of the window, and wondered how much longer he'd have to wait before putting the kettle on for Jonas Turner. The old man would be surprised to find him at home, he guessed, but that wouldn't prevent him from downing his second-favourite tipple. Alondra wandered through to the lounge, her devoted companion at her heels. Nash noticed she had removed her smock, a clear sign that work had been suspended, even if temporarily. 'I thought Jonas was here today?' she asked.

'He is, but he was going to the allotment first, so he won't get here until after lunch, when he's finished tickling his tomatoes, cuddling his cauliflowers, or patting his parsnips.'

Alondra chuckled. She liked the elderly gardener — his rustic courtesy charmed her. She was about to speak when Nash's mobile rang. He glanced at the screen. 'It's Clara,' he said.

However, he was wrong.

'Ayup, Mr Nash, ah've bin robbed. Buggers 'ave nicked all mi gear.'

Nash blinked with surprise. 'Jonas, is that you? What are you doing on Clara's phone?'

'She gev it mi. Ah'm in thy office. Sergeant Miniver telled mi to call ye. Ah kem in ter report a theft. Seems ah'm not t' only one — 'ang on, ah'll pass y'over.'

'Mike, all hell's breaking loose. So far we've had Jonas the gardener, Gareth Roberts from Wintersett Grange, Netherdale Parks and Gardens, Bishopton Bowls and Lawn Tennis Club, and Helmsdale Cricket Club, all reporting thefts. Everything from lawn tractors to chainsaws has been taken from their sheds or lockups. Not only them, but Jonas telled me . . . er . . . told me, every hut on the allotment has been burgled. The list of missing items goes on forever. Luckily, they didn't take Esmeralda.'

'Esmeralda, that's Jonas's pet goose, isn't it?'

'Yes, he found her safe and well, shut in one of the huts. Jonas thinks they were scared she would create enough noise to raise the alarm.'

'Hang on. Did you say one of the places targeted was Helmsdale Cricket Club?'

'Yes, their groundsman was on the phone a few minutes ago.'

'OK, here's what I want you to do.' Nash explained, and then added, 'By the sound of what they've taken, the thieves will have needed a large van to put the gear in. With a bit of luck, we might be able to solve this case quickly, which will make a refreshing change.'

An hour later, Clara rang back. 'You were dead right, Mike. I think you're about to be made an honorary life member of Helmsdale Horticultural Society, and several other local clubs. Uniform branch have just arrested the perpetrators. Better still, by what they've just told me, they've recovered all the stolen equipment. How did you know Helmsdale Cricket Club had CCTV, and one of the cameras covered the car park and tackle shed?'

'I took Daniel there last winter. They organize a junior indoor cricket league in the sports hall alongside the pavilion. Daniel was desperate to play. Unfortunately, he only managed a couple of weekends during the school break. Naturally, I stayed to watch. I actually saw them installing the CCTV system. Did you get a result from their camera footage?'

'We certainly did — big time. We got the van used by the thieves, including the registration number. Added to that, we've got the men, clearly identifiable, in the act of committing the robbery. We were able to trace the vehicle to an address in Netherdale. Uniform are currently taking the suspects back to the station there to complete the formalities.'

'That's excellent news.'

'How's Alondra?'

'I've never considered it before, but I reckon painting must be a great way to alleviate stress. It certainly works for her. She's feeling much better, so I'll be back at work tomorrow. Can you pick me up on your way in, please? You can update me then.'

'That's good news. I won't trouble you again today unless I have something momentous to report.'

* * *

As requested, Clara pulled up outside Smelt Mill Cottage in Nash's Range Rover, and relinquished the keys. 'I could get used to driving this. I suggested to David we should buy one.'

'And his reaction?'

'He didn't need to speak. His face said it all.'

Nash kissed Alondra goodbye, and gave strict instructions that should she have any problems, no matter how small, she was to phone him.

During the journey, Clara updated him about the gardening equipment thefts of the previous day. 'Steve Meadows sent his lads to the address DVLA supplied. They spoke to a woman, the common-law wife of the registered keeper. She told them her partner was at work at his warehouse. Apparently, he runs an online wholesale outfit selling second-hand agricultural and horticultural equipment.' Clara smiled before adding, 'I think that firm is about to cease trading. They arrested the owner, his brother, and one other man, who were in the act of unloading the stolen goods from a large van. They booked them and conducted the interviews at Netherdale. The van owner opted for "no comment" throughout, but his brother and the third man more than made up for it. Steve reported they'd told him "singing like canaries" would be a massive understatement.'

'That's an excellent result.'

'It is and it isn't. The rightful owners of the property were delighted. They were slightly less enthralled when they were told they couldn't have them back until they'd been catalogued and photographed for the prosecution. And we would also need proof of purchase wherever possible.'

'They should be grateful they don't have to fork out for replacements.' Seeing Clara wince, he apologized. 'Sorry, bad pun. Judging by what you told me yesterday, that could have cost them or their insurers thousands.'

'I tried telling them so, but the only one to accept it was Jonas.'

'That's because he still fancies you,' Nash teased her. 'You only have to look at him and he's putty in your hands.'

Clara blushed slightly, but smiled as she replied, 'He told me he had a spare fork and spade at home, and has enough work to keep him going at his allotment until he gets his mower back. Even so, he still can't get my name right.'

'I think that's a great result. Anything else to report — *Sergeant Miniver*?'

'Only that Forensics division are going wild about the mountain of work being thrust upon them. They'd only just begun examination of the vehicle from the Riven Scar incident, when they got dragged away to photograph that gardening equipment as evidence. Their team leader told me, thankfully, they've finished at All Alone Cottage. Anyway, more importantly, how's Alondra this morning?'

'Back to normal, as far as I can tell. She's staying at home working on the landscapes she started prior to the crash. She's got Teal for company, and she told me the two of them would be fine, and that I must go and do some work, rather than getting in the way at home.'

'She's doing wonders for you, Mike. Between them, Alondra and Teal have got you tamed. Nobody but Alondra could boss you about like that and get away with it.'

Nash smiled contentedly. 'I know that, and the weird part is I'm actually starting to enjoy being hen-pecked.'

* * *

When they arrived at the office, Nash remembered something from his day at home and told the team: 'I read an advert in the *Netherdale Gazette* yesterday, and it gave me an idea about those house burglaries.'

He explained about the travel company, adding, 'I'm not suggesting HTS supplied information about their clients' itineraries, but it might be worth checking if our victims booked their holidays via the same source. Alternatively, what we're looking for might not be one common denominator, but two. Perhaps whoever got called to each incident could follow up with the people concerned, maintaining the existing contact.'

He also added he would be leaving early that afternoon. 'I know Alondra said she was OK, but I'd rather play it safe.'

Clara brought him a coffee and reported that, so far, none of the team had been successful in raising the robbery victims. 'Keep on trying,' Nash told her.

Minutes later, Nash received a phone call from Jackie Fleming. 'I've just been talking to the head of our Forensics team,' the superintendent told him. 'Apart from whining about their workload, he told me they'd been able to rule out mechanical defects as a cause of the Riven Scar fatal accident.'

'If it wasn't a vehicle malfunction, what did happen?'

'I understand the driver was under the influence, and had passed out before the crash.'

'Drunk? In the middle of the afternoon? That doesn't seem like normal behaviour for a solicitor.'

'No, she wasn't drunk. Petra Stevens had ingested, intentionally or otherwise, a huge dose of extremely powerful sedatives and painkillers. I've got Professor Ramirez's post-mortem findings in front of me. In his opinion, the amount she had in her bloodstream was sufficient to have been fatal, even without the car going down that cliff. His actual phrase was, "The combination adds up to a lethal cocktail."'

'I guess that leaves only one outstanding question — did she fall or was she pushed?'

'I think we might be able to rule out suicide. Petra Stevens and Gavin Mitchell weren't just business partners, they were an item. When interviewed, Mitchell said Petra had been recovering at home, having suffered injuries during a skiing holiday at Easter, which was why she wasn't at the office. He also said Petra had dropped him off at Netherdale Crown Court, where he was to defend a client. From there, Petra went to her bank, then visited HTS and booked a holiday in Marbella for her and Gavin during September. That doesn't exactly seem like the action of someone suicidal, does it?'

Jackie paused while she read more of Mitchell's statement, then added, 'This is interesting, Mike. Mitchell said he'd arranged to phone Petra when the court session was over, so she could come and collect him. He said she sounded a bit odd when he spoke to her, almost as if she'd been drinking, but that couldn't be right because Petra Stevens was virtually a teetotaller.'

'All that seems to rule out suicide. So, unless Ms Stevens took the overdose accidentally, the only remaining alternative I can see is either the pharmacy made a huge blunder, or she was deliberately poisoned.'

'I agree, Mike, so I think we'll have to hand the inquiry over to you and your team. I'll bring the chief up to date and send you the file. Most of it's available online. Good luck with it.'

* * *

Nash studied all he could and sat thinking, before returning to the general office. But before he could speak, Lisa said, despairingly, 'I'm not surprised these people were so easy to rob. The first people who were burgled are now in London visiting relatives, and have decided to take in some visits to art galleries and a couple of West End shows. The other couple are at a race meeting in Newmarket until Friday.'

The others reported similarly, with visits to a test match and a tour round Castle Howard explaining their absences.

Once they had been tracked down, the replies to the key question were disappointingly mixed. Although three couples confirmed that they had booked their vacations via HTS, two out of three didn't have their milk delivered via Helm Dairies. Of the others, although they did have their milk delivered, they didn't have the same roundsman and they did not use HTS to book their holidays.

'Well, keep trying, but now we've got a tough assignment ahead,' Nash shook his head. 'I'm sorry, but depending how things progress, it may mean no weekends off. Although I had all next week booked off, I'll only take Monday, as we've got too much on our plate. I'm collecting Daniel tomorrow — I can't expect him to walk home from boarding school for the summer holidays. He'll be fine at home with Alondra. Besides, we're taking him to stay with his aunt in France soon.'

They all nodded their acceptance of the situation, as he then explained what Jackie had told him, and the interpretation derived from the post-mortem.

'Our first task is to visit Gavin Mitchell and question him about Petra Stevens. Clara, that's you and me. We'll also need his cooperation in order to collect the medication she was taking. In light of the post-mortem findings, it's imperative we send them to the laboratory for testing.'

'Are you convinced it wasn't self-inflicted, Mike?'

Nash looked surprised by Pearce's question. 'I don't think for one minute she took the overdose deliberately. Is she *had* wanted to commit suicide, she could simply have remained at home and waited for the drugs to take effect. She certainly wouldn't have taken her car out and driven along a notoriously dangerous stretch of road. Regardless of what actually happened, there was the possibility of her being involved in an RTA and getting carted off to hospital, where they would have found the drugs in her system and taken remedial measures.'

'Apart from that,' Clara added, 'booking an expensive holiday in Marbella on the morning of her death isn't exactly the action of someone who has decided to end it all. Added to which, she didn't leave a note. I know that people taking their own lives don't always leave suicide notes, but if we string all the evidence together I think Mike's quite right, and Ms Stevens' death was not of her own volition.'

Pearce was silent, reflecting on the overwhelming evidence put forward by his colleagues.

'What we need to determine,' Nash told them, 'is how that medication, which Mexican Pete referred to as "a lethal cocktail", came to be in her body — whether it was simply a terrible accident, or something more malicious.'

He turned to Clara. 'Will you phone Gavin Mitchell's secretary and find out if he's at work? We need to interview him and get hold of that medication ASAP.'

'What do you want us to do, Mike?' Viv asked.

'We need to gather all the information we can about Petra Stevens, including her background, family, education, everything we can glean. That's down to you, Viv. Unfortunately, computers can't answer all our questions, which is where you come in, Lisa. I need you to go to Netherdale Crown Court, ask about Petra Stevens *and* Gavin Mitchell. Then I want you to approach anyone who might have had business dealings with Mitchell & Co. You'll need to be discreet. I'm talking other law practices, plus accountants, estate agents, and so forth. Literally, anyone you can think of.'

He turned back to Pearce. 'I want you to do the same checks on Gavin Mitchell as you're doing for Petra Stevens — and include Mitchell & Co. as well,' he added as an afterthought.

CHAPTER TEN

Nash and Mironova were en route to Mitchell's house on the outskirts of Bishop's Cross. As they travelled, Clara reported on her conversation with Mitchell's secretary. 'Apparently, Mitchell's so distressed by Ms Stevens' death that he hasn't been into the office since it happened. She called me back after she'd spoken to him. He was extremely reluctant to allow our visit, but in the end she managed to persuade him.'

'What's happening to all the legal work?'

'The firm's junior partner is trying to handle it all. And she's tearing her hair out because she's attempted to consult Mitchell several times, but he's just hung up on her.'

'That doesn't sound good.'

'I agree, and it raises an interesting point. I wondered if you were going to use this interview to bring up the topic of All Alone Cottage, and the owners of the property. I know you were intending to speak with him, especially after the second skeleton was discovered.'

'I was pondering the idea, but in light of what the secretary told you, I think it might be inappropriate to stray from the main topic of the interview. I'll make a decision when we're face to face.'

Their meeting turned out to be every bit as difficult as they'd anticipated. The first indication of Mitchell's state of mind came from his appearance. He was unshaven, his hair tousled, his eyes reddened, and as he stepped aside to allow them to enter the house, Clara caught the unmistakeable smell of body odour combined with stale whisky.

These obvious signs of his lack of care extended to his reaction when Nash asked if he would allow them to take Ms Stevens' medication away with them.

'What for?' Mitchell asked, his tone lacklustre.

'The post-mortem indicates that Ms Stevens had ingested a lethal dose of painkillers and sedatives. We don't believe she did this intentionally, so we must have the medicines laboratory tested, to discover if the dispensary made a fatal error. There could be serious legal consequences if that turns out to be so.'

'What good will that do? It won't bring Petra back.' Even the mention of Petra's name caused Mitchell such distress that his eyes filled with tears.

Clara, who had been watching the solicitor, turned her head away to avoid embarrassing him. She wondered if they would be able to persuade him to cooperate, but the man's mood changed abruptly after Nash's follow-up question. 'Do you know of anyone who might have wished to harm Ms Stevens? Someone she might have crossed swords with at work, perhaps, or who had threatened her?'

Mitchell's head came up, and he stared at the detectives in astonished disbelief. It was a moment before he gathered his wits sufficiently to respond. 'Is that what you believe? Do you think Petra was murdered?'

'It is a possibility. But without background information, we can't say for certain. There are many factors to be considered before we can make a judgement. Put it this way — we can't rule out foul play at this early stage.'

There was a long pause before Mitchell replied, 'I can't think of anyone who would want to harm Petra. She dealt mostly with the property side of the practice — tenancy agreements and conveyances, that sort of stuff.'

'Let's look at it from another angle. In your profession, you become the repository of many secrets — things that your clientele would definitely not want to become public knowledge. Is there any chance that Ms Stevens was in possession of something, perhaps information she learned accidentally, that others might consider dangerous?'

There was a much longer silence, before Mitchell answered, 'I don't know of anything like that.'

The possibility of foul play had changed Mitchell's attitude sufficiently for him to allow the detectives to collect all the medication they could find.

As they drove away, Clara returned to the topic of Nash's final question of the solicitor. 'I think Mitchell was lying,' she suggested. 'When you asked him about dangerous information, he took a long time to answer — too long in my opinion. And when he did, he looked away, avoiding eye contact so you couldn't see his expression.'

'Yes, I noticed that and reached the same conclusion. However, without knowing the information he refused to reveal, we're no further forward. We'll have to await the lab result on the medication, then we might be in a position to apply more pressure.'

'What's our next move?'

'I suggest we call in at HQ and drop these tablets off with Tom Pratt, providing he isn't still busy digging up the golf course. He can get them to the lab and ask for a rush job. At the same time we can update Jackie. Then we can go back and see what Viv and Lisa have unearthed.'

As they were leaving the headquarters building, the forensic team leader hailed Nash. 'I've emailed our report about All Alone Cottage through to you.'

'Is there anything spectacular to add to our meagre store of knowledge about the crime scene?'

'Not really, certainly nothing worth calling the fire brigade about.'

Nash frowned, baffled by this strange remark. 'What does that mean?'

'Oh sorry, I thought you knew. One of my team found a toy fire engine in a corner of the small bedroom. He dated it to the 1960s because of the shape, so I guess it's way before the time you're interested in.'

* * *

On the drive back to Helmsdale, Clara asked, 'Have you anything special planned for Daniel over the school holidays?'

'Other than his annual visit to France, nothing special, other than on Monday. I'm taking him to Scarborough for a day. Yorkshire's playing a limited-over match, and you know how dead keen Daniel is on cricket. He doesn't know yet. Let's just hope the weather is in our favour.'

'I remember the day I met Daniel's aunt Mirabelle when she brought him to England. And Daniel, he looked so small and unsure of what was happening.' She laughed at the memory. 'You were in a state of shock.'

'Yes, it's not every day you find out you have a six-year-old son.'

Daniel was born in France, from an earlier relationship. His mother, Monique, had returned to her family home, unable to remain in England, which held many sad memories. She was ill, and before she died, Mirabelle, her aunt, helped to raise Daniel, fulfilling her promise by taking him to his father. Daniel knew everything about Nash, as told to him by his mother. Nash did not know of his existence.

'I never thought you'd marry, either.' Clara laughed again. 'The Great Lothario!'

Nash pulled the car to a halt in the car park. 'OK, *Mrs Sutton*. Get out of the car, and for that remark, you can get me a coffee.'

Having given Viv and Lisa a brief account of their discussion with the solicitor, Nash and Clara listened to what their colleagues had discovered. Viv began with his précis of the internet research he'd carried out.

'Petra Stevens was born and brought up in Keighley, West Yorkshire. Her father was a solicitor with a practice in Bradford, with branches in Keighley and Skipton. Her mother was a librarian. They died several years ago. Petra was educated at Keighley Grammar School, and went on to study law at Leeds University. She has no siblings.

'Similarly, Gavin Mitchell is the third generation of his family to practice in Netherdale. His parents are both dead, and he is also an only child. He was educated at Netherdale Grammar School, and went to Leeds University, which I assume is where he met Ms Stevens. Although there is nothing on the PNC about either of them, not even a speeding ticket, I did find a couple of CCJs registered against Gavin Mitchell four years ago.'

'County court judgements? That doesn't sound good. I thought all lawyers were rolling in money.'

'They were settled immediately, and in full. They will vanish from his record in eighteen months or so, when the six-year period is up.' Pearce looked up from his notes and nodded to Lisa, who took up the tale.

'I asked around, and what I was told more or less bears out what Viv has just said. Mitchell & Co. has a good reputation, apparently, although one of the lawyers I spoke to was a little reluctant to pass on an opinion. When I pressed him, he commented that around the time of those CCJs being handed down, he'd experienced a great deal of difficulty obtaining money from Mitchell & Co. in settlement of a civil suit for his client — even though the amount involved was relatively small.

'Apart from that, the people I spoke to about Ms Stevens were all happy to confirm that she was well thought of. I got that opinion from three estate agents and a couple of fellow solicitors. Apparently, Ms Stevens concentrated on property transactions, plus matters of probate settlements. She did little other civil work, and didn't handle any criminal cases whatsoever.'

'OK, thanks to both of you for that. We'll now have to sit back and await the lab results. Just keep digging for anything related to either case we have on. So much for my early finish — get yourselves off home. Who's on call?'

'That will be me,' Viv said.

'OK, let's all take this as a normal weekend, unless anything else breaks. I'll see you on Tuesday.'

* * *

On Saturday morning, Nash and Alondra set off for Harrogate, accompanied by Teal, in her usual place in the luggage compartment of the Range Rover. As they approached their destination, Nash glanced in the rear-view mirror and then nudged Alondra. 'Take a look at Madam. She's been fast asleep throughout the journey, but not so now.'

Alondra glanced back. The Labrador was standing up, her nose pressed close to the window, tail wagging furiously. Alondra reached the obvious conclusion. 'She knows where we're going — and why. She's excited because she'll be seeing you-know-who, soon.' Alondra was careful not to get the dog even more agitated by mentioning Daniel's name.

'Absolutely correct, but don't ask me to explain how she knows all that.' Nash grinned. 'One thing for certain, he won't need to wash the back of his neck tomorrow. She'll do it for him on the way home.'

'I'm still amazed how well behaved Teal is. I've noticed a lot of people who own dogs, particularly big ones, have to put a grille across the back seat to keep their animals from jumping over it, but she's never even tried to do that.'

'That's because she's a Labrador, and is quite content on the comfortable dog bed provided for her. I reckon she thinks of the luggage compartment as her kennel.'

They arrived at the school and Nash opened the tailgate, commanding Teal to 'stay'. Within seconds, Nash was grabbed around his waist in a hug before Daniel hugged Alondra, then jumped into the boot, sitting alongside the dog and cuddling her. He grinned at Alondra. 'I'm packed and ready,' he said. 'I've said my goodbyes, can we get going, Pa?'

Nash stared at his son. 'Pa? Where did that come from?'

'Oh, come off it, Pa. Do you really want me to call you Papa forever? I am twelve, you know.'

Nash looked at Alondra, who was trying to keep her face straight. She shook her head. 'He's your son.'

Having loaded the luggage, they set off. They had passed through Helmsdale and were en route for Wintersett, when a confluence of events occurred that would later cast doubt on Nash's disbelief in coincidence. He was reflecting on how enjoyable the next few days would be, with what he now classed as his family unit together.

He glanced at Alondra alongside him, before looking in the rear-view mirror, where he could see Daniel stroking Teal. As he looked, Nash's attention was drawn to a rapidly approaching emergency vehicle, its lights flashing and sirens blaring. He pulled off the carriageway to allow the vehicle to pass. As the fire engine raced past, the driver gave a single toot on his horn to acknowledge the courtesy. Nash smiled and glanced at the signpost on the side road he was using as a lay-by. The lane led to Drover's Halt, but it was much later that he made the connection— and even then, he was reluctant to entertain the wild idea.

* * *

The house, on the outskirts of Gorton, was at the upper end of the village. It was a large, detached property, set in its own grounds. A further measure of the owners' affluence came via the two expensive German motor cars parked side by side in the double garage.

Although the owners were sunning themselves on a beach in Hawaii, the building was not unoccupied. The person inside, albeit a strictly unofficial visitor, had gained entry via his usual method, a brick applied with force to a pane of glass on the back door.

The intruder had already rifled the double bedroom he guessed to be the master, and had turned his attention on the expansive dressing room. He wasn't sure he would discover anything worthwhile concealed in there, but it would be slapdash for him to leave without searching every possible hiding place.

He was in no hurry. He knew the official residents weren't scheduled to return from their vacation for at least another fortnight. He had almost completed his search when he reached the farthest end of the wardrobe that covered the whole of one wall. The last door resisted his attempt to open it. Using the torch facility on his mobile phone, he identified the problem. Unlike the others, this section was locked. That seemed promising. He argued there was no reason to lock a door unless there was something inside worth stealing.

Abandoning any attempt at subtlety, the burglar took out the multitool he invariably carried, and prised the lock open. The door slid back, and he stared in astonishment at the garments hanging in the open space above the drawers.

'Well, well, well,' he muttered. 'You naughty boy and girl.'

The wardrobe contained clothing, certainly, but it was of a type he would never have associated with the apparently respectable couple who owned the house. The garments were of a specific nature, used primarily for a variety of sexual acts that achieved gratification with the assistance of bondage and similar sadomasochistic behaviour. The leather costumes, masks, hoods, whips, and dildos were unmistakeable indications of perverted activity. Once he'd recovered from the shock, the intruder wondered what else he might discover.

Switching his attention to the drawers, the burglar's efforts were soon rewarded. He moved a pile of socks to one side, and as he did so, noticed something below that definitely didn't belong among the hosiery. He removed the set of photos and immediately recognized the householders from the snapshots he had seen in other parts of the house. None of those images, however, were anywhere near as explicit as these.

Among several striking poses of them wearing bondage clothing was one of the man of the house, clad in his High Court judge's wig and gown — and nothing else. The next, equally revealing shot was of the lady of the house. She was also dressed legally, in her barrister's wig and gown. What she was doing as she knelt on the bed in front of her husband, however, was definitely not part of court procedure.

The intruder removed his mobile from his pocket and took shots of the photos, plus some of the bondage clothing from the space above the drawers. As he moved one of the costumes aside to get a better viewpoint, he noticed something tucked at the back of the unit. He reached inside and removed a camera case, leaving the adjacent tripod *in situ*. Inside the case was a very high-tech digital camera. He switched the device on and began flicking through the photo gallery, before watching the videos also recorded there.

What he'd seen earlier was mild, compared to the activities revealed by the stills and the movies. Obviously the couple had mounted the camera on its tripod, and then used the remote control facility to record their wilder intimate moments — or, as he thought with a grin, hours. That had no doubt been achieved with the help of the blue pills he'd also discovered in the sock drawer.

The burglar removed the memory card from the camera and placed it in one of his pockets, securing it with the zip, returning the camera and case to its rightful position. He then sent the images of the snapshots he'd taken earlier via SMS to his colleague, along with the message, 'Check these out and I'll phone you.'

'What do you think of those?' he asked, minutes later.

'Those are the people who live there, aren't they? The judge and the barrister, right?'

'They certainly are. I'm going to make copies of those images, and when they return from Hawaii I'll send them to the owners, along with a request for contributions towards our pension fund.'

'You mean you're going to blackmail them? Won't that be dangerous, particularly with what they do for a living?'

'I think that's all the more reason for them to keep quiet and pay up, don't you?'

'They might claim these photos were only posed for a bit of fun.'

'That's true, but the photos and videos on the memory card I've just taken from their camera will be a lot more difficult to explain. And if you think what you've just seen is hot stuff, the content of those videos is dynamite and Semtex combined. Put it another way, there are six videos, and if I posted just a clip from any of them online, it would go viral immediately.'

CHAPTER ELEVEN

When Nash arrived at Helmsdale later than usual on Tuesday, he hadn't chance to reach his office when the message given him by Sergeant Meadows signalled the end of his weekend off, in no uncertain manner.

'I know you're looking into Gavin Mitchell,' Meadows began, 'so I thought you should be aware that we've received a request for a welfare check to be carried out. His secretary rang Netherdale control after she tried to contact him before she set off for work this morning. Says she's been trying to reach Mitchell over the weekend to see if he's OK, but without success. He hasn't answered her phone calls, or replied to texts and emails. She even sent their intern to the house yesterday, but he couldn't get any response.'

'That doesn't sound good. Let me know what they find, will you?'

When he entered his office, Nash glanced at his desk and was relieved to see there were only two folders on it. On top of them was an email Clara had printed off, with the annotation, 'Mike, check the details below.'

The email contained the results of the lab tests carried out on Petra Stevens' medication. The items Clara had highlighted were the dosages of the painkillers and sedatives. The variance between the strength shown on the labels attached to the bottles and the contents of the capsules within was stark.

The medication prescribed by Ms Stevens' GP had been switched for tablets of a much greater strength, which confirmed the post-mortem findings. The problem still remained, however, as to who had substituted them, and why.

He had barely finished reading the message when Mironova walked in. He was about to tell her about the welfare check when his phone rang. 'Yes, Steve, what now?'

'Our guys went to Mitchell's house, but there was nobody inside.'

'Did they have to use the big red key?'

'No, the front door was unlocked.'

'OK, Clara and I will head straight there.'

* * *

At approximately the same time as Nash and Mironova were pulling out of the car park in Helmsdale, the maintenance crew, assigned the task of repairing the crash barrier on Riven Scar, arrived at the scene.

'Oh no, that's bloody marvellous,' the foreman muttered. He reached for his mobile and phoned their depot in Netherdale. When the manager answered, the foreman told him, 'We've got to Riven Scar but we can't start work.'

'Why not?'

'Because some pillock, with more money than sense, has only gone and parked a whacking great Porsche Carrera right across the stretch of broken fencing. No way can we start flinging lengths of metal around without risking damaging their precious paintwork — unless you're happy to foot the bill for a respray, that is.'

The foreman grinned at the invective coming down the phone, and when the manager had run out of steam, asked, 'So what do you want us to do? Sit here supping tea until the owner turns up?'

'Give me the reg number and I'll try and raise someone to get it shifted. Wait there until I call back.'

'Don't worry. I hadn't anything else planned for this morning.'

The foreman smiled again at the manager's valedictory message. The word was definitely not goodbye.

* * *

Nash and Mironova were almost halfway to Bishop's Cross when his mobile rang. He signalled to Clara to intercept the call. She listened, before switching it to speakerphone. 'It's Steve,' she explained.

'We've just taken a call from Netherdale Highways Department. They sent a crew to repair the fence on Riven Scar, but they couldn't start work because there was a Porsche obstructing the broken section. They asked us to check the number on the plate — the registered keeper is Gavin Mitchell.'

'OK, Steve, we'll divert to Riven Scar. Ask the officers at Mitchell's house to wait there until we arrive. You might also alert our neighbours, we might need paramedics and a fire crew on standby. Given what our men found at the house, this is starting to sound very ominous.'

They turned off the main road onto the lane leading to Cauldmoor and again Clara shivered superstitiously. 'Do you think a particular area attracts evil?' she asked. 'There has been so much tragedy round here, so much misery and unhappiness, and now these new problems.'

'A jinx, is that what you mean? I'm not sure the area has anything to do with it, more likely it's the evil that people bring to it.'

'As far as Cauldmoor is concerned, I'd be happy if I never had to pass this way again. We both have more than enough reason to want to forget what happened here.'

They reached Riven Scar, the site of Petra Stevens' fatal accident, and pulled to a halt behind the maintenance crew's pickup truck. The three-man team was sitting in the cab drinking tea.

'Have you taken a look round?' Nash asked the foreman.

'No, we're awaiting instructions from base.'

As they were speaking, Clara walked across to the Porsche. 'Mike, the keys are still in the ignition.'

Nash strode across, but before he reached the car, Clara had moved to peer over the edge of the precipice. 'You'd better phone Steve back and ask him to despatch the other services, ASAP.'

Nash joined her and stared down the near-vertical drop. At the foot of the cliff they could see the prostrate form of a body, undoubtedly human.

After calling Meadows, Nash rang Netherdale and told Jackie Fleming what had happened. 'Officers went to Mitchell's house to carry out a welfare check. The house was unlocked, and they found what appears to be a suicide note on the desk in his study. Then his car was discovered at Riven Scar. There's a body at the foot of the cliff, just where his partner, Ms Stevens, died. I think we can assume Mitchell fell to his death here.'

'You reckon he threw himself off?'

'Certainly looks that way. We'll have to wait and see. Now his lover's death's beginning to look like murder, it would be natural to assume Mitchell killed her, and was overcome by remorse, but I have my reservations.'

'Why might that be? Is there a solid foundation for thinking that way, or is it more of the famous Nash intuition working overtime?'

'A bit of both, maybe. Petra Stevens was fed a lethal cocktail of painkillers and sedatives. The dosage was far stronger than the one prescribed by her doctor, which leaves one huge unanswered question.'

'And that question is?'

'How would a solicitor, with no known connection to health professionals, manage to acquire those drugs? They're certainly not available over the counter, and I very much doubt if they can be bought over the internet, or on a street corner.'

'Yes, I take your point. Well, keep me in the picture.'

After Nash ended the call, Clara asked him, 'You told Steve Meadows to instruct our men to treat Mitchell's house as a crime scene. Is that because you believe he was murdered?'

'Suicide or murder, it's still a suspicious death. Suicide might no longer be classified as a crime under English law, but there is always the possibility that he was assisted, and that is an illegal act. On the other hand, if it isn't suicide, then the house is definitely a crime scene. I think we should keep an open mind, despite the suicide note.'

* * *

Meadows had despatched more officers and Nash instructed them to liaise with the other emergency services and report developments. He and Mironova continued their interrupted journey to Mitchell's house.

Their first priority was to examine the suicide note. As he entered the large study, Nash inspected the room. Everything appeared normal. There were two desks, each bearing a laptop, plus a filing cabinet and a separate table with a printer on it.

As they looked at the typewritten note, Clara asked, 'What do you make of it? The wording seems a little odd to me.'

Nash picked up the single sheet of A4 paper with his gloved hand. Before placing it in an evidence bag, he read the content aloud.

'*I cannot continue. I am unable to live with what I have done. I now admit that I caused Petra's death. My mistake has cost me the one thing in life I treasured. I am sorry. Gavin Mitchell.* I'm far from convinced by it. As you said, the phrasing is strange. He doesn't say he killed Petra — merely that he caused her death by his misconduct, which is a totally different thing. Given his state of mind when we met him, I find it curious this note has been typed and printed off, rather than being handwritten. Even the signature is typed, which again, I find rather suspicious.'

Nash paused and then said, as if thinking aloud, 'Why was it printed off?'

Clara frowned. 'I don't follow you. Mind you, that's difficult at times when you go wandering off picking up ideas.'

'I wondered why Mitchell bothered to print the note off. Why not write it by hand, or simply leave it on his laptop screen? The computer's connected to the mains, so he couldn't have been worried about the battery dying.' Nash paused before adding, 'Unless, of course, the note wasn't typed on one of these laptops in the first place.'

'Where else would Mitchell have typed it?'

'That's the point. I'm beginning to wonder if Mitchell typed this note at all — or whether he'd seen it, or knew of its existence, before he died.'

'You're not convinced Mitchell committed suicide, then? You think he was murdered?'

'I'm beginning to believe that's what happened. The problem will be finding out who killed him and Ms Stevens — and why. Admittedly, there are many people who have wanted to kill lawyers from time to time, myself included. But I don't reckon they carry out that wish. Put it this way, I'll be interested to see what the post-mortem on that body from Riven Scar reveals, if it does turn out to be Mitchell's, and if it was the fall that killed him.'

Nash took out his phone. 'Steve, I want you to order a forensic team to Mitchell's house. Tell them I need the building examined closely. And ask them to pay particular attention to the two laptops and printer in the study. I'm not talking simply checking for fingerprints and DNA, I want the recent usage history of all three devices reported in detail. We also have to arrange for the Porsche to be uplifted from Riven Scar and taken to Netherdale, for them to examine that as well.'

'Will do. By the way, the fire crew at Riven Scar have reported to our guys. The person at the base of the cliff is dead, and ID in his wallet shows it to be Gavin Mitchell. I've asked Mexican Pete to attend once the corpse has been recovered. I haven't heard such colourful language since I encountered an angry, drunken Spaniard in Ibiza.'

'OK, Steve. I'll phone Netherdale and report developments.'

When he'd repeated what he knew to Superintendent Fleming, she asked Nash, 'I take it you're not convinced that Mitchell killed himself, right?'

'Far from it. I had my doubts before I saw the supposed suicide note. Now I'm even more convinced this was foul play.'

Ending the call, Nash went in search of his colleague. Clara was wandering downstairs as he entered the hall. 'I've been checking the bedrooms and bathroom,' she explained.

'Anything of interest?'

'Only one item I noticed that might support your wild idea. There was one of those fancy shaving stands in the bathroom, the ones that you hang your razor and shaving brush on? Alongside it was a mug containing shaving soap. Both the surface of the soap and the bristles on the brush were damp. That suggests Mitchell had a shave recently, and it led me to wonder why he would take such pains over his appearance if he was determined to commit suicide.'

It was a minor point, Nash thought, but it did fit his developing theory. 'I don't think there's anything to be gained by remaining here. We'll ask our uniform lads to remain on site until the forensic crew get here. Steve's sending them as I speak. We've now got confirmation that the body was Mitchell's. Steve told Mexican Pete, who sounded to be on top form, so I reckon we should avoid Riven Scar and return to Helmsdale to brief Viv and Lisa.'

CHAPTER TWELVE

Although Nash anticipated the post-mortem would be straightforward, the pathologist's remarks, once the procedure was over, cast a different light on the events surrounding Mitchell's death, and in so doing, confirmed the accuracy of Nash's theory.

'There is no doubt as to cause of death. That is due to the fall, but there is one anomaly I'm not happy about. Until I can clear it up, I shall reserve my decision.'

'What sort of anomaly, Professor?'

'There is an unexplained puncture wound on the back of the man's neck. In the light of this, I have taken a blood sample, which I will send off for analysis. That's routine procedure anyway, but in this instance, the results could prove very enlightening.'

'Would you care to enlighten me? Even if it is only guesswork at this stage.'

'The wound is exactly the sort that would result from the use of a hypodermic needle. If the blood test yields a positive result for some unexplained substance, we might be looking at a different verdict than suicide.'

'Are you implying that Mitchell was drugged, and then thrown off that precipice?'

'It's entirely possible. Put it this way, from the location of that needle mark it would have been physically impossible for it to have been self-administered, even if the dead man was double jointed.'

Ramirez paused before adding, 'The body was severely damaged by the fall, I guess from hitting rocks several times before coming to rest. However, there are some unexplained abrasions I find curious. There is every possibility the victim of this fall was restrained in the period before his death. Finally, I am also curious about the time of death. Although there is no set time for people to commit suicide, I venture to suggest that around five or six o'clock in the morning is one of the least probable parts of the day. There again, if I'm proved correct about that puncture wound, then we're looking at a case of murder, and I don't believe any such inhibitions apply.'

* * *

Nash returned to CID, where Lisa and Viv had returned from Netherdale High Street to report the outcome of their visit to Ward's Pharmacy, the name on the medication supplied to Petra Stevens. 'We spoke to the owner,' Pearce began.

'Mr Ward, I presume,' Clara guessed.

'No, he's long gone, apparently. The current owner is also the senior dispenser, but he wasn't on duty the day the prescription arrived from Ms Stevens' doctor, so he didn't make up the medication. He was quite happy to show us the record. Then we went to the home of the locum who actually made up the medication and interviewed him.'

Lisa told them, 'He acts as stand-in for several pharmacies in the area. He was shocked rigid when we told him why we'd gone to see him, but couldn't explain how such a thing could have happened.'

Pearce took up the story again. 'We couldn't find anything remotely suspicious about the prescription, the medication, or any connection between the owner, the dispenser, and either Mitchell or Ms Stevens.'

'That leaves us with one outstanding question. How did the medication get switched?' Clara asked.

'Actually, Clara, it's two questions.'

'What's the other one, Mike?'

'Who switched the tablets — and injected Mitchell before throwing him off Riven Scar.' Nash thought for a second or two, and then asked, 'Did you get the guy at Ward's Pharmacy to show you the medication? It would be interesting to know if there's any difference in size, shape or colour between the ones Ms Stevens was supposed to take and the substitutes.'

'We thought of that, Mike, and there is no difference, other than the manufacturer's imprint. And I don't suppose you look at that when you're taking your tablets. Otherwise, they're absolutely identical. To prove it, the guy took one tablet out of each bottle to demonstrate.'

Nash looked at Clara. 'Can you recall our interview with Mitchell, and whether he told us who collected the prescription from the surgery, and who collected the medication from the pharmacy?'

'I can answer both those questions,' Lisa told him. 'The prescription was initially sent through by email, but couldn't be dispensed until the hard copy, delivered by courier the following day, arrived. That's standard procedure for some of the more powerful or addictive drugs, such as barbiturates. Gavin Mitchell collected them the next day. We inspected the pharmacy's copy of the prescription form, and it had Mitchell's signature as the patient's representative.'

Nash thought for a while. 'That raises another issue, or a possible solution. If Mitchell collected them on a day when he was in court, they might have been left unattended. Alternatively, he might have taken them to his office. Either way, that gives a window of opportunity in which the substitution might have taken place. However, until we can identify someone with the motive, means, and opportunity to harm Mitchell or Ms Stevens, we're getting nowhere. It's a bit of a long shot, I suppose, but just for form's sake, will you check out both pharmacists online, Viv? Leave it till morning. It's been a long day — get yourselves off home.'

* * *

The pathologist had requested the laboratory treat the blood sample from Mitchell as a priority, and the next morning Ramirez phoned Nash to inform him of the results.

'Mr Mitchell received a subcutaneous injection of Midazolam, one of the more potent, fast-acting drugs in the benzodiazepine range.'

'Thank you for that information, Professor. Is there an English translation of what you just told me?'

'Midazolam is a powerful sedative, stronger than Diazepam, the one people are more familiar with. Therefore, I will recommend that the coroner returns a verdict of wilful murder by person or persons unknown.'

'I was already moving towards that conclusion.'

Ramirez was sufficiently intrigued to ask, 'What led you in that direction?'

'I'd received the results from the forensic team we sent to Mitchell's house. He'd left a suicide note, or so we were supposed to believe, admitting responsibility for the death of Ms Stevens, his partner. However, the wording of the note made me suspicious, as did the fact that it was typed, not handwritten. When our boffins examined the paper, they found a complete absence of fingerprints, not even Mitchell's. They then responded to my request to check Mitchell's computers and printer. The devices hadn't been used for a week prior to Mitchell's death, and there was no history of that note having been either typed on them or run off by the printer.'

'I think the person responsible made a serious blunder by failing to appreciate the level of your detective prowess, Mike.'

It wasn't often that Ramirez stunned Nash into silence, but that compliment certainly did.

Nash lost no time in updating Superintendent Fleming.

'So we're now looking at a double murder, correct?' she asked.

'True, and that means our running total is four murders, including All Alone Cottage, and at least four burglaries, maybe more to be discovered yet, all unsolved. What is even worse, as things stand, we haven't a clue as to who committed any of these crimes.'

'Haven't you got any leads, Mike?'

Nash laughed, but without humour. 'At present, the only lead I have is the one I use to walk my dog.'

Nash briefed the team, who were equally dismayed by their lack of success. Clara attempted to dispel the gloom. 'Look at it this way — things can't get much worse.'

Nash remembered the old saying that things have to get worse before they get better, but in the interests of morale, decided to that it would be beneficial not to mention it.

'I know they call it a "bobby's job", but I don't recall anyone claiming a detective's work was easy,' Clara commented. 'Nor do I remember anyone saying that sometimes it's a fruitless task.'

They all stared at Lisa Andrews, who had begun humming a tune. It was a few bars in before they recognized the theme music from *Mission: Impossible*. Nash smiled slightly, wryly acknowledging the frustration they all shared.

Lisa's impromptu rendition might have lightened the mood, but only temporarily.

Later that day, when Pearce reported his findings on Petra Stevens' pharmacists, it seemed that this was yet another dead end. 'The owner is single, and as far as I can discover, unattached,' Viv told Nash. 'There's nothing against him in the PNC, and when I asked about locally, his reputation is excellent. The only slight whiff of scandal I got was about his brother. He was married, but apparently he hooked up with another woman and they eloped several years ago. That's everything, I'm afraid. As for the locum, clean as a whistle.'

* * *

As Nash was leaving the office, Sergeant Meadows stopped him. 'You'll have to go the long way round to reach Wintersett, Mike.'

'Why's that?'

'The main road is blocked, so we've had to set up a diversion via the Drover's Halt road.'

'Has there been accident?'

'There's been an accident, right enough, and I'm sure it's going to be serious for the farmer whose bales of silage came off his trailer, overturning the tractor in the process.'

'Not good. Is the farmer OK?'

Meadows grinned. 'Apart from a sudden need to change his underpants, you mean? Yes, he's not hurt. Whether he'll be OK when he gets fined for having an insecure load is a different matter.'

Nash reached the Drover's Halt junction and turned off, acknowledging the greeting from the uniformed officer charged with maintaining the roadblock. As he swung the Range Rover onto the side road, Nash recalled the previous occasion he had taken this road. That had been when they collected Daniel from school. There had been a trauma on that journey too, as he had to pull off the road to allow a fire engine to pass. The memory of the emergency vehicle triggered something in Nash's mind. For some reason, a fire engine should be important, but no matter how hard he tried, he couldn't think why.

It was almost a quarter of an hour later when Nash pulled up at home, but as he got out of the car, he was no closer to identifying the source of that elusive memory. Seconds later, he was greeted passionately by Alondra, enthusiastically by Teal, and with a 'Hello, Pa' from Daniel.

He promptly forgot about his random recollection.

CHAPTER THIRTEEN

The lack of progress in the cases all changed via a sensational development, which they acknowledged was solely due to modern technology, and had nothing to do with their detection skills.

Nash was in bed when his mobile rang in the early hours.

Alondra stirred, muttering, 'What's wrong?'

'It's Control,' Nash told her. 'This can't be good news.'

For once he was wrong, even though it meant his plans for getting a decent night's sleep would have to be put on hold. 'Nash,' he said. 'What's the problem?'

'Actually, I think it's more of a solution than a problem, sir. Sorry to disturb your beauty sleep, but I believe we've just arrested one of your most wanted, the guy Viv Pearce referred to as the vacation burglar.'

'You have him under arrest? How did that come about?'

'We got a call from Cyprus, of all places. A couple from Helmsdale are on holiday in their villa. Before they jetted off to the sun, they invested in one of those Wi-Fi CCTV systems they advertise on telly. The ones you link to your mobile and monitor activity from wherever there's a hotspot, if you know what I mean.'

'Er . . . yes, I think so.'

'Anyway, they were alerted to someone breaking into their house, and phoned us. We sent a four-man team to the property, and arrested him as he was rifling through the contents of the bedroom. They're bringing him in now.'

'I'm on my way.'

He looked at Alondra. 'Looks like I'm going to be an hour or two. You may well be up before I get back.'

* * *

Dawn was breaking as he arrived at Netherdale HQ, just as a pair of police vehicles pulled into the car park. One of the officers gestured to the van. 'This character gave us a bit of trouble. He tried to make a run for it, but when he realized he was cornered he turned nasty, and tried to fight his way out of trouble.' He indicated the dog handler's vehicle. 'Luckily he amended his behaviour once our mate showed him Hannibal.'

Nash waited for the officers to haul the arrested man from the van and hustle him into the building. As they escorted him towards the booking desk, the prisoner began to resist. What followed was more like a comedy than a drama. Despite being handcuffed, he lashed out, using his fists, knees, and feet, even attempting to bite one of his escorts. Seconds later, a single bark alerted him that the police dog had entered the building. The handler had the German Shepherd on a leash, despite which, the dog was straining forward, obviously keen to get to grips with his target. The prisoner's last show of defiance ended abruptly as he backed away, whimpering, 'Get him away from me. Keep him away.'

The handler ignored him. Speaking to Nash, he suggested, 'Any further trouble from this character and I'll put the dog in the cell with him, OK? You can collect the remains in the morning.'

He turned to the prisoner. 'Hannibal hasn't been fed today, he's really hungry.' He grinned. 'Hannibal isn't his real name. It's the nickname our lads gave him — after

Hannibal Lecter. But perhaps you've never seen *The Silence of the Lambs.*'

Nash looked away to avoid laughing aloud. Unfortunately, that meant making eye contact with the desk sergeant, who was also struggling to contain his amusement. As there was no likelihood of further trouble, Nash said, 'This character's caused us enough bother already. Get him booked in and stick him in a cell. I'll interview him later, after I've been home and had my breakfast. Can you get someone to collate all the burglary files and have them ready for when I get back?'

* * *

At home, having showered and eaten his breakfast, Nash sent Clara a text, asking her to meet him at Netherdale. When he entered the headquarters, she was in conversation with Jackie Fleming.

'Morning, Mike,' the superintendent greeted him. 'I understand we've got some good news at last.'

'So I believe, but it's early days to be getting excited. Hopefully, we'll know more once we've interviewed him, but up to press we haven't even got an ID.'

'Why's that?'

'There was nothing on his person. No wallet, no driving licence, no bank cards. All they found in his pockets was a packet of tissues, two spare sets of latex gloves, one of those multitool kits, and a pay-as-you-go mobile.'

'What about car keys? He would have needed transport to get away from the scene of the crime.'

'No, he either lives nearby, or someone dropped him off. Maybe he's an Uber customer.'

'Is there any call history on the mobile?'

'We haven't examined it yet. We've turned it over to Forensics, and once they've checked it for prints and DNA, I've instructed them to send it to Pearce. It's highly likely the device will be password-protected, and I don't want all the data wiped because of someone's lack of IT skills.'

The interview yielded no fresh information. This was down to the detainee's complete lack of cooperation — even to the extent of refusing to divulge his name. The only time the prisoner spoke was to utter all detectives' least favourite phrase, 'No comment.'

Nash suspended the interview. He and Clara returned to the desk in the custody suite and Nash told the waiting sergeant, 'The man refuses to give his name. However, I hope that will soon change, and if I'm right, I'll be able to supply you with all the necessary details. With luck, I should have the information ready within the hour.'

Clara stared at Nash, completely astonished by what she thought was his outrageous claim. 'I like your confidence, Mike, but I'm not certain where you think we'll get his details from. Not unless you've suddenly taken up mind-reading without telling me.'

Nash smiled at Clara's joke, but told her, 'I think the best way would be to ask his employers, don't you?'

'What employers? Did you recognize him from somewhere, or has he a secret symbol somewhere on his clothing that only you can see? A company logo, from a firm run by the invisible man, maybe?'

Nash shook his head in mock sorrow. 'Now you're getting silly. What I suggest is, you go outside and clear your head with a breath of fresh air. While you're outside, why not phone Viv Pearce and ask him to put a call into Helm Dairies. He should ask which of their roundsmen failed to turn up for work this morning. Unless there's more than one, we should have our felonious friend's name and address soon.'

'You believe he works for Helm Dairies? How do you work that out? We know there's no connection between the homeowners.'

'When he was brought in, I saw he had splash marks on his trousers. I didn't think anything of it at the time, but when we were in the confined space of the interview room just now, I noticed a familiar, if faint, aroma. Not body odour, but equally unpleasant. A few years ago, I spilled a carton of milk in the footwell of my car. I didn't have chance to clean it up immediately, and the car stank horrendously for months afterwards. Once it's seeped into the fabric, it's extremely difficult to get rid of. The burglar's clothing had the definite smell of stale milk about them.'

Less than twenty minutes later, Nash and Mironova re-entered the interview room. Clara made the announcement of the resumption of their interview, before Nash said, 'Perhaps we can now have a more meaningful discussion than previously, Mr Thompson. You initially refused the services of a legal representative. Would you care to change your mind?'

Ian Thompson stared at Nash, clearly appalled by the ease with which he'd been identified. There was a long silence before he replied. 'I want a solicitor.'

'I think you need one. Have you anybody in mind?'

'I don't care.'

'Would you settle for the duty solicitor?'

'I suppose so.'

'OK, we have to suspend this interview until your legal representative is available and has consulted you. In the meantime, you will be charged with one offence of breaking and entering, with the option to add further instances.'

Now, after days of frustration, they finally had work to do.

* * *

They were greeted with smiles when they entered the CID suite, a marked change from the recent gloom over their lack of success. As they briefed their colleagues, Nash was keen to prevent the euphoria from taking over, and emphasizing there was still a lot of hard work to do.

'Our first priority must be to establish Thompson's guilt beyond doubt, not only for this offence, but also the other burglaries we suspect he committed. Therefore, we need to apply for a search warrant ASAP. We also need to ascertain how Thompson knew all these houses would be unoccupied. The Helm Dairies connection alone is not sufficient. Some of his victims didn't use the dairy, and those that were customers had their deliveries carried out by different roundsmen.'

Nash paused to allow them to mull this over, before continuing, 'I think Thompson must have an accomplice. That would probably explain where he obtained the information. We need to nail that down, and ensure we not only pursue Thompson for the burglaries, but also tie him into the associated offences. I'm referring to the assault on Mr Firth — ' Nash smiled slightly — 'plus the criminal damage and assault in smashing a valuable vase over Firth's head, resisting arrest, and assaulting a police officer.'

'Might a good defence lawyer question the police version of that last accusation?' Lisa objected. 'The only witnesses to the alleged assault were fellow officers. He might imply that our account of the event was prejudiced.'

'Fortunately, two of our uniform guys were wearing bodycams. They captured the incident clearly enough to negate that argument.'

* * *

Later in the day, having obtained a search warrant, the detectives entered Thompson's flat. Any hope they had of obtaining incriminating evidence, via property stolen in the course of the burglaries, was soon dashed. Viv and Lisa, who had been tasked with attempting to match any items discovered to those on the list they had brought, reported their failure to Nash. He, along with Clara, was searching Thompson's bedroom as they delivered their findings — or lack of them.

'That doesn't altogether surprise me. I believe Thompson's partner in crime got wind of his arrest and spirited the incriminating evidence away before we got here.'

'How can you be certain Thompson had an accomplice?'

'I'm fairly sure of it.' Nash reached into the drawer of the bedside cabinet he had just opened, and pulled out a pair of scanty, lace-trimmed, pink knickers. 'I appreciate you haven't met Thompson, but I have, and I can't imagine him buying something like this, let alone wearing it.'

'Much as I hate to admit it, Mike's right,' Clara told them as she emerged from the en-suite bathroom. 'I found several items of feminine toiletries. Even if Thompson is into cross-dressing, I don't believe such a fetish would extend to the use of tampons.'

'So how would his accomplice have got wind of Thompson's arrest?' Pearce asked.

'I think she might have been close at hand when Thompson was detained. Remember we were puzzled as to how he got to and from the burglary sites? And some of the stolen items were large, too heavy to be carried away. I reckon his lady friend acted as chauffeuse, and probably saw the police cars racing to arrest him.'

Nash thought for a moment before adding, 'Alternatively, even if she didn't witness the arrest, she might have been spooked by Thompson's failure to return. She could have assumed the worst, especially if they had an action plan that went along the lines of, "If I'm not home by a certain time, take the gear and scarper." That would make sense as a contingency measure. The problem we now have is discovering who she is, and where she's vanished to.'

'One thing we did find,' Pearce told them, 'is a laptop. Maybe we should take it.'

'Good idea, Viv. We don't know who it belongs to.'

'There's another item, and I don't quite know what to make of it. Alongside the laptop was an envelope, and inside was a memory card taken from a digital camera. Thompson doesn't appear to be into that level of photography. From what I've seen around this place, he seems more likely to use the photo app on his mobile. I've had a good look round, and guess what — no camera.'

'That is puzzling, I agree. Keep it safe, Viv, and we'll take a look at the images stored on the card when we have chance. However, I reckon we've more urgent matters to deal with.'

* * *

They returned to Helmsdale, and once they were back in the CID suite, Nash asked Pearce to revisit the personnel working at Helm Dairies and Helmsdale Travel Services. 'I feel sure there must be a connection somewhere, we simply haven't seen it yet. It might be someone working at one place, with a relative at the other firm.'

Viv soon reported another failure. 'I can't find anyone with links to both companies. I've checked every member of staff and looked for common surnames, but got nothing.'

'That's disappointing. I thought it must be there, even if it was a cleaner or a temporary member of staff.'

'There aren't many people employed on a permanent basis by either company. With the dairy it's only the delivery men, plus a couple of directors. HTS, of course, is a seasonal business, so apart from the sales people in their shops, there are no full-time clerks. They rely on agency . . .' Pearce's voice tailed off as he realized the significance of what he was about to say. 'Of course,' he muttered, 'why didn't I think of it before?'

He looked at Nash apologetically. 'I'm sorry, Mike, I should have twigged earlier. Both HTS and Helm Dairies supplement their regular staff by employing temps supplied by an agency. That might be where the link comes from. I'll go check it out.'

Twenty minutes later, Pearce returned accompanied by Clara. 'There's one person on the agency's books who fits our criteria,' Pearce informed them. 'Her name is Kathy Parker, and she works as a clerical officer on a temporary basis wherever the agency sends her. Because the agency is a regional outfit with headquarters in Leeds, they only have one representative in this area. Ms Parker has been employed by both

Helm Dairies and HTS over the past fifteen months. I have her address here.'

'I think it's high time we paid Ms Parker a visit. Did the agency tell you if she's working at present?'

'They said not. She's due to return to HTS in a couple of weeks, but they have nothing for her before that.'

'Then I think we should see if Kathy's come home.' Nash grinned as Clara groaned at his joke.

'This could be a late finish,' he said. 'We'd better all phone home.'

They were about to leave, when Nash asked Pearce, 'Before we go, do a DVLA check, will you? I want to know if Ms Parker owns a car. If, as I suspect, she does, we might get lucky and pick up images of it lurking near the various crime scenes. Admittedly, there are very few street cams around here, but a lot of houses have CCTV systems, and if so, they could have recorded her vehicle in the vicinity at the time the burglaries took place. It's circumstantial, but might prove useful backup.'

An hour later, Clara and Viv listened as Nash delivered the statutory caution, the first stage of Kathy Parker's arrest process. The evidence recovered from her flat, including a television, along with smaller items contained within three Good Buys shopping bags, was sufficient to detain her. Fortunately for their investigation, much of the property taken from the various burglaries was easily identifiable, via serial numbers that matched the stolen items. Equally damning was the presence of both Thompson and Parker's fingerprints on the goods.

CHAPTER FOURTEEN

On Saturday morning, with both suspects released on bail pending further enquiries, Viv Pearce was preparing to examine the laptop and Thompson's mobile. Although he was intrigued by the cryptic note enclosed with the devices from the forensic officer — which read, 'Check pics!!!' — Viv's first priority was the call log, emails, and SMS messages.

Having found one or two texts that might prove incriminating given their dates and times, his curiosity got the better of him, and he turned to the mobile's photo gallery. Seconds later, Clara and Lisa were startled when he exclaimed, 'Hell's bells!'

'What's the matter, Viv?'

'I'm checking Thompson's photos. They're quite interesting, to put it mildly. I'll show you them in a minute, but first, I'm going to look at the pictures on his laptop.'

They waited, their curiosity roused. Before long, Pearce muttered again, 'Hell's bells and buckets of blood.'

'What now, Viv?'

Pearce ignored the question, and called through to Nash. 'Mike, come here, you've got to see these!'

The detectives crowded round Pearce's desk as he flicked through the gallery. After viewing several photos, Clara asked, 'Is that who I think it is?'

'I'm absolutely certain of it, Clara.' Nash, like the others, was stunned by the images.

As they pondered the implication, Pearce told them, 'If you think those are bad, wait until you watch the videos.'

'If they're worse than the photos, I'm not sure I want to,' Nash replied, 'I'm far too young and innocent to be exposed to such things.'

The photos left the team with two important questions to answer. The first was, how had Thompson acquired such graphic images of a High Court judge, and his barrister wife, indulging in a variety of highly unusual sexual practices? The second, equally baffling, was what, if anything, they should do with the information now in their possession?

Later that afternoon, Steve Meadows wandered into the CID suite, mug in hand, en route to the coffee machine. As he passed Nash's office, he paused in the doorway, keen to impart an interesting item of news he had picked up.

'I've just been talking to my opposite number in Netherdale,' he said. 'He told me our Bonnie and Clyde couple have not one but two legal representatives. When they were in custody, their solicitor visited them, along with a high-ranking barrister. Apparently, she's been retained by the defence — and they reckon crime doesn't pay.'

Meadows was surprised that Nash seemed unperturbed by this startling development. 'Let me guess,' Nash replied, 'was it Lucinda Hartley, QC, by any chance?'

When he'd recovered, Meadows said, 'Yes, it was, but how on earth did you know that? Did someone from Netherdale tell you?'

Nash smiled. 'I could claim it was down to my detective skills, but let's just call it inside information.'

* * *

Nash had told the team to take Sunday off and spend it with their partners. On Monday, he and his colleagues reviewed the situation. 'Although we've got them fair and square for the burglaries via the evidence we collected, that isn't the whole picture.'

'Why, what's missing, Mike?' Viv asked.

'It's all very well nicking a load of expensive gear, such as the stuff we recovered, but how were Thompson and Parker planning to get rid of the goods? Assuming that they're not obsessive collectors, they must have had an outlet in mind. I don't for one minute believe they were going to flog such expensive items at the next car boot sale, do you? And where's the rest of it?'

Nash paused as they digested his comments, and then asked, 'What do we know about our suspects? Apart from their prolific purloining of peoples' property, we've found out very little. I'm thinking about their background. We should make their back stories our next priority. It might give us some insight into what caused them to turn to crime, and where they intended to dispose of the loot.'

As they were pondering this, Nash said, 'Most of the research will be down to you, Viv, with Lisa's assistance. Don't allow anything else to distract you, because I want this case put to bed as quickly as possible. Let me know as soon as you have anything. Once we've finished with it, we can devote our full attention to the murders. We've made little or no headway with them, and I, for one, am beginning to get irritated by our lack of success. Clara, you and I can go over what we've got so far on the murders.'

* * *

Later, Andrews and Pearce presented the results of their enquiries. 'Thompson and Parker are both locals, both twenty-three years old, and both born and raised in Bishopton. They attended Bishopton High School, which is no doubt where they met. Ian Thompson's parents are dead, and he has no siblings.'

Lisa looked at Viv, who took up the story.

'Kathy Parker's parents got divorced when she was seven years old, following her father's long-term affair with another woman. She had already borne him a son, who is effectively Kathy's half-brother. After the divorce, Kathy's father moved with his mistress and child to Birmingham, where he opened a business. When he died of pancreatic cancer eighteen months ago, his son Tony took over. Once Kathy reached eighteen, her mother sold the family house in Bishopton and moved with her new husband to live in Spain. Kathy was pretty much abandoned the moment she ceased to be a child in the legal sense.

'Despite the estrangement of her birth parents, Kathy remained in contact with Tony, her half-brother. When I checked Kathy's mobile and tablet, I found regular phone calls, text messages, and emails, some of them proving highly informative. I also got Forensics to check the satnav on her car, and this revealed regular visits to Birmingham.'

Viv paused, clearly leaving the most dramatic revelation until last. 'I believe the trips weren't only sentimental — the business Tony Parker runs is that of a pawnbroker. There are a fair number of emails from Kathy to Tony that contain attachments, with photos of watches, rings, and other items of jewellery.'

'That is excellent work. Well done, both of you,' Nash told them.

Clara suggested, 'I think a phone call to Birmingham CID, together with a list of missing items from the burglaries, might pay dividends.'

'Good idea, Clara. I'll leave it to you to make the initial contact.'

'And what are you going to do?'

Nash looked shocked. 'Brew some coffee, of course. Nobody else seems keen to volunteer.'

* * *

Next morning, Nash received a visit he was half-expecting. Neither the caller's identity nor her reason for coming to see him was a surprise. Meadows rang through and told him,

'Mike, I have Lucinda Hartley, QC, in reception. She's asked if she can see you in private. Shall I put her in an interview room?'

'Certainly not! She's not a suspect. Escort her to my office, will you?'

As he waited, Nash removed a small envelope from his desk drawer and placed it on the middle of the blotter. He watched as the barrister approached. There was no doubt Lucinda was a very attractive woman for her age, which he knew to be just the wrong side of fifty. He'd encountered her in court a couple of times, and although she was defending clients he had arrested, Nash had always found her to be reasonable and fair. Once she entered his office, Nash shook her hand, before he walked across and closed the door. As he returned, he said, 'Given the topic you want to discuss, I thought it would be less embarrassing if we conduct the conversation in complete privacy.'

Lucinda stared at him for several seconds, her surprise apparent. Eventually, she smiled, wryly, and said, 'I should have known better than to try and hide anything from you. I'd forgotten how good a detective you are.'

'Please, take a seat. I have to say I'm surprised that, in the circumstances, you're representing Thompson.'

'Hmm, yes, he specifically requested my services. I believe he thinks he has something he can use to his advantage.'

'Shall I try and make it easier for you? We have Thompson and Parker's laptops, and their mobiles. From which, texts and emails will be used as evidence at their trial. Copies of those messages will be printed off for court use. There are also items on those devices that have nothing to do with the offences with which they have been charged. I have issued strict instructions to my colleagues that on no account must they be allowed to become part of court proceedings. The phones and laptop will remain in evidence and *not* be returned. Does that set your mind at rest?'

For a moment, it seemed as if the barrister had lost the eloquence she was renowned — or feared — for. 'Inspector Nash . . . if I could explain . . . those photos were stolen.'

Nash held up one hand. 'There's no need for explanation. What you and your husband get up to in the privacy of your home is none of my business — unless, of course, you're breaking the law.' He smiled, wryly. 'If you ask my colleagues, they'll probably tell you I'm the last person to sit in judgement on someone else's private life.'

Lucinda recovered her composure a little. She smiled as she replied, 'I think "sit in judgement" is a singularly appropriate phrase, don't you? Thank you for being so understanding. I was concerned that the meeting might take a totally different course, or that you might have misinterpreted my motive for wishing to see you.'

'Not at all, I was fairly certain I knew the reason — unless, of course, it was to seek my assistance in recovering items your client stole when he broke into your home.'

'How did you know Thompson had broken into our house? He certainly hasn't confessed to that offence.'

'How else could he have obtained the photographs? I couldn't believe someone like Thompson obtained them legally.'

'It's no wonder your superiors think so highly of you, Inspector Nash. You're absolutely right, of course.' Lucinda paused. Her nervous expression returned as she said, 'There is one item I am particularly keen to recover, but I'm not certain whether you have it or not. It certainly isn't among the list I was given at disclosure.'

Nash handed her the envelope from his blotter. 'Would that be the item you're referring to?'

Lucinda peeped inside the envelope, saw the memory card, and then looked at Nash, her face registering a variety of emotions. Nash guessed these were relief, tinged with acute embarrassment, and a degree of suspicion.

Keen to put at least one of them to rest, he told her, 'There is no *quid pro quo* involved here. I was going to wait until the trial was over, and then deliver them to you at your home, but you jumped the gun.'

'Thank you for keeping this safe — and also for being so understanding.'

'That's not an issue. I'm glad to be of assistance.'

As he was ushering Lucinda out, Nash smiled wickedly at her, and whispered something that made her blush. When she had left, Nash told Clara in strict confidence about the reason for the meeting.

'What was it you said that made her blush?' Clara asked. 'It was as you were showing her out.'

Nash laughed. 'I couldn't resist the temptation. It's definitely the first, and most probably the last, time I've told a barrister what a nice bottom she has.'

Later that day, they heard the outcome of the raid carried out on the pawnbroker's shop in Birmingham. Clara updated her colleagues. 'I've had an email from the DI leading the investigation there. Several items were recovered that match pieces on our list. In addition, they also recovered proceeds from other robberies committed elsewhere, offences that are not connected to our villains. As a result, Tony Parker is now in custody, charged with receiving stolen property.'

'I think that wraps everything up rather neatly,' Nash told them. 'Well done, everyone.'

CHAPTER FIFTEEN

Nash and his colleagues were now able to concentrate on the four murders on their books.

'Right, today, I suggest we concentrate on the recent deaths, the solicitors. At least with them we know the identity of the victims. We now have to discover what made them into targets. Accepting this isn't the work of a psychopathic poisoner, there has to be a motive behind the crimes. We can only hope to discover that by digging into their personal lives and professional activities. When we researched our burglars' backgrounds we came up trumps, so let's hope the same happens here. I reckon our best option is to begin with Mitchell & Co., where both victims were partners. If we can gain access to the solicitors' offices, we may find something worth following up.'

He looked round. 'Clara, will you and Viv go there? Talk to Mitchell's secretary and any others who worked alongside him and Ms Stevens. We also need to look through both partners' case files.'

'And what will you be doing while your foot soldiers are on the march?' she asked.

'Lisa and I will be going through all the forensic reports gathered in respect of both murders. It'll be boring, admittedly, but necessary, in case we spot something our foot soldiers missed first time round. Of course, if you want to swap duties, I'll quite understand.'

Clara had seen enough paperwork over the past few days to last a lifetime. 'Come on, Viv. Let's go to Mitchell's offices.'

The last sound Clara heard as she left the CID suite was Nash's laughter. Viv was trying to keep his face straight.

* * *

The drive to Netherdale didn't take long, and they soon arrived at Netherdale Hall, the building that housed the solicitors' offices. 'Wow,' Pearce exclaimed, 'who was it said crime doesn't pay?'

'That's a slanderous thing to say about a respectable law practice,' Clara rebuked him. 'But I can see what you mean.'

The premises were on the outskirts of the town, in an area of mixed occupation. Alongside other commercial properties were several which were purely residential, like those in the immediate vicinity of Mitchell & Co.'s building. Some of the adjacent houses had been converted into flats, some had nice garden areas, but none was on as grand a scale as Netherdale Hall.

The three-storey property was set back from the road, and as they drove into the grounds, Clara noticed the building name etched into the stone gateposts, below which was a brass plate advertising the law practice. Clara drove at a snail's pace along the gravel driveway, admiring the lawns, shielded by a variety of mature trees. She spotted a wooden bench of the type usually seen in public parks alongside the grass. Obviously it wasn't all work and no play here.

As she pulled to a halt in front of the building, Viv said, 'I wonder how old this place is? I reckon someone with a load of money had it built. It's like a young mansion.'

He was puzzled when Clara burst out laughing.

'What's so funny?'

'I was talking to Tom Pratt just before we left, and I mentioned we were coming here. He told me the history of Netherdale Hall.'

Tom Pratt, formerly a senior detective, had taken the post of civilian support officer following his retirement on health grounds. He, along with Jack Binns, their retired desk sergeant, were twin founts of knowledge on the area.

'Go on, then, tell me what Tom said.'

'Apparently the building dates back to the early nineteenth century. It was constructed on behalf of Netherdale Parish Council and was designed for use as an almshouse.'

'I've heard the name before, but I've never known exactly what an almshouse is, or what purpose it served.'

'An almshouse was designed to provide accommodation for people who were poor, homeless, and in need, or disabled, or too ill to work. I suppose it's a bit like the homeless shelters of modern days. That's in contrast to a workhouse, where the destitute worked long hours for little reward, other than a bed and basic food.'

They headed for the door, but minutes later they began the return journey to Helmsdale.

* * *

For a long time, it seemed as if the scrutiny of the forensic files from the crime scenes and Mitchell's house would yield nothing new. Nash and Lisa had barely started on the reports from their home in Bishop's Cross when Clara and Viv returned, far earlier than expected.

'How did it go?' Nash enquired, although he thought he could guess by the scowl on Clara's face.

'It didn't go at all,' she replied. 'As wild goose chases go, this was a prime example. We were greeted by Mitchell's secretary, who informed us she had been forbidden to discuss the case, or the activities of the law practice, with anyone — including the police. That embargo extends to all other staff members, and also precludes us from examining any files on the partners' desks, or in filing cabinets.'

'Who issued those instructions?'

'The locum solicitor appointed by the Law Society. Apparently, when something like this happens, they send a qualified solicitor to oversee the running of the firm, until such time as the disposition of the practice has been agreed.'

'What does that legal mumbo-jumbo mean?' Lisa asked.

'It means until someone else inherits the business, or it gets wound up,' Nash explained. He smiled sweetly at Clara as he added, 'Since you have nothing better to do, perhaps you or Viv will make coffee while Lisa and I continue our work.'

Nash returned to his examination of the report he was holding. Clara and Viv had interrupted just as he reached the section referring to Mitchell's study. The break in concentration obviously worked, because he almost immediately spotted something in the section detailing the contents of that room. Although this interested him, he was more intrigued by what was omitted from the list. He flicked over the remaining pages, but failed to find any reference to what he was seeking.

At that moment, Clara returned bearing a tray of mugs. She presented this to Nash, much in the style of a hand-maiden serving her master. 'Pearce has gone for refreshments for our lunches, my lord. He didn't wish to disturb your light reading,' she explained.

Despite smiling briefly at her comedy routine, Nash asked her, 'Would you do me a favour? Phone Mitchell's secretary, and tell her we accept the embargo for the time being, but also ask her if she would be able to supply one piece of information. Explain that we understand the need for confidentiality, but we don't believe this will impinge on her vow of silence. What we need to establish is whether Mitchell or Ms Stevens kept their personal paperwork at home or at the office.'

Clara blinked with surprise. 'Isn't it listed there?'

'No, according to Forensics, the filing cabinet was only half full, the contents dated back many years, and mostly concerned Mitchell's father and grandfather. The same goes for the desk in the study. There are no bank or credit card statements, no cheque books, or recent financial information of any description for either of them. Not even regular household bills for services, such as council tax, gas, water, telephone, or electricity.'

'That's weird — unless, as you say, they kept it all at work.'

Five minutes later, Clara reported back. 'Mitchell's secretary was reluctant to reveal anything, but when I explained all we needed was confirmation one way or the other, she told me neither of them kept any personal papers at the office. She said Mitchell was very cagey about his private life. It was a year or so after Ms Stevens joined the firm that the secretary found out they were living together. That's how secretive Mitchell was.'

'That's interesting, because it means he either has another address we're not aware of — or there's part of the building we haven't searched, like an attic or basement. I think our next task must be to return to Bishop's Cross and give Mitchell's house a thorough going-over. If we don't find anything, we'll be up against a brick wall — again. I suggest we have lunch, then we can all go. Clara, we'll take our own cars, in case we're needed elsewhere. Viv, can you bring Lisa in yours?'

'No problem, boss.'

'In the meantime, we'll make more copies of these reports, and everyone can study them later.'

They were about to leave when Clara asked if he'd made arrangements for getting inside Mitchell's house. Nash smiled and dangled a bunch of keys in front of her. 'Forensics returned these, along with the reports.'

'I won't be far behind you,' she said.

* * *

When Clara arrived at Mitchell's house, Nash's Range Rover was parked on the gravel forecourt, but there was no sign of him. Assuming him to be inside the building, she ducked under the incident tape strung across the facade, suspended from metal stakes driven into the gravel by their CSI team. She went to the front door, only to find it locked.

'Breaking and entering. Don't you think there's been enough of that lately?'

Clara turned and saw Nash standing by the corner of the house. 'Where have you been?'

'I was checking the lie of the land — literally. Come with me, I want to show you something.'

Five minutes later, they returned to the front of the building to find Andrews and Pearce standing by the entrance, looking slightly bemused. 'There's nobody in, unless you believe in ghosts,' Nash told them.

As he unlocked the door, Nash explained what he'd discovered. 'The house is built on a slope. The back garden is stepped, and there's a waterfall feature on three levels, leading to a large fish pond. The area at the rear of the house is approximately eight to ten feet lower than at the front. We also noticed a small window, no more than two feet square, on the back wall, below ground-floor level. We believe there might be a basement we failed to spot earlier.'

As they entered the building, Clara stooped and picked up an assortment of mail from the mat. She examined the various items, before placing them on the hall table along with another pile of unopened envelopes.

'Anything of interest?' Nash asked.

'Mostly junk mail and flyers, which might be of some use if you like Chinese food, or pizzas, or if you want to change your broadband supplier. Apart from them, there are a couple of what look like bank statements, one for Mitchell, and the other for Ms Stevens.'

'Those might be worth looking at. The statements, I mean, not the flyers. We'll take them back with us. Who knows, they might reveal something relevant to the case.'

Knowing a basement existed was a promising development, but finding an entrance was quite another matter. The detectives spent a long time fruitlessly examining the interior of the property as they searched for a means of ingress, until Pearce made the discovery — purely by chance.

As he was walking from the kitchen, along the short corridor leading to the dining room, Pearce vented his frustration by kicking at the mat which served as a runner between the rooms. The edge of the rug flicked over, and as he bent to straighten it, Pearce noticed a thin line cut across the floorboards. He peeled the mat back, and saw that it concealed a trapdoor. He called out for his colleagues, who crowded into the narrow gap, staring at the floor.

'Go on, Viv, you found it, so you should have the honour of leading the way into the dungeon,' Nash encouraged him.

Pearce grasped the ring pull handle, and turned it as he tugged at the trapdoor. It yielded easily, guided by the concealed hinges lying flush with the flooring at the opposite end of the framework. When the trapdoor was fully open, the detectives peered into the gloom below.

The hidden entrance led to a short flight of steps, no more than ten in number. Alongside the top step was an electric switch, screwed into one of the joists supporting the ground floor. Pearce flicked it, dispelling the darkness as a fluorescent tube sprang to life. One by one, the detectives walked carefully down the stairs and looked around the subterranean space.

As cellars go, it was a miniature edition, little bigger than a box room. One wall contained a floor-to-ceiling wine rack, and Nash noticed almost every compartment was full. Obviously Mitchell didn't believe in running short of essential supplies. He picked a bottle at random and inspected it. The solicitor was clearly a connoisseur, judging by the vintage.

Below the window they had observed from outside was a small desk and office chair. The desk was a cheap one, of the type sold in their millions by DIY stores. Nash assumed it had arrived as a flat-pack and been assembled inside the basement. On the fourth wall was a two-drawer filing cabinet Nash guessed would contain Mitchell's personal paperwork. What puzzled him was the need for secrecy amounting almost to an obsession. There was only one way to find out. 'Let's examine the contents of that.'

It seemed that Mitchell believed the measures he'd taken to conceal the existence of the cellar were sufficient security, for the keys to the filing cabinet were hanging from the lock. The top drawer contained a series of files, within which were bank and credit card statements going back a number of years. Nash selected one of the files, and took out several statements at random. Almost immediately, he noticed that, until a few years ago, the documents showed an overdraft at the end of the period in question. Later statements all showed substantial credit balances, so Mitchell must have found some means to turn his fortunes around.

Behind these, other folders explained Mitchell's earlier need to rely so heavily on substantial bank borrowing. The files showed details of accounts in Mitchell's name with several firms of bookmakers. Nash showed these to Clara. 'I think we can work out why Mitchell got those county court judgements. He clearly had a gambling problem, which at one point threatened to overwhelm him. Whether he cured himself, or had a stroke of fortune, I'm not sure, but judging by the bank statements, whatever happened took place in the region of three to four years ago.'

The contents of the lower drawer, all pertaining to Petra Stevens, showed nothing untoward.

Meanwhile, Viv and Lisa had been concentrating on the desk, but apart from two current account cheque books, and some stubs from earlier ones, plus a number of credit cards, they didn't find anything that seemed relevant to their enquiry.

Clara had begun scrutinising Mitchell's gambling activities. Mitchell, it seemed, had favoured a local bookmaker over the more well-known national companies. 'He seems to have placed most of his wagers with Better Bets in Netherdale,' she told them.

'Wasn't that the firm owned by the guy we put away a couple of years ago?' Pearce asked.

'Yes, but it's been renamed and given a revamped image by the new owners,' Lisa responded. 'They've taken out a series of adverts in the *Netherdale Gazette* and on Helm Radio emphasizing the new look and promising fairer treatment for their customers.'

'They've got a hard job trying to persuade people to overlook the unsavoury reputation left behind by the previous owner,' Clara replied.

'That's beside the point. I don't think it's standard practice for bookies to go around bumping off clients because they haven't paid up. It wouldn't get them their money back. Anyway, whatever his problems were, they seemed to be in the past. His recent bank statements indicate Mitchell was fairly affluent. What we still don't know is what led to his sudden change of fortune. One minute he's deep in debt, his overdraft's at its limit, his credit cards maxed out — then, almost overnight, he has a five-figure balance at the bank and his cards have been paid off in full.'

'Perhaps he won the National Lottery,' Lisa suggested.

'That's a possibility, given his predilection for gambling — however, the enormous odds against such a win make it highly improbable. Failing that, or a hugely successful string of bets on the horses, what other reason could there be? An inheritance, perhaps, or a massive payout from a grateful client following a successful lawsuit or . . .'

'Or what, Mike?'

'The only other alternative I can think of would explain Mitchell's reluctance to divulge any information to us. That would be misappropriation of funds from a client's, or group of clients', accounts — more commonly known as embezzlement.'

As they dwelt on the implications of Nash's suggestion, he told them, 'I think we ought to remove everything from this room, and take it to Helmsdale for safe keeping. I'm referring to the paperwork,' he added with a smile, 'not the Château Lafite. We don't want confidential documents such as these to fall into the wrong hands, especially when they might later prove pivotal.'

'Might that locum solicitor handling Mitchell's affairs need them?'

'He might do, but he isn't going to get them. That's what I meant by the wrong hands. If he asks, I'll tell him they contain evidence pertinent to a murder enquiry. If he won't allow us to look through Mitchell's business files, he can't expect us to give him access to the personal ones.'

Once they had loaded all the documentation into his car, Viv asked Nash if he should close the trapdoor. 'No, leave it open. People will need to be aware of the basement's existence. Potential buyers will want to inspect the cellar. Apart from that, there needs to be access to the wine racks.'

Although he didn't mention it to the others, Nash had an ulterior motive behind his decision. At some stage, the locum solicitor would doubtless visit the house in search of any other files that might have been stored there, or Mitchell's personal documentation. Finding no trace of them would provoke a reaction, or so Nash hoped. That was why he had placed his visiting card on the desk in the basement.

As Nash drove away from Mitchell's house, he believed they had removed anything relevant. It would be a good while later when he realized how wrong that supposition was.

CHAPTER SIXTEEN

The following morning, Nash conferred with Clara. 'I'm intending to speak to that solicitor sent to deal with Mitchell's law practice. I want it clearly understood that by preventing us from accessing Mitchell's files, he is impeding the murder inquiry. Naturally, being a lawyer, he'll probably later deny the conversation ever took place. To be on the safe side, I'll use the landline and put it on speaker, so you can witness our discussion. Again, being a lawyer, he'll probably allege that we are in collusion, so for good measure, I'll use the app on my mobile to record every word spoken.' Nash paused and smiled. 'Er . . . that'll have to wait until Viv's shown me how to use it.'

Now at the offices of Mitchell & Co., Henry Court had only been in Netherdale for twenty-four hours. Over the years as a practising solicitor, Henry had taken a lot of ribbing about his occupation and surname. The task handed down to him now, however, was no laughing matter. Almost as soon as he'd arrived, the secretary had informed him of the police requests to view all outstanding case files, and asked what she should do if they asked again.

'Don't tell them anything. Put them through to me and I'll deal with it.'

Henry was annoyed by the police action. Throughout his training, and during his career, he had been strict in his application of lawyer–client privilege, and was a staunch defender of the right to privacy enjoyed by those who were paying for his services. Minor local officials, such as the police in a small rural unit, who attempted to breach that golden rule would get short shrift from him.

It was almost lunchtime when the call came in. The secretary interrupted Henry's meeting with the intern, to inform him that Detective Inspector Nash was on the phone asking to speak to him. Henry was determined to nip any intrusion in the bud, even if it meant making life difficult for the police officer. A small-town plod, with no knowledge or respect for the workings of the legal system, warranted no special treatment.

'Tell him I'm in a meeting and cannot be disturbed. Take his number and say I'll call him back when I'm free.' Henry almost added, *Tell him not to hold his breath*, but decided against going that far.

When the secretary relayed this information, Clara, who was listening as instructed, was surprised by Nash's response. 'I understand how busy he must be. I'll speak to him when he's ready, always provided I'm available.'

Having ended the call abruptly, Nash buzzed through to Steve Meadows. 'If a guy by the name of Henry Court, or anyone from Mitchell & Co., phones and asks for me, tell them I'm out, even if I'm standing alongside you, OK?'

He smiled at Clara. 'Obviously this comedian is playing hard to get. No problem. Two can play at that game.'

* * *

In Drover's Halt, Louise had soon become accustomed to having Robert around. Moreover, she quickly realized that the former soldier had a strong work ethic, and combined this with an affinity for the animals under their care. As he had commented when he volunteered to help her, he had no previous expertise or experience in this area, so the bond he established with the various species must be a natural one.

Not only was it with the animals that Robert bonded. The friendship from their childhood resumed as if uninterrupted. As they grew steadily closer, Louise began to wonder where the natural affinity between them would lead, if anywhere. Apart from a couple of short-term relationships when she was in her late teens and early twenties, she had not been interested in male companionship. Now, she wondered what her reaction would be if Robert showed signs of wanting to take their friendship to another level.

That might never happen, Louise conceded, because she knew from the snippets he'd revealed that Robert had been badly hurt by the catastrophic outcome of his ill-fated marriage. The emotional damage caused by the betrayal of his wife and the man he thought was his friend would take a long time to recuperate from. That recovery could also be hampered by the after-effects of his earlier battleground traumas.

In the event, it was those experiences that were responsible for a shift in Robert and Louise's relationship. Almost three weeks after the horrific discoveries at All Alone Cottage, Louise was awakened in the early hours of the morning by Robert calling out from his room across the landing. Although she had heard similar sounds soon after he'd arrived, this sounded far more urgent. Louise switched her bedside light on, grabbed her dressing gown, thrust her feet into her slippers, and hurried to find out what was wrong.

Although she switched his lamp on, he didn't wake up. Robert was lying on his back, twitching and mumbling, the words indistinguishable, until he suddenly called her name. It was clear he was dreaming, and that dream was more of a nightmare.

'It's OK, Bobby, I'm here. Everything's all right.'

Her voice seemed to calm him, but only momentarily, because he soon began to thrash around, his voice strengthening as he mumbled a strange litany of unknown words.

Louise decided he needed a calming influence. Flicking the light off, she sat in the chair alongside him, and put her hand on his shoulder. Robert shuddered, his muscles tightening with anxiety, and Louise knew he needed reassurance. She began to whisper, repeating the phrases until they became a mantra. 'It's all right, Bobby Bear, nobody's going to harm you. Lulu-Belle says so. I'm here beside you. I won't let anyone hurt you.'

Slowly, imperceptibly, Robert's breathing eased, and he ceased his disjointed ramblings. Soon, he had drifted off into a deep, comfortable sleep. Louise was conscious of the risk of recurrence should she leave him, so she remained in the chair beside the bed.

Robert woke early, in part due to his army training, but also as a result of his new occupation. He could hear the gentle sound of someone breathing — clearly he wasn't alone. His alarm receded when he glanced sideways and saw it was Louise, sitting in the chair, smiling gently at him.

'What happened?' he asked.

'You were having a nightmare, jerking about and calling out. You shouted my name a couple of times, so I came in to try and settle you down. It worked, but then I fell asleep.'

'Thank you, but you didn't have to go to all that trouble. You should have just woken me. I'm sorry for disturbing you and for being such a nuisance.'

'Don't be silly, of course you're not a nuisance. Anyway, I stayed because I didn't want you to get upset again. What was the nightmare about, can you recall?'

'Strangely enough, I can. I don't usually remember my dreams, but this was really vivid. I was searching for you, but every time I got close, someone snatched you away. I knew you were in danger, and if I didn't get to you soon, it would be too late.'

'That sounds horrible. What we need to do is to think of a way to prevent the nightmare returning.'

* * *

Once the animals had been fed and watered, Robert and Louise had a belated breakfast. As they sat close together at the kitchen table, Louise brought up the subject of their future. 'I don't know what you're feelings are, Bobby, but I'd like you to stay here with me —' she hesitated — 'permanently. I know it's all very sudden, but I've been thinking of asking you for a while.' She smiled. 'I hope you might want the same.'

There was no hesitation before Robert replied, a clear sign that he, too, had thought the matter over. 'So much has gone wrong in my life, but the only good parts have been when I'm with you. If you feel able to put up with me, and the relics of my past, I can't think of anywhere I'd rather be than at your side.'

That evening, instead of parting on the landing, Louise took Robert's hand, guiding him towards her bedroom. 'From now on, we share this room. That way I'll be able to deal with any nightmares you have.' She smiled as she added, 'That isn't the only reason, not by any means. This is where my parents used to sleep, and the bed is where I was conceived. Who knows, if we're lucky we might even be able to raise some bear cubs here in the future.'

Robert didn't need any more encouragement.

* * *

Twenty-four hours after Nash's call, Henry Court decided he'd made the copper sweat long enough and dialled the number he'd been given.

'Is it urgent?' Sergeant Meadows asked. 'Detective Inspector Nash has court hearings he must attend, and I believe he also has a meeting scheduled with the chief constable, so I can't see him being free until tomorrow, or even the day after. I can put you through to Detective Constable Pearce if it is something that needs dealing with before then.'

Court declined the offer. Being denied the chance of putting the police officer in his place began to irritate the solicitor, so he tried three times during the course of that day, only to be told on each occasion that Nash was still unavailable. Eventually, Court said, 'Then ask Inspector Nash to call me when he *is* free.'

Five minutes later, Meadows reported the conversation to Nash.

'Haven't you made him suffer enough?' Clara asked.

'I certainly hope so. We'll see when I ring him back.'

Eventually, having dragged out the charade as long as possible, Nash made the call, with Clara listening intently, and his mobile recording. She noted Nash didn't bother to apologize for the delay, but went straight in. 'I've got a few minutes to spare,' he began, 'so I want to clarify the position regarding Mitchell's files, and those of Ms Stevens. I was told you were unwilling to allow us access to them. Is that still your attitude?' Nash's tone angered Court — precisely what it was intended to do.

'That is my attitude, and it will remain so. I cannot believe that you actually made the request in the first place. Activity between a lawyer and his clients is privileged.'

Court was about to deliver a lecture on the sacrosanct nature such information, but Nash cut him short before he began. 'I'm not interested in that baloney. We're investigating four murders, including those of Mitchell and his partner, and I believe the files contain evidence pertinent to those crimes. By preventing us from inspecting them, you are inhibiting our efforts to solve them.'

'Nevertheless, I cannot give you access to those files, and neither can I allow you to interview any members of Mitchell's staff, which I believe is the other request you made.'

'Very well, your attitude is noted. I must inform you, however, that you are sailing very close to the wind. Your reaction could be seen as obstructing the police in the execution of their duty, which, I am sure you are aware, is a criminal offence. Not only that, but I should also inform you that Gavin Mitchell refused to give information to one of my colleagues.'

'That merely underlines the fact that my decision is the correct one.'

'Only as long as you're prepared to take the risk. I assume you know that your decision could put your life in danger.'

'Danger, what danger? Why might I be in danger?'

Nash heard the alarm in Court's voice and pressed home his advantage. 'I don't know why you might be in danger. Perhaps if I'd been able to look at Mitchell's files, I might have been able to tell you. However, if you should feel threatened, be sure to call me, and I'll do my best to assist — always providing I'm available. All I can say for certain is that shortly after Gavin Mitchell refused to cooperate with us, both he and Petra Stevens were murdered. Good day to you.'

Seconds later, as he heard the disconnect tone, Henry Court glanced nervously around Gavin Mitchell's office, as if expecting to see an axe murderer lurking in the shadows. Only when he was convinced the danger Nash had intimated was only inside the detective's mind, Henry resumed his task. His priority was contacting the clients on the list provided by Mitchell's secretary, and assuring those with active cases that the previous level of service would be maintained. It was routine, or so he believed. Henry could have no premonition of the disastrous consequences of his actions.

CHAPTER SEVENTEEN

The day after his spat with the solicitor, Nash got a call from Henry Court. He knew instantly by the bristling tone of voice that the lawyer was angry, even before Court demanded, 'What have you done with Mitchell's private papers?'

'Why are you asking? What makes you think I've done anything with them?'

'Mitchell's secretary informed me that you'd been enquiring about them. When we went to his house I found your visiting card in his basement office, so it's obvious you removed his personal documents. I must have them back.'

'Did you remove anything from the house when you entered it without permission?'

'No, because apparently you'd already taken it all. And I don't need permission to enter that property.'

'That's where you're wrong, Mr Court! Mitchell's house is a crime scene. The incident tape across the building should have told you that. You had absolutely no right to enter that building without consent. Did you wear protective clothing?'

There was a long enough silence for Nash to guess the answer. 'I assume not. So by crossing that incident tape you have possibly contaminated evidence in a murder case. I shudder to think what a *good* defence lawyer would say about your irresponsible actions. If you intend to return there, you can only do so with my approval, and you must be under the supervision of a police officer at all times. That situation will remain unchanged until Mitchell's murder, and that of Ms Stevens, are solved.'

Clara was surprised when Nash raised his voice slightly, which was very unusual for him. 'Of course,' he continued, 'we might be able achieve that much quicker, if we were granted access to his business files.'

Nash paused to let that sink in before telling Court, 'In answer to your question, yes, we did remove Mitchell's personal documentation. We are holding the paperwork as potential evidence in a double murder case, so there is no way I will allow anyone to view it, let alone release it, until I am satisfied it is no longer germane to our enquiries.'

Nash replaced the receiver, ending the call as abruptly as Court had begun it. He looked across at Clara and smiled. 'Another satisfied customer — or maybe not. Now, with no chance of getting access to anything that might help us solve the recent murders, I suggest we go over the forensic reports of the other crime scene again. Who knows, one of us might have a brainwave.'

Despite his words, Clara recognized Nash's downbeat tone. The phrase 'clutching at straws' came to mind. And their subsequent perusal of the reams of documentation provided by the scientific officers provided no further enlightenment. Or so it seemed at the time.

It was late afternoon by the time they had finished reading, and as he was preparing to leave, Nash told Clara, 'I won't be in first thing tomorrow. I've to go through to Netherdale for a meeting with Jackie. She wants an update, and as I've been given some shopping to do by Mrs Rembrandt, I'll deliver the report in person. Given our lack of progress all round, the meeting will only last a few minutes.'

'What has Alondra asked you to buy?'

'Some pre-stretched canvasses. She's so productive she's almost run out. At least one member of the family is achieving something. She's also allowing Daniel to try his hand. All I can see on his attempts are paint splashes.'

'Cheer up, Mike, things will get better soon.'

'I certainly hope so, but I'm also aware of the saying "Things have got to get worse before they get better," and that's the last thing we need.'

* * *

Nash was driving to Netherdale, his thoughts on the forthcoming meeting with Superintendent Fleming and the purchases Alondra had asked him to make, when he heard the sound of sirens behind him.

He glanced in the rear-view mirror and saw a fire engine hurtling towards Netherdale. He moved over onto the verge to allow the vehicle to overtake, and a second fire truck also came racing past.

Knowing that Netherdale had its own fire station and equipment, Nash guessed the Helmsdale crews must have been called on to assist in what could only be a major incident. Not a good start to the day for somebody, he thought, unaware that the event might concern him.

Long before he reached the town, Nash could see the source of the emergency. The plumes of smoke billowing into the air were clear evidence of the severity of the blaze. Nash hoped nobody had been in the building when it caught fire. If there had been someone inside, he gave little chance for their survival.

When he approached the roundabout on the ring road, Nash joined a queue of motorists all waiting their turn to proceed. The tailback was considerable, so it was a while before he reached the head of the queue. The delay was extended by the road into the town centre being blocked by two police vehicles parked across the carriageway, their emergency hazards flashing.

Right of way at the roundabout had been temporarily suspended, traffic being controlled by uniformed officers.

Nash managed to attract the attention of the constable nearest him, who was holding his hand up to prevent his progress.

'What's the problem?' Nash asked the young officer, wondering if the man had begun shaving yet.

'Major fire on the road into town.' The reply was curt, dismissive.

'Where exactly?' Nash could do curt too.

'Netherdale Hall.'

Nash knew the building contained Mitchell & Co.'s offices. 'OK, I need to get there. Shift one of the squad cars and let me through.'

'Didn't you hear what I said? The road's blocked off to all traffic. That includes you. No way can we make exceptions just because you've got a fancy car. Use the ring road like everyone else.'

'Perhaps I didn't make myself clear, young man. I assume you must be new to the area, and you've no idea who you're talking to.' As he was speaking, Nash pulled his warrant card from his pocket, and held it up for the constable to read.

The officer's face went pale as he stammered, 'I'm . . . I'm sorry, sir, I didn't know. I thought you were a member of the public.'

'Fine, but you might want to bear this incident in mind. Soften your approach, and use a bit more tact to begin with. If that doesn't work, then it's time to get tough. Now, give your colleagues a shout and let me through, I need to get to Netherdale Hall.'

Five minutes later, having parked as close as he could behind several emergency vehicles, Nash rang Clara and told her, 'If you've nothing better to do, why not come through to Netherdale and join me in front of a nice warm fire?'

'Mike, have you been drinking?'

'Certainly not. The fire is the blazing inferno currently in the process of destroying Netherdale Hall.'

'I heard the fire engines leaving from next door and wondered where they were going. Hang on, did you say Netherdale Hall? That's where Mitchell's offices are.'

'I think the term should be *were*, not *are*. Despite the fire brigade's efforts, that building is past saving.'

* * *

Clara reached Netherdale almost an hour later. Her arrival coincided with that of Superintendent Fleming, who had also been contacted by Nash. They set out together in search of him, and found him standing alongside his car watching events taking place near the site of the conflagration. He greeted the new arrivals, telling them, 'I managed to grab a quick word with Doug Curran. He's a bit preoccupied, as you can imagine.'

Doug Curran, as Clara and Jackie knew, was the area's chief fire officer.

'Even with crews from both stations tackling the blaze, there's little they can do to save the building. Their main priority now is to prevent the fire from spreading to nearby properties. Those trees are presenting a bit of a worry.'

'I don't suppose they've been able to identify the cause yet. My guess would be an electrical fault,' Jackie said.

Nash shook his head. 'No, it wasn't. This was an arson attack. Curran told me they believe the person responsible poured huge quantities of petrol through the letter box in the front door, then went to the back of the building and did the same there. For good measure, they then went to the left-hand side, broke a window, and added even more fuel to the fire. The only positive news to come from all this is that there was nobody inside the building when the fire was started.'

'You said something on the phone about this possibly being linked to the murders, right?' Jackie looked confused.

'I think the connection is a fairly obvious one to make. Gavin Mitchell and Petra Stevens were murdered. Now their offices have been torched.'

'But what would that achieve, if the partners were already dead?'

'I've believed from the start of our investigation that the key to their murders was something they knew, something

143

the killer was desperate to avoid coming to light. If that information was contained in the files within these offices, the murderer might have been concerned that we would gain access to them. Then we could work out why they were murdered. I also believe they now consider themselves safe, having severed all links with the law firm, but there is one connection still remaining.'

'What's that, Mike? If all the files have gone, surely there can be no outstanding link?'

'Who says the files are gone?' Nash said. 'It's my understanding that solicitors use fireproof safes or lockboxes. They may be salvageable. But there is another link, and it all stems from what kicked off this chain of violence. This is only my opinion, but I believe the recent murders and this fire are a direct consequence of Robert Pickles finding the first skeleton at All Alone Cottage — and then the discovery of a second victim.'

Jackie shook her head. 'There's a flaw in your logic, though, Mike. None of the events at the cottage have been made public, so how would someone like Mitchell, or the killer, know about them?'

'Other than Viv phoning Gavin Mitchell and asking about ownership of the cottage, the information might have been leaked, either deliberately or accidentally. Sometimes it only takes a bit of casual gossip to trigger such a reaction. A few years ago, we were able to solve a string of murders that took place round here because of something a barmaid in a London club overheard. She passed the information to her lover, who just happened to be a Scotland Yard detective, and he fed it back to me.'

'OK, I take your point, Mike. So perhaps there isn't a flaw in your theory.'

As Fleming was speaking, Nash glanced around, and his gaze rested briefly on one of the fire engines. Although he was apparently concentrating on the vehicle, his mind was elsewhere, trying to grasp an elusive memory. The harder he tried, the less success he had.

Clara drew Nash's attention to a woman standing nearby. 'That's Gavin Mitchell's secretary,' she told him.

Nash looked at the woman and the man alongside her. 'Then I guess the bloke she's talking to — the one with the briefcase and the supercilious expression on his face — must be Henry Court, the stand-in lawyer. If so, I want a word with him. In fact, I want a word with both of them. Care to join us, Jackie?'

Seeing the grim set of Nash's features, Fleming laughed. 'Wild horses couldn't keep me away.'

'Excuse me. Are you Henry Court?' Nash's guess was clearly accurate, because the solicitor turned abruptly at the mention of his name.

'Yes, I am. Who are you?'

Nash showed his warrant card and nodded towards the building. 'What do you have to say about this?'

'It's a dreadful accident. Why are you here?'

'I came with my colleagues, Detective Superintendent Fleming and Detective Sergeant Mironova, to investigate a crime. This was no accident. This was a wilful, well-planned arson attack, committed by someone desperate to destroy the building and its contents. So determined, they poured petrol in via three locations and ignited it.'

Nash paused to let the bad news sink in, and then continued, 'If you recall, I did warn you of the potential danger. I can only assume their intention was to destroy evidence.' He looked Court straight in the eye and said, 'Evidence, might I remind you, that should have been available to our murder inquiries, had it not been for your stubborn, intransigent attitude. Without that evidence, our chance of catching the killer, or killers, of Mitchell and Ms Stevens, plus two as yet unidentified victims, have possibly gone up in smoke. It's only fortunate the building was unoccupied at the time the fire was started. Had anyone been in there, they would have died in unspeakable agony — and you would have had their death on your conscience.'

Nash paused again, but only to draw breath before adding, 'Will you at least now cooperate with our investigation by allowing us access to those files, if they are recoverable? Or, if necessary, reveal the names of the clients Mitchell was working for, or allow Mitchell's staff to speak with us?'

Court might have been humbled by Nash's tirade, but, Clara thought later, he was made of strong stuff. 'I'm extremely sorry if this hampers your inquiry, Inspector Nash, but my decision remains unaltered. I cannot, and will not, reveal such information. No matter what the consequences might be. I told you before that lawyer–client privilege is sacrosanct, and I hold firm to that principle, come hell or high water.'

'Be careful what you wish for,' Nash warned him. 'In view of this latest development and your earlier uncooperative attitude, I will now report your actions to the chief constable, and recommend that a complaint of your behaviour be passed to the Law Society.'

Jackie Fleming interrupted at this point. 'That's all right, Inspector Nash. I'll speak to the chief constable when I get back to HQ, and see it is dealt with immediately.'

Nash nodded his acknowledgement, and then turned to Court's companion. 'I believe you were Gavin Mitchell's secretary, correct?' He held up a warning hand to deter Court, who was about to interrupt. 'The question I am about to ask you does not transgress any so-called sacrosanct confidences, or overstep any boundaries. It is merely to establish one aspect of the office's working practices.'

Ignoring Court, she asked, 'What do you want to know, Inspector Nash?'

'I merely want to know if Mr Mitchell backed up data from his office computer. We checked the laptops at his house and there was no cloud storage on either of them.'

Clara turned away to mask her smile at Nash's apparent familiarity with IT. She guessed, correctly, that Viv Pearce and Nash's son Daniel were the sole sources of his knowledge.

'No, he didn't. I've mentioned before that Mr Mitchell was an extremely private person. He felt that putting confidential information on anything such as you're suggesting might be extremely unsafe. He didn't even share details of cases he was working on in the office, unless it became absolutely essential.'

'Thank you. That *has* been most helpful. If either of you think of anything else you might be able to share with us, without breaking any Masonic vows, please feel free to contact me. In addition, you should be aware that I consider the danger to be far from over. With both partners dead, you and your colleagues represent the only obstacles to the perpetrator. Therefore, please call us immediately if you feel threatened, or you see someone acting suspiciously.' With that, Nash handed them both his card and walked away.

'You certainly put the frighteners on them,' Fleming said when they were out of earshot. 'Did you mean that last bit, or were you ensuring you got your point across?'

Nash smiled. 'A bit of both, really. I don't think there's much we can do here until we get a report from the fire service, and that might not tell us anything we don't already know.'

CHAPTER EIGHTEEN

When Nash returned to Helmsdale, Viv Pearce entered his office and placed a sheet of paper on his desk. Nash studied the document with increasing interest, and then looked up at the tall Antiguan.

'Viv, that's absolutely brilliant. I'm a bit annoyed, though, because I should have thought of this.' He signed the application for a warrant, and then told Pearce, 'This might just provide the breakthrough we've been looking for.'

He watched Pearce leave, a broad smile on his face, and then summoned Clara. 'Did you know about the warrant Viv's applying for?'

'No, I didn't. All he said was he needed you to sign something.'

'It's an application for a warrant to obtain Gavin Mitchell and Petra Stevens' mobile phone records, plus those from their landline at their home. Obviously, we can't do anything about the one for Mitchell & Co. without incurring the wrath of Henry Court, and having the Law Society breathing fire and brimstone. But the ones we *can* get our hands on might yield us what we need. If Mitchell and Ms Stevens *did* have something to hide, I reckon it's far more likely they'd use their mobiles than a landline, don't you?'

When Clara left, Nash sat at his desk, staring into space thinking back to his arrival at the station earlier, after the fire. As he'd driven past the rear of the fire station to reach the police station car park, he'd glanced sideways, and noticed that two of the three bays that usually contained the fire engines were vacant, their crews still combating the blaze at Netherdale Hall. The third bay contained the only other vehicle, a far older model kept for training, and as standby.

Seeing the old fire truck triggered Nash's memory from earlier that morning. This time it was supplemented by the comment made by the forensic team leader after the search of All Alone Cottage, the connection raising a huge question in his mind. After considering the idea for several minutes, Nash dismissed the notion as far too fanciful, even for him.

He succeeded in forgetting it for the rest of the day, until he was leaving for home and saw the fire crew cleaning one of the engines that had been in operation. That brought the outlandish idea back, and no matter how hard he tried, he was unable to shake it off.

Several times during the evening, Alondra noticed her husband was preoccupied, and eventually asked if there was something troubling him.

Nash smiled. 'Is it that obvious? I was told something a while back, and I got reminded of it today, and that in turn sparked a wild idea. Clara says I get them regularly, but this one seems a bit extreme, even for me. I accept that occasionally my weird mind comes up with off-the-wall theories, and later, they turn out to be accurate, but at other times they're way wide of the mark. I think this might well be one from the latter category.'

'Hang on, though, Mike, if you hadn't got one of what you called your "wild ideas", I wouldn't be here with you now. In fact, but for you I'd probably be dead. So don't dismiss it out of hand. It's obviously troubling you. Why not run it past me? What's the English expression? "A trouble shared is a trouble halved," isn't it?'

Nash hugged her. 'I'm so lucky to have you. I count my blessings every day because you're with me. OK, here goes.' He explained, and when he'd finished, he sat waiting for Alondra's verdict.

'I agree that on the surface it seems far-fetched, but I don't think you should dismiss it. How would you feel if you ignore it, and later it turns out to be correct? Knowing you, I think you'd beat yourself up for being careless.'

Next morning, as Nash was preparing to leave home, Alondra asked him if he'd given the matter further thought.

'I was mulling it over as I walked Madam here,' he replied, nodding towards Teal, 'and I've decided to tell Clara, and see what she thinks.' He smiled wryly. 'Whatever her opinion is, she won't be shy of voicing it.'

* * *

Nash was the first to arrive in the CID suite, but after a few minutes Clara walked in.

'Grab a coffee and come into my office, I've something I need to talk to you about.'

Clara did as instructed, wondering what Nash had in mind. Later, she reflected that she could have guessed for ages without getting close to the answer. When she was seated, Nash explained his idea and what had prompted it.

She stared at him, dumbfounded for what seemed an age, and eventually asked, 'Let me get this straight. You believe there might be another body at All Alone Cottage, one we haven't yet found, correct?'

'That's right. I know it sounds like a wild idea, so I wondered what you thought.'

'You're basing this outlandish theory purely on the discovery of a toy fire engine, nothing more. A toy that, by your own admission, was made over half a century ago. That means it could have been left at any point since then. We don't know what the cottage was used for before it was deserted. It might have been a holiday let, and that could mean thousands of families have stayed there over the ensuing period.

You described it as a wild idea. I'd say it was way beyond outlandish, even for you, Mike.'

'It wasn't only the toy itself. There was another factor to take into consideration. If the toy is connected to the bodies found there, we might be looking at a family unit. Think about it, Clara, a man and woman between thirty and forty years old, plus a dog, and also a child's toy. Three bodies discovered, one family member possibly missing.'

There was another long silence before Clara responded. 'I have to admit, there does seem to be a small element of logic in what you say, but haven't you overlooked one highly important fact?'

'OK, what have I missed?'

'We searched those premises from top to bottom before handing the crime scene over to Forensics, and they also went through the cottage with a fine-toothed comb. Then, once they discovered the second body, the one in the well, you ordered a comprehensive sweep of the grounds, during which, I believe, they brought in cadaver dogs to assist. Despite the extensive search, there was no trace of a third body.'

'I appreciate what you're saying. But I still think it would be worthwhile going back and taking another look, this time with my "outlandish theory" in mind.'

'OK, I'll tag along, Mike, as long as you promise me one thing. Will you try to stop having these weird ideas? You know it's bad for you — and therefore bad for me.'

Having outlined their reason for going back to the cottage to Andrews and Pearce, whose scepticism clearly outstripped Clara's, they set off for Drover's Halt. 'Do you want me to come along?' Pearce volunteered as they were leaving. 'I'm a dab hand at chasing wild geese.'

'Certainly not! We wouldn't want to waste valuable resources on such a wild theory. Besides which, who's going to refill the coffee machine and go for our sandwiches, if you're not here? You can do that after you've got some more work done.'

* * *

If anything, All Alone Cottage looked even more derelict than her memory of it, Clara thought. Perhaps that was fanciful, fuelled by her recollection of the recent grim discoveries. That was OK — she was in the right company for fanciful ideas.

'What exactly are we looking for?' Clara asked as they approached the cottage door.

'That's the problem. I haven't the foggiest idea.'

'You've no idea, Mike? Are you sure you're feeling well?'

Nash smiled, but told her, 'Look at it this way, we went over Mitchell's house, then Forensics searched it, but we didn't discover that basement room until we went back for another look. And we found it almost by accident. I'm not suggesting there's a hidden cellar here, but there could be a place we've missed.'

Despite paying close attention to every space within the cottage, their prolonged examination yielded no results.

'I have to admit I'm glad that on this occasion you've been proved wrong, Mike,' Clara told him, as they drove back to Helmsdale. She glanced at him and, with her insight into Nash's mindset, realized he still wasn't prepared to relinquish his theory. 'You're still not convinced, are you?'

'No, I'm not, because all the time we were inside the cottage I got this strange feeling that there was something we were missing. Something was staring us in the face.'

'OK, accepting that, what do you intend to do about it?'

'I don't really know. At the moment I've run out of ideas.'

Clara sighed. 'Well, that's a relief.'

* * *

The following morning, Clara could have been excused for believing she'd wandered onto the set of *Groundhog Day*. As soon as she entered the CID suite, Nash called her into his office and told her, 'I had another idea last night.'

'Mike, I warned you about getting ideas. What is it this time, UFOs, Bigfoot, or the Loch Ness Monster?'

'Nothing quite that exciting. Actually, it was your mention of cadaver dogs that set me thinking, so I rang the handler and asked if his dogs had become agitated at any point during their search of the grounds.'

'What did he say?'

'He told me the only time they showed any interest was when they were near the well, or passing the front door of the cottage. He dismissed their reaction, believing it to be due to the bodies we'd already discovered in those locations. However, I now reckon they might have been agitated because they sensed there was another body concealed within the cottage.'

'Are you going to ask him to take his dogs back there for another try?'

'I can't do that at present. He's been called in by West Yorkshire Police to assist in the search for a body supposedly buried in upper Wharfedale. That means he could be away for a few days. I was brought up in that area, and there are immense tracts of wild moorland to cover. Anyway, I digress. I intend to return to the cottage, and this time, I'll take someone along who has a better knowledge of the building layout, if he's willing to go with us.'

'Who are you thinking of?'

'I thought Robert Pickles would be able to give a better opinion than anyone. He stayed there regularly as a child, and if anyone can spot any changes, he'll be the one. My only reservation is that he might be reluctant, given his fragile state of mind.'

If their colleagues had been sceptical the previous day, Nash's decision to return to the cottage was greeted with incredulity. Even their planned inclusion of Robert Pickles in the search team did nothing to dispel their belief that it would prove to be yet another waste of time and effort.

* * *

Clara put a call in to Louise Gough, who assured her that Robert would be at Simeon House, and would be quite willing to talk to them.

'We want to enlist Robert's help,' Clara told her, 'but it might be something he'll be unhappy about. In which case, we quite understand. We'll explain what we have in mind when we get there.'

When they reached Louise's house, she waved to them, pointing towards the back door. She preceded them into the kitchen, having asked if they'd like coffee. Robert was seated at the table, and as Clara looked at him, she noticed a marked difference in the ex-soldier's demeanour. All the stress and anxiety seemed to have vanished, and he looked cheerful and relaxed.

As they waited for the kettle to boil, Robert said, 'Louise told me you wanted me to assist with your enquiries. Does that mean I need a lawyer?'

Nash was surprised, but then realized Robert was joking. 'Not in the usual meaning of that phrase,' he responded. 'I need to ask a favour. But I quite understand if you feel unwilling to undertake what I have in mind, given your previous experiences. I don't want you to feel obliged to help.'

Nash explained what he needed, and both he and Clara were astounded by his instant reply, 'Of course I'll help, if I can. I remember the building well — and so does Louise, for that matter, so perhaps it would be even better if we both go with you.'

He paused and looked across the room. 'What do you think? Are you up for it?'

Louise nodded her agreement.

When they had drunk their coffee, the augmented party set off on the short journey, using Nash's Range Rover. Although Clara watched for signs of reluctance in Robert's attitude on reaching the cottage, there was only slight hesitation as he walked up the path to the front door. The fact that Louise was holding his hand no doubt helped. Inside, he didn't seem perturbed on entering the dining room where he had found the skeletal remains. He examined the room, and despite his close scrutiny of the building's interior, he could find nothing suggesting changes had been made — until they climbed the stairs to the upper floor.

'This is where my mother and father slept,' Robert said, as they entered the larger bedroom. 'It seems exactly the same as I recall, as does the bathroom. All that remains is the bedroom I used. I remember it well enough, don't you, Louise?'

'I seem to think the only room I saw up here was the bathroom. I certainly don't think I ever went in your bedroom when I was little.'

Nash opened the bedroom door and stood to one side. Robert took two paces inside and then stopped abruptly.

'Oh, they've boarded up the alcoves.' He pointed to the wall on his left-hand side and explained, 'The centre part is a chimney breast. When the fire is lit in the lounge it keeps this room lovely and warm. On either side of the chimney stack there were alcoves. One contained a chest of drawers, and the other had a hanging rail for clothing in it.'

'That's interesting. Are there any other changes?' Nash glanced at Clara as he spoke. He saw Clara nod, and knew she had got the unspoken message.

'No, that's the only difference I can see.'

'Is it important?' Louise asked.

'We're just following up on all the reports we've received, that's all,' Clara replied, knowing they did not want to cause Robert any further distress.

'OK. Now we've finished looking round, Clara, why don't you run Robert and Louise back home. I'll wait here.' Clara caught Nash's hidden meaning immediately.

* * *

Nash watched them leave before reaching for his phone. When Clara returned a few minutes later, he was on his mobile, and she knew from the gist of the conversation that he was speaking to Jackie Fleming.

Once he'd ended the call, Nash told her, 'I've ordered Viv here, Lisa can mind the shop. He'll set off once he's located a couple of crowbars. I looked at those false walls after you'd gone, and I reckon they're only plasterboard, so they shouldn't take much shifting.'

Clara gave voice to the question that had been troubling her since they learned of the altered structure. 'Why do you think they boarded both sides up?'

'I assume it was to avoid anyone noticing that the room looked odd — it seems to have worked. Let's face it, we've inspected the property twice without giving that room a second glance, and we were keeping an eye out for anything untoward.'

Pearce arrived, opened his car boot, and removed a pair of sledgehammers. 'When you described the walls as plasterboard, I thought these would be ideal for the job. I borrowed them from the fire department.' He then handed out pairs of thick gardening gloves. 'I called at the garden centre as I passed.' He looked directly at Nash. 'I've kept the receipt!'

Nash and Pearce took one section each, with Clara removing the broken pieces of plasterboard as they worked. The task of opening up the recesses only took a few minutes, but as the detectives examined the interior of one, they knew it would be a long time, if ever, before they could cast the horror of what was concealed within from their minds.

Nash rested his sledgehammer against the window sill, took out his mobile, and pressed a short code. 'Jackie, would you please get Mexican Pete and a CSI team out here ASAP?'

He listened for a moment, and then said, 'No, Jackie, it isn't one body, there are two. I'm extremely sorry to have to tell you . . . two small skeletons. Two little infants were walled up in one of the alcoves.'

* * *

They had moved outside, keen to be away from the dreadful sight. Viv had been sent back to Helmsdale, and Nash and

Clara were awaiting the arrival of the pathologist and CSI team. Nash's mobile rang. The caller was Superintendent Fleming, and she began by asking if she'd rung at a bad time. 'Not especially, we're twiddling our thumbs until Mexican Pete and the boffins get here. You could say any time was bad, after what we just found.'

'When you can get away, I'd like you to come through to Netherdale. I told the chief what you found, and she thinks we ought to discuss the way forward. Clara should come along as well, given the gravity of the situation.'

'I'm up for that, but it could be mid-afternoon before we're free.'

'OK, let's switch the venue to Helmsdale.' Fleming paused, and then asked, 'Is it bad there?'

'Yes and no. We've all seen some fairly grim sights in our time, and at least this one isn't a bloodbath. On the other hand, seeing those pathetic remains conjures up horrific mental images of what those innocent little mites must have suffered.'

'How old do you think they were?'

'Our worthy professor will be able to give a better estimate, but judging by the size of the skeletons, I'd guess they can't have been more than two years old, if that. Both of them were crouched, huddled up, as if they were terrified. Come to think of it, if they were conscious, that might have been true. There was insufficient space for them to move around, and they would be in complete darkness. Our only hope is that they were put to sleep before being placed in their dungeons. However, someone capable of such unspeakable cruelty probably didn't bother putting them out of their misery.'

As Nash was speaking, he saw the pathologist's vehicle pull up. 'Mexican Pete's arrived,' he told Jackie. 'I'd better go. I suppose I'll have to brace myself for another outbreak of sarcasm.'

Professor Ramirez had only just got out of his car, when he was confronted by DS Mironova. 'Before you start,

Professor,' Clara told him. 'I want you to promise not to say anything about Mike's predilection for finding corpses. Believe me, he isn't in the mood. In fact, neither of us are. I'm sure when you see the poor little souls, and the place they were killed, you'll understand what I mean.'

Ramirez placed his hand on Clara's arm, a reassuring gesture, no more. 'I get the picture. Given what Superintendent Fleming has told me, I certainly won't say anything out of place.'

He greeted Nash, who led him inside the cottage, and Clara accompanied them as they climbed the stairs. Ramirez took one look at the scene, and gave vent to his feelings. As he spoke in Castilian Spanish, Clara looked towards Nash for a translation.

'I didn't follow it all, but basically I think he was saying what he'd like to do to the person, or persons, who did this. Said he hoped to meet them — on his mortuary table.'

The professor's two assistants arrived, and the detectives took the opportunity to remove themselves from the scene. Ramirez expressed his understanding, and added, 'I only wish I could go with you, or that I hadn't been called here in the first instance.'

Nash pondered the pathologist's remark. He had rarely seen Ramirez so visibly moved by a crime scene before. That was hardly surprising, given what was inside the cottage.

CHAPTER NINETEEN

When they returned to Helmsdale, Lisa Andrews greeted them, apologizing for her lack of belief in Nash's theory.

'Don't worry, Lisa, you weren't the only Doubting Thomas, and on this occasion I wish I'd been wrong.' Without even a sideways glance at Clara, he added, 'It does happen, occasionally, despite people believing I'm a genius.'

Clara's scornful laugh was curtailed by the entrance of Chief Constable Ruth Edwards and Detective Superintendent Fleming. The senior officers were keen to begin the meeting, but Nash told them he required coffee beforehand. 'We've only this minute got back, so Lisa can make it as a penance for failing to believe in my uncanny ability.' The gallows humour was continuing.

This time, Clara's laughter was echoed by the others.

Ruth Edwards began by asking Nash and Mironova to describe the crime scene. 'I want to know why the two latest victims weren't found earlier, given that CSI had been examining the cottage and surrounds so carefully.'

'That's partly my fault,' Nash responded. After outlining the location of the bodies, he added, 'When I asked for the cadaver dogs to conduct a search, I told their handler to concentrate on the area surrounding the cottage. I should have requested a further check on the interior. I spoke to him later and he told me the dogs showed interest in the building, but he, like me, assumed that was purely their reaction to the woman's body we'd already found.'

'Don't beat yourself up over it,' Ruth told him. 'At least the bodies have been found now. And after all this time, a few weeks is hardly going to make any difference.'

'I feel as if I've let the team down, though. Clara, for one, used to believe I was perfect, and now she's disillusioned.'

The chief disguised her smile. 'What we should concentrate our thoughts on is the best way to take the investigation forward. We now have four unidentified victims, with absolutely no clue as to the motive behind their murder, let alone a suspect.'

'I think it's actually six victims in total,' Nash corrected her. 'We believe Gavin Mitchell and Petra Stevens were murdered because they knew too much. Our theory is that the killer was desperate to avoid what happened at All Alone Cottage becoming known, and silenced them to eliminate anyone who might spill the beans.'

Edwards and Fleming pondered this for a while, and then the chief constable suggested, 'I think it's time to consider revealing what we know about the cottage victims. Granted, that isn't very much, but it might just prompt someone to come forward with information that could prove vital. Let's face it,' she added with a grimace, 'even a snippet is more than we've got at present. I'm not suggesting the informant will be someone associated with the killer, although that is possible. But it could equally be someone who recognizes what we believe to be a family unit, and can therefore provide us with possible identities.'

'Publicity might do that for us,' Nash replied, 'but I'm concerned it could also provoke even more violence. If our theory is correct, the killer has already not only eliminated the two people who could link him to All Alone Cottage, he has also burned down their offices. If we go public, it might lead to even more mayhem.'

'Do you honestly believe that's likely?'

Nash answered Jackie Fleming's question immediately. 'I'm not sure, but I'd be reluctant to take the risk. Look at what's already happened. We asked Mitchell about the ownership of the cottage, and within days Petra Stevens, the partner who handled property transactions at Mitchell & Co., was murdered. Less than a week after her death, Mitchell was also killed. Both deaths made to look like suicide. What disturbs me is that if the killer finds out exactly what we discovered at the cottage, including the one solid piece of evidence we have, they could well go on the rampage. Overall, I reckon we should hold off from revealing what we've found — at least until the post-mortems have been carried out on the children. We need to establish that the five victims *were* a family unit. That will enable us to narrow down the search criteria considerably.'

'Don't you mean four victims?' Fleming asked.

'It's five, if you include the dog.'

'Ah, yes, I'd forgotten about the pooch. You also said something about a solid piece of evidence. What was that?'

'The extremely unusual, and highly expensive, piece of jewellery found at the cottage by Robert Pickles. That could give us a clue as to the identity of the female victim, and from there we might be able to connect the dots and put a name to the others.'

'Have you any thoughts on the way forward?'

'Without DNA to support our theory, we can't assume the victims were a family unit, although that remains a strong probability. Our revered pathologist tells me this will happen, but it's going to take time.' Nash saw Ruth Edwards wince as he added, 'He also warned me the procedure will be very expensive.'

After giving further consideration to what Nash had said, and noticing that Mironova seemed in total agreement, the chief constable said, 'OK, we'll put the publicity machine on hold for the time being. As to the immediate tasks before us, I've asked Jackie to act as the attending officer at the autopsies on the two children.'

She saw Nash was about to protest, and held up her hand to stop him. 'I think you should step aside on this occasion, Mike. You and your colleagues have had more than enough horrors to cope with already. I'd rather not add to them when it can be avoided. I'd also like you, Clara, and Viv to go home immediately. Spend time with your loved ones, and that might help you regain a sense of perspective, knowing there is more goodness in the world than evil. And finally, simply because I'm sending you home early this afternoon, that doesn't mean you've to rush into work tomorrow. Those are orders, by the way.'

* * *

Alondra was looking out of the lounge window, when she saw her husband's car pull in alongside hers. She glanced at her watch, a reflex action prompted by his much earlier than usual return home. She'd been alerted to Mike's impending arrival by Teal, whose sensitive hearing had identified the car engine sound, long before the Range Rover came into view.

As Mike stepped out of the car, Alondra noticed his sombre expression. She asked Daniel to go to his room, telling him, 'I think your father has had a bad day. Give him some time. I'll call you when he is settled.'

She hurried to the front door and opened it as he approached. Her greeting was accompanied by a warm embrace that lasted several seconds. She took hold of his hand, led him inside, and guided him towards the lounge. 'Come along, sit down, and tell me all about it,' she ordered.

Nash smiled. 'That obvious, is it?'

'It is to me, and to someone else who cares about you.' Alondra gestured towards the Labrador, who was trying to attract her master's attention. 'And Daniel has gone to his room to give you some space, so tell me.'

She waited until Mike sat down in his favourite chair, then perched on the side. With Teal leaning against his leg, her head on his knee, and with Alondra's arm around his shoulders, Nash told her what they had discovered at the cottage. No matter how he told it, the terrible atrocity, and the effect it had on those compelled to witness the dreadful sight, could not be disguised.

'The chief sent us all home early, told us to spend time with our loved ones.' He smiled, a trifle sadly, as he added, 'I'm so glad this didn't happen a few years ago, when I had no one at home. That makes me appreciate how lucky I am.'

'Do you have any suspects, or is it too soon to go down that road? Oh, I forgot — perhaps you're not allowed to discuss it.'

'I don't think there are any such restrictions between husband and wife. Let's be fair, for all I know, I might talk in my sleep.'

Alondra bent over and kissed him lightly. 'You do,' she told him with a smile.

'Really, what do I say?'

'Usually it's just one word, and that's fine by me.' She saw his puzzled frown and told him, 'You say my name.'

Nash smiled, and then admitted how little evidence the team had.

'Don't let it get you down, Mike. You've told me before of instances where the least likely scrap of information turns out to prove crucial. And let's be fair, you've got a great team working with you, so don't try and shoulder all the responsibility. If anyone can do it, you, Clara, and your colleagues can.'

Alondra's encouraging words and the comfort provide by Teal's obvious concern had the desired effect and Nash began to relax.

Daniel joined them, asking, 'You OK, Pa?'

'I am, now I'm home,' Nash replied.

'Good. My bike's got a puncture and I need some help.'

Later, after they retired to bed, Nash found sleep difficult to come by, and when he did eventually doze off, his rest was disturbed by a nightmare such as he had not experienced for a long time. It was a jumble of images portraying the two innocent victims being trapped in a dark place, stifled by lack of air and terrified by their inability to see or move, with their cries going unheard.

Woken by her husband's restlessness, Alondra put her arm about him, comforting him in the hope that he would relax. Mike woke up, and comfort soon became passion. After they made love, he went back to sleep. This time, his rest was undisturbed.

* * *

Next morning, obeying the chief constable's instructions, Nash took his time before setting off for work. He made the most of the opportunity to eat the cooked breakfast Alondra served him, and chat to Daniel about his forthcoming trip to France.

It was late morning when he arrived at Helmsdale, and he had only been there a few minutes when his phone rang. The caller was Superintendent Fleming, reporting the results of the post-mortems. 'Hang on, Jackie,' Nash told her. 'I'll put you on speaker so Clara can hear.'

'It was very much as you feared, Mike. The victims were little more than infants. One was a boy, the other a girl, and Professor Ramirez estimates them to have been somewhere between eighteen months and two years old when they died. As they were kept inside such a confined space with little access, there was far less scavenging than with the adult victims.'

Out of his eye corner, Nash saw Clara shudder at Fleming's statement, but concentrated on her next comment. 'As a result of that, Professor Ramirez is confident they'll be able to get DNA. Cause of death was similar to the adults, a combination of dehydration and malnutrition. There is no way of telling whether they were sedated prior to being walled up. The only minute crumb of comfort is that owing to their much smaller stature, their suffering would not have been as prolonged as that of the adult victims.'

'It's cold comfort at best, Jackie. Thanks for updating us, and for stepping into the breach. It can't have been easy. I only hope you didn't find it too distressing.'

'It wasn't easy, but the PMs didn't take long. When I came out of the mortuary, I was more angry than distressed. Now, all I feel is a fierce determination to find whoever is responsible, and put them behind bars, preferably for the rest of their miserable life. All we can do for those poor innocent little bairns now is to bring justice on whoever did this to them.'

* * *

Later that day, Viv Pearce was able to report the outcome of his research into Mitchell and Stevens' mobile phone records.

'There were very few calls, or text messages, on their devices, and most of these were to and from each other. However, there is one incoming number I found on Mitchell's phone that could prove interesting. There might be an innocent explanation for the call, but it definitely warrants investigation.'

'Why, who does the number belong to?'

'The call took place nine days or so before Ms Stevens was killed. It was from a mobile belonging to Bob Greenwood.'

'Bob Greenwood?' Nash asked.

'Yes, you remember, the civilian support officer who at the time was standing in for Tom Pratt and Maureen Riley.'

Nash stared at Pearce in surprise, and then glanced at Mironova. He could tell by Clara's expression that she was equally shocked by the news.

'Unless he's a client, I think this is a matter for investigation by Jackie Fleming, or the chief constable. There might be disciplinary measures to be taken, if not worse. One way or the other, Mr Greenwood could have some very awkward questions to answer. Viv, will you phone Jackie, tell her what you've discovered, and then forward your evidence to her?'

Nash turned in the direction of his office, but stopped. 'Did Gavin Mitchell ring anyone directly following Greenwood's call?'

'No — at least if he did, it wasn't from his mobile.'

'OK. And the date and time of Greenwood's call to Mitchell . . . was that before or after we sent our reports about All Alone Cottage to Netherdale?'

'It was the same day, Mike. I checked that.'

Once Pearce was out of earshot, Nash told Clara, 'Viv's on top form these days. I wonder what's changed.'

'Maybe now that little Brian is older, Viv's getting a full night's sleep.'

CHAPTER TWENTY

Nash sat at his desk, pondering the implications behind Pearce's revelation about Bob Greenwood, when his phone rang. He glanced at the screen. 'Good afternoon, Professor, what can I do for you?'

Ramirez, it seemed, was in business mode. 'I have two pieces of information for you. The first is regarding the infants at the cottage. I suspect they are twins — DNA analysis will confirm that. I'm not sure if that fact alone is helpful, given that there are on average more than twelve thousand sets of twins born in the United Kingdom every year. However, the second piece of information might help to narrow your search for them down a little. The laboratory tested the dog hair from the unfortunate animal's corpse. The analysis reveals it belonged to a mature Borzoi bitch.'

'Did you say "Borzoi"? I don't think I've ever heard of such a breed.'

'That's hardly surprising as we're in Helmsdale, not Leningrad. The breed is used extensively for game hunting throughout Russia.'

'I didn't realize you were an expert on dog breeds, Professor.'

'I'm not, but Google certainly is.'

'Thank you for the information. It could be extremely useful.'

Nash called Clara into his office, and relayed what Ramirez had told him. 'Normally, I'd ask Viv to do this, but he's a bit tied up at present, so would you go online and discover what you can about Borzoi dogs. See if you can find out who breeds and owns them in this area. Borzoi is a Russian breed, apparently. The name—'

Clara cut him short, 'Means "sight hound", and the word is a corruption of *Borzoya*. They're also quite common in Belarus.'

'I keep forgetting you hail from that neck of the woods, originally.'

'Why are you asking about a Borzoi? Was that the breed of dog we found near the cottage?'

Nash nodded, before adding, 'Mexican Pete just told me, and also agreed with what we suspected, that those two little ones were twins. Combine that with a dog breed that, unless I'm very much mistaken, is as rare in these parts as rocking horse droppings, and I think we might at last be starting to make some progress. Oh, and ask Viv to pop in when he's free, will you? I've another job for him. That's why you're in charge of research for now.'

It was ten minutes before Pearce entered Nash's office. 'Sorry, Mike, I was on the phone.'

'No problem, Viv. Now, this is what I want you to do.' Nash explained what he had in mind, adding, 'And don't let Forensics sidetrack you. They'll probably moan about workload, and try to tell you they can't get round to it until next Christmas. Remind them the instruction came from me, and has the highest priority, so they must leave anything else they're working on. If they don't like it, they can explain why to the chief constable.'

* * *

Viv was glad of the additional work Nash had given him. Keeping his brain occupied with the new task helped to distract him from the terrible discoveries at the cottage. As father to a boy slightly younger than the latest two victims, he was finding it difficult to come to terms with the appallingly cruel deed. Trying to shelve his emotional response, and dedicate his efforts to finding the killer, was no easy task, but he knew it was the only way he could help those infants now.

Such was his determination to advance the investigation that he overrode the objections from Forensics that Nash had so accurately predicted, and was thus able to present his findings to the team only twenty-four hours later.

Pearce smiled at Nash. 'Once I'd got Forensics on board, we examined the data from the satnav memories in Mitchell's car, and also that of Ms Stevens. I couldn't find anything untoward on either device. The only journeys of note were a month or more ago. One was to London. The others were to York, Leeds, and Scarborough.'

'What about more recent journeys?'

'Nothing I could pinpoint as exceptional, Mike. There was zero activity from the Range Rover device until the day of Ms Stevens' fateful last journey. I assume that was because she was recuperating at home after her skiing accident.'

'What about Mitchell's car?' Clara asked.

'Again, nothing out of the ordinary. The Porsche only travelled to and from Netherdale during the working week, and remained inactive at weekends. All the trips were to Mitchell's office, with the exception of one.'

'What was different?'

Pearce smiled at Clara's persistence, guessing that she, like all of them, was trying to focus on this rather than dwelling on events elsewhere. 'The journey was to Netherdale, and it took place four days after Ms Stevens was killed.'

'So, where did he go apart from his office?' Lisa asked.

Viv grinned. 'Sorry, Lisa — remember, Mitchell didn't go to his office at all after Ms Stevens' death. Fortunately, the satnav installed in the Porsche is a high-end spec, and is extremely accurate, so I was able to pinpoint the exact location of the only places he visited. The Porsche was parked for an hour outside Anderson & Holden, another firm of solicitors in Netherdale. Then it moved to the other end of the high street, and stopped again for about twenty-five minutes, in the yard to the rear of Shires Bank. The car then returned directly to Mitchell's house — so, sadly, unless we can obtain information from the solicitors, or the bank, I think that's another dead end.'

Nash winced at Pearce's dreadful, albeit unintentional, pun, but thanked him for his efforts, even though they appeared to have been in vain. Pearce's assumption was a natural one to make, but then, he hadn't seen how distressed Mitchell had been following his partner's death.

'One question before you go,' Nash said.

'What?'

'Who was driving?'

Viv grinned again. 'Mitchell, of course. I knew you'd ask that, so I checked the CCTV on the high street around the time of the journey and saw him at the wheel.'

'I've had a thought,' Clara said, and began rummaging in the files. Moments later, she had a sheaf of papers spread out on her desk.

'OK, so what is it?' Nash asked.

'That journey Mitchell made to the solicitors and the bank in Netherdale. It seems a bit odd, given that when we saw him four days earlier, he was in no fit state to go anywhere.'

Nash nodded. 'Just what I was thinking.'

Clara held up the paperwork she had been examining. 'These are the bank statements we removed from Mitchell's house. The latest page covers the period up to the Friday following that journey. According to his bank statement, Mitchell neither paid into, nor withdrew from, his account during that week. In fact, the last transaction shown on here is a direct debit payment for council tax, made a week prior to Ms Stevens' death. The question I've been trying to answer is, why would someone visit a bank if not to make a deposit or withdrawal?'

It was a simple, straightforward question, but the answer was by no means easy to come by.

* * *

That evening, as they were sitting down for dinner, Alondra asked, 'Mike, what does "all to cock" mean?'

Daniel grinned, and Nash blinked with surprise. 'It means everything's gone wrong. Where did you hear that expression?'

'Jonas rang to apologize for not having been to do the gardening before now. He's been waiting for the return of his equipment, and then, of course, last week it was raining. He said he'll be here on Saturday, weather permitting, if that's convenient.' Alondra smiled. 'At least, I think that's what he meant. As far as I can remember his actual words sounded something like, "Ah'll be up at thy place cum Sat'day. Allus providin' it ain't chucking it down. Trouble is, them thievin' sods an' last week's rain 'ave thrown mi all t' cock".' She smiled. 'Does that make sense?'

Daniel burst out laughing at Alondra's attempt to mimic the old man's broad Yorkshire accent with the Spanish infection in her voice. Nash, having given him a warning glance, stifled a chuckle, but agreed her translation was accurate. He wasn't to know that the gardener's delayed visit would prove pivotal in providing some of the information they were seeking to solve the case.

Alondra returned to the topic of Jonas Turner's impending visit. 'I usually make sandwiches for Jonas's lunch, although you wouldn't know that, as he normally comes during the week. He likes cheese and pickle, although the way he prefers it, I think a more accurate description would be pickle and cheese. I've run out of pickle, so as I'm not planning on going to town before the weekend, would you mind nipping into Good Buys and getting a couple of jars tomorrow? While you're there, could you also get half a dozen bottles of Theakston? That's Jonas's favourite brew.'

'No problem, darling. After all, we've got to keep the workers happy.'

* * *

Nash was in business mode the next morning, hoping they might all get a weekend off for a change. He called Viv Pearce into his office. 'Viv, I've got a job for you. I want you to go through to Netherdale and talk to that firm of solicitors Mitchell visited after Ms Stevens' death. See if you can get them to tell you the reason for Mitchell's visit. When you're talking to the solicitor, make a point of telling them you're looking into Mitchell's murder and that of his partner, plus the arson at their offices. Put the frighteners on them by explaining that we tried to get information from Mitchell, but he refused, and shortly afterwards he was murdered. You could even mention in passing that we believe lawyers withholding information from us is becoming extremely unhealthy. It might not have the desired effect, but it's worth a shot.'

A couple of hours later, Viv returned. 'I went to the lawyer's office and they stonewalled me for a while, but when I intimated that reluctance to cooperate was proving injurious to lawyers' health, they changed their attitude slightly. Not enough to give us what we need,' he added swiftly, seeing the look of expectation on his listeners' faces, 'but sufficient to confirm Mitchell did go to see them, not simply use their car park. Unfortunately, the partner Mitchell saw, Paul Holden, is in court all day today, so even if he's prepared to be forthcoming, it will have to wait until he's free. According to his secretary, his diary is full with court appearances, so we might have to wait a while. She did say something that puzzled me, because I couldn't work out the meaning at first. She told me they were still acting on Mitchell's behalf, and I wondered how that could be if he's dead. Then I realized she might have meant they were the repository of his will and had been tasked with carrying it through to probate. However, that's only a guess.'

'I'd say it's probably a fairly good guess,' Nash replied. 'And it would explain the timing of his visit. Prior to Petra Stevens' death, I would imagine she would have been the main beneficiary, but you can't leave a bequest to someone who is already deceased.'

CHAPTER TWENTY-ONE

Fortunately for Jonas Turner's peace of mind, Saturday dawned bright and clear. When Nash and Daniel returned from their morning walk with Teal, the gardener's van was already parked on the drive.

Nash greeted the old man, while Daniel watched with amusement as Teal frolicked with Pip, Turner's Jack Russell terrier.

'Nah then, Master Daniel, 'ow's tha doin'?'

'Fine, thank you, Mr Turner.'

'That's good.' He turned to Nash. 'Thought ah'd mek a start on t' borders, afore ah get lawn trimmed, an' by gum, it needs it. Can't do wit' pitch bein' unfit fer young Len Hutton, 'ere.'

Nash laughed. 'Don't call him that, he thinks he's the next Ian Botham. I'll leave you to it, Jonas.'

He wandered inside and went into the conservatory, where Alondra was cleaning some brushes. A painting was on the easel, one he hadn't seen previously. Nash was surprised, knowing her reputation had been built on landscape images, whereas this was a portrait. He stared admiringly at the depiction of a small, frisky dog.

Alondra glanced over her shoulder, gesturing to the portrait. 'Do you think it looks like Pip?'

'I do. I think you've captured the little fellow perfectly. In fact, I'm not sure someone could do better with a camera.'

'I thought I'd give it to Jonas as a present. I just hope he likes it.'

'I reckon he'll be over the moon. Anyway, I just came to tell you I'll be in the shed, if you need me. I've work to do with Daniel.'

'What work is that?'

'More bicycle maintenance. I've got to make sure they're in tip-top condition — otherwise I'll be in trouble. He wants to take his with him to France this year.'

'I'm glad you mentioned that, because I've been wondering if we ought to get another bike. I'm concerned that I'm not getting enough exercise.' Alondra smiled mischievously. 'Except at night, of course. I thought it would be nice if we all went cycling together.'

'That's a great idea. Why don't we visit the bike shop tomorrow? I think the Netherdale store is open on Sundays — I'll check.'

* * *

Nash, under Daniel's supervision, finished attending to the bikes shortly before lunchtime. Having washed his hands, he wandered through to the kitchen, where Alondra was preparing sandwiches. 'I wouldn't mind one of those,' he told her. 'But don't go too heavy on the pickle.' He eyed the ones she'd made for Jonas and added, 'I doubt whether you could taste the cheese in those.'

Nash carried a tray containing the plates of sandwiches outside. Alondra followed, one hand behind her back concealing the portrait she was carrying. Before handing Turner his lunch, Alondra told the old man, 'I have a present for you, Jonas. I hope you like it. It's to say thank you for all you do for us.' She produced the painting she'd been hiding.

Turner gazed on the image, his eyes misting over as he saw the representation of his faithful companion. It was several seconds before he could bring himself to speak. 'By 'eck, Mrs Alondra, tha's done t' old feller proud. Ah'm reet suited wi' it. Thank ye ever so. Sithee, Pip, cum an' look at thee sen. Tha's proper famous nah.'

They adjourned to the picnic table on the terrace, with its spectacular view of Black Fell. After Turner had taken a couple of bites of his sandwich, he said, 'By, but this 'ere pickle's a bit of all reet, ah can tell thee. Ah'd say it's near on as good as Barty's, and that's sayin' summat.'

Alondra looked at Mike for enlightenment, but he merely shrugged his shoulders, clearly as baffled as her. 'Barty? What is a Barty?' she asked.

The gardener looked at her, then at Nash. 'I reckon tha's both far too young ter remember Barty's Pickles. They were reet champion, nowt better in my book. Course,' he laughed, 'ah might have been prejudiced as ah worked for Barty reet after ah left school.'

'You mean Barty's was a firm that made pickles, is that it?'

'That's reet, Mrs Alondra, an' they were best in t' business. Shame it all went ter pot after Barty died.'

'What went wrong?'

'Barty were a secretive sort at best o' times. Mind you, from what ah were told about t' way 'e carried on as a youngster, ah'm not surprised. Anyroad, 'e kept recipe to 'issen, never let on about quantities, an' t' 'erbs an' spices 'e put into t' mix, so without anyone t' put t' ingredients together, firm died along wi' 'im.'

'Barty is an unusual name. What does it stand for?'

'It's short fer Bartholomew — but 'e couldn't fit it on t' label.' Jonas chuckled.

Nash hadn't been paying close attention up to that point, but he sat up straight in his chair, stared at Turner for several seconds, and then asked, 'Was his Christian name Bartholomew?'

'Nah, it were 'is surname. Roland Bartholomew were 'is full name.'

There was another long silence as Nash digested what Turner had told him. He laughed before saying, 'That's different. What else do you know about him?'

Alondra listened as her husband, apparently showing only casual interest, extracted what little information Jonas was able to supply.

''E were allus secretive abaht 'is private life, were Barty.' Turner glanced sideways and winked at Alondra, before adding, 'That were likely cos ah 'eard tell, as 'e allus 'ad a different lady friend on 'is arm when 'e were younger. Like some others round 'ere ah cud mention.'

Nash ignored Alondra's giggle, but he looked disappointed. 'He wasn't married, then?'

'Ah can't say one way or t' other fer certain if 'e tied knot.' Turner grinned wickedly. 'But Barty certainly 'ad a daughter, that ah do know. 'Er name were Christine, and she were a reet cracker.'

'Did he have any other family?'

'No, I reckon 'e were . . . oh 'ang on, 'e did 'ave a sister, much younger than 'im. She were a schoolmistress, I reckon. 'Anged if I can remember 'er name, though. Anyroad, why the sudden interest in Barty? I reckon 'e must have been dead close on fifty years, if not more.'

'Just professional curiosity, I suppose. Once a busybody, always a busybody. I like to keep my hand in and refresh my interview technique.'

'Hah, ah reckon there's next t' no chance of tha gettin' rusty the way crime is these days, even round 'ere.'

Nash's glib explanation might have satisfied the old man, but Alondra wasn't taken in by it.

After a moment, prompted by the look in Turner's eyes when he mentioned Bartholomew's daughter, Nash asked the old man casually, 'Something leads me to think you and Christine were a bit more than casual acquaintances, am I right?'

Jonas smiled reminiscently, 'Ay, yer could say that, an' no mistake. Ah were reet taken wi' Christine and she felt t' same abaht me, or so ah reckoned. Ah often wonder what might 'ave 'appened if ah 'adn't 'ad t' go away. Ah were a terrier, tha' knows, an' ah got called up. Still, what's past is past, an' no use frettin' abaht it.'

Alondra was puzzled. 'What do you mean, you were a "terrier"? Is that to do with dogs?'

It was several seconds before Jonas brought his laughter under control sufficiently to explain. 'Nah, Mrs Alondra. Terriers is t' slang name fer t' Territorial Army. Mi dad were a soldier, and ah wanted 'im t' be proud o' mi, so ah joined t' TA soon as ah could. Got sent ter Cyprus in 1962 along wi' a couple o' mi mates, t' stand in fer reg'lars who'd been sent t' other places. We weren't told straight out, but we reckoned it were summat t' do wi' yon Fiddle Castro and t' Russkies, wi' them missiles the Yanks got their knickers in a twist ower. Anyroad, ah were away gettin' on fer two years. When ah got back, everything 'ad changed. Barty were dead, an' Christine 'ad got 'ersen hitched. That med mi sad fer a while, cos she thought ah were dead.'

'Why did she think that?' Alondra asked.

'There were a training accident at garrison where ah were stationed, just afore ah went to Cyprus, an' t' press gev out as one o' t' casualties were a Private Turner. Christine thought it were me, but it were a guy from Wiltshire wi' t' same surname. Course, when I kem back, she got t' shock o' 'er life, but by then, it were t' late fer us. Ah moped ower 'er for long enough, but then ah 'ad other fish ter fry.'

* * *

Later, after Turner had left, proudly carrying the portrait of Pip to his van, Alondra asked Mike about what she'd heard. 'What was your real reason for asking a string of questions about a pickle manufacturer who died over half a century ago? Don't try and convince me with that nonsense you told

Jonas about brushing up your interview technique. Was it connected to a case you're dealing with? Because if so, I can't see how, given the number of years since the man was alive.'

'I can't be sure if it's connected to a case or not. Bartholomew's Pickles might be relevant, but on the other hand, it might be pure coincidence.'

'I thought you didn't believe in coincidences?'

'I don't as a rule, but I'm willing to admit that they do happen from time to time.' Nash smiled. 'Just don't tell Clara I said that.'

'You told me Jonas's wife died a few years ago, was that what he meant by having other fish to fry? It's an expression I've never heard before.' Alondra laughed. 'Like quite a few Jonas uses.'

'Yes, they were married a long time, not too happily towards the end. But I suppose that's understandable, given what happened to them.' He saw Alondra's puzzled expression and explained, 'Jonas and his wife had one child — a son — but, tragically, he was killed in a road accident when he was in his twenties.'

* * *

As soon as DS Mironova entered the CID suite on Monday morning, Nash told her, 'Your boyfriend came to our house on Saturday to do the garden, and Alondra made him a sandwich as usual. That led to a very interesting conversation, all because of the sandwich's contents.'

Clara smiled at Nash's reference to Jonas Turner, but the rest of his statement made no sense whatsoever. 'Sorry, Mike, you've lost me completely. Were you talking about chicken mayonnaise, or egg and cress? Because, if so, I'll have to pass. I'm not a great expert on sandwich fillings. I can't even begin to think how you could find it an interesting topic of conversation.'

'It wasn't anything like that. It was pickles.'

'Pickles? As in piccalilli?'

'That sort of thing, yes. Jonas reckoned the jar I bought at Good Buys was top notch.'

'I know it's early, Mike, but we are here to work, aren't we? Or have you decided we deserve a day off, and we should spend the whole of our time discussing food?'

'Ignoring food, Clara, tell me what the word "pickles" brings to mind?'

'If it's about work, then it's obviously Robert Pickles, the guy who found the first body in the cottage. Unless, of course, you've reverted to discussing sandwiches. Which is it?'

'Actually, I think it's both — or possibly neither.' Deciding he had wound Clara up enough, Nash added, 'Let me explain, and then you'll understand why I found the conversation interesting.'

As Nash told Clara what Jonas Turner had said, she made the same inference as he had. 'You believe the reason we couldn't find any reference to Robert's father is because the name Bartholomew Pickles was invented?'

'That's my theory, and I believe the idea was to throw anybody who enquired off the scent. However, thanks to Jonas, I also believe the man who fathered Robert Pickles was a descendant of Roland Bartholomew, or someone close to him. There could be quite a few of his offspring around, because according to what Jonas was told, Roland Bartholomew was an insatiable womanizer, a real Jack-the-lad, until he settled down later in life. What we don't know is if he settled down because he got married, although that sounds highly probable. I think it might be worth getting Viv to check out Roland Bartholomew. It might be yet another dead end, but if nothing else, it might throw some light onto the ownership of All Alone Cottage back when Robert was born.'

* * *

Viv Pearce accepted the task gladly, and by late afternoon he was able to report his findings, such as they were. Initially, these seemed to point to yet another frustratingly unsuccessful effort.

'The information I was able to discover about Roland Bartholomew is disappointingly sparse,' he told the other members of the team. 'I was unable to find any record of him having got married, nor is he listed as father of any offspring. The only relative was a younger sibling, a sister named Agatha Bartholomew.'

'She'll be long dead by now, I suppose,' Clara suggested.

'Actually, she isn't, according to the BMD registers. She was born in 1928, which makes her twelve years Roland's junior. She's ninety-two years old, and now lives in St Cecilia's Care Home here in Helmsdale.'

Clara was impressed by the extent of Pearce's knowledge. 'How did you find that out?'

'I used the wonders of the internet, and found an article in the *Netherdale Gazette* about her. Apparently, Agatha Bartholomew was headmistress of Helmsdale Primary School. When she retired, the school governors not only presented her with an expensive leaving present, they also organized a lavish dinner in her honour. Having read that, I took a chance and phoned the school. I managed to get through to the current headmaster, who began his education as one of Agatha's pupils. Apparently, he's still in touch with her and provided me with her whereabouts. He also said something I'm not sure I understand. He said, "Agatha's still got all her chairs at home, despite her age" — whatever that means.'

Clara was equally baffled, and they both looked at Nash for enlightenment.

'The expression means she's still in possession of all her mental faculties.'

'Sometimes you need a translator for Yorkshire dialect and slang,' Clara grumbled.

Nash glanced at his watch. 'It's a bit late for us to go visiting Ms Bartholomew this afternoon. I've to go through to Netherdale for a meeting with the chief and Jackie, so I suggest we leave it until tomorrow. Clara, will you call St

Cecilia's, and ask them what time of day would be most suitable? I'd suggest late morning, which will give the staff time to sort out residents, and we'll be able to avoid clashing with breakfast and lunch.'

'OK, will do, Mike. What's your meeting about?'

'Next year's budget.' Nash sighed. 'And isn't that going to be fun?'

CHAPTER TWENTY-TWO

Having been advised by the manager of the care home that eleven o'clock would be the most opportune time to visit, Nash and Mironova left the CID suite, intending to walk the short distance to St Cecilia's. They were surprised to find a visitor in the station reception area, chatting to Steve Meadows. Jack Binns, their retired uniform sergeant, was in deep conversation with his successor.

'This is a pleasant surprise. What brings you to this den of iniquity?' Nash asked.

Binns grimaced. 'The wife's gone shopping for new clothes. She warned me it could take several hours, so, rather than trail round shop after shop, I decided to pop in here and kill a bit of time.'

'No change there,' Nash retorted. 'Have you brought some sudokus and crosswords, like you used to?'

'No, I thought you lot must have a stack of them upstairs, to help you while away the boredom, so I'd be able to raid those. Anyway, where are you two going? Off to catch a big-time criminal? That would make a change.'

Nash laughed. 'Hardly, Jack, we're going to St Cecilia's to interview a retired schoolmistress by the name of Agatha Bartholomew.'

'Agatha Bartholomew, the lady who was headmistress at Helmsdale Primary? I didn't realize she was still with us. She must be a fair age now.'

'I think Viv said she was ninety-two. How do you know her?'

'She used to teach me, that's how. A damned good teacher she was too, and a very nice lady. It would be a real pleasure to see her again. I don't know if it's appropriate or not, but I'd love to tag along, if you don't mind.'

Nash winked at Meadows as he told Jack, 'We could take you with us, I suppose. At least it will get you out of Steve's hair for a while. I know how busy uniform branch can be — after all, you told me so often enough.'

They timed their arrival at the care home to perfection, and after identifying themselves to the receptionist, they were conducted through to the resident's lounge, where they found Agatha Bartholomew seated in an armchair, reading a thriller by the author Joy Ellis.

'I'm Detective Inspector Nash, from Helmsdale CID, and this is my colleague, Detective Sergeant Mironova,' Nash told the old lady, before gesturing to the third member of the visiting party. 'And this is a former pupil of yours, retired sergeant Jack Binns.'

Agatha glanced at each of the detectives in turn before her gaze fixed on their companion. 'Did you say Jack Binns?'

'That's correct, Ms Bartholomew.'

'Do you mean to tell me that Binns is a retired police officer?'

She saw Nash nod, and continued, 'I must say that is extremely surprising. The way he behaved at school, I'd have been more inclined to believe he would finish up on the wrong side of the law. Whoever thought that little Dusty Binns would turn out to be an honest, upright citizen?'

By now, Nash recognized the humour in Agatha's voice, the twinkle in her eyes, and responded, 'I'm not sure I'd go that far.'

Clara glanced at Binns, who she could tell was acutely embarrassed, his discomfort increasing as Nash continued, 'We'd love to hear about some of the things Dusty got up to at school, but before that, I'd better explain the main purpose of our visit. We are investigating a crime, and during our inquiries, someone mentioned your brother's name. It might be totally unconnected, but we thought you might be in a better position than anyone to tell us about Roland. We've been unable to discover much, apart from the fact that he became a pickle manufacturer. We're particularly keen to know about his family. We did hear that he had a daughter, and I believe her name is Christine. We'd also be interested to find out if he had any connection to a cottage near the village of Drover's Halt.'

Agatha looked at Nash in astonishment at the mention of her brother's name, and it was a long time before she answered. When she did reply, Clara winced at the unintentional pun the old lady used. 'I think you'll have to provide me with a good reason for your interest, Inspector Nash. Because I'm not at all comfortable revealing the skeletons in our family closet — things that have remained secret for many years. It had better not be anything trivial, because if so, there are some matters I would prefer to remain buried in the past.'

'We're anxious to discover the current owners of a derelict cottage close to Drover's Halt, where certain extremely serious crimes have been committed.'

Seeing the appalled expression on the old lady's face, Nash hastened to add, 'Those crimes were committed recently, probably no more than four or five years ago, but we cannot find any details about the current owners of the property. All the Land Registry search gave us was the name of a local firm of solicitors, and they were unable, or should I say unwilling, to provide any information. I'm afraid lawyers take their responsibility regarding client confidentiality extremely seriously, and that has proved to be an impenetrable barrier to our inquiry.'

Given Nash's reassurance, Agatha began to reveal, albeit with marked reluctance, what she knew about her family's history. And in so doing, confirmed what Nash had suspected about the past use of All Alone Cottage. Clara, who had been given the task of taking notes, wondered whether the information divulged by the old lady would be of any use in their investigation. Eventually, when she had told them all she could, Agatha looked at Nash and asked, 'Will that be of any help?'

'I can't honestly say at this stage. It might be, or then again, it might be nothing more than a coincidence. I can assure you that everything you've revealed will be treated with the utmost confidentiality, and however our investigation turns out, either Sergeant Mironova or I will bring you up to date with the result.' Nash leaned forward, his expression eager as he asked her, 'Now we've got that out of the way, what can you tell me about the misdemeanours committed by Dusty Binns?'

Eventually, they stood up, preparatory to leaving, having thanked her for her time and cooperation.

The old lady smiled. 'It was nice to feel useful again, Inspector Nash. Thank you for giving me that chance — and also for bringing Dusty Binns along with you.' She looked at Jack and added, 'Perhaps I didn't do such a bad job teaching you after all.'

* * *

As they were walking back to the station, Clara remarked, 'I'm really surprised by how alert Ms Bartholomew is. Quite obviously, her mental faculties haven't decreased one iota, despite her age.'

Nash glanced at her, and Clara saw him wink before he responded, 'I totally agree. I think she's a remarkable old lady, don't you, Dusty?'

'Hey, enough of the "Dusty", if you don't mind. I've been trying to live that nickname down for most of my life.

And I wouldn't want the other stuff Miss Agatha told you spreading about, either.'

'That's all very well for you to say, but you must know that we're duty bound to record every scrap of information revealed during that interview — word for word, where possible. Your name will have to go into that report, together with what she told us about you. Luckily for you, I think she held back on some of the things she could have told us. I'd love to know what they are. My guess is they must have been really bad for her to think you'd end up on the wrong side of the law. What she did tell us was enlightening, though. Don't you agree, Clara?'

'It certainly was, Mike.'

Nash continued, 'I can remember many occasions, Clara, when Dusty teased me about my love life, but at least I didn't start chasing girls when I was in primary school, like he did.'

Binns remained silent for once, unable to come up with any means of retaliation.

When they reached the station, Nash said farewell to Binns, shaking his hand as he said, 'It's good to see you looking so well. Don't leave it too long before you pop in to visit us again — Dusty.'

* * *

When they entered the CID suite, they found Superintendent Fleming on an unscheduled visit. 'I thought I'd come and find out if you've made any progress with the murder case — or should I say, cases?'

'Then you're either very lucky, or psychic,' Nash replied. 'I believe we've just been given our first potential clue as to the owners of that derelict cottage. Actually, it isn't the first clue, it's the second one, but the first clue hasn't got us anywhere yet. I'd like to claim this was down to good detective work, but I reckon it owes more to chance than skill.'

'Would you care to explain that? Sometimes talking to you is like struggling with a cryptic crossword.'

Nash grinned, but told her, 'First, I think we should all have a coffee, because the explanation could take a while. Viv, would you organize the refreshments, please? And include one for our friend Dusty, who's downstairs talking to Steve Meadows. Lisa, while Viv's making the drinks, would you ask Dusty to come and join us?'

'Dusty? Who's Dusty?' Viv and Lisa asked in chorus.

'According to his former headmistress, "Dusty" was Jack Binns' nickname when he was at primary school. Jack doesn't like the name, so I think we should use it at every opportunity. That, by the way, is by no means the only thing his ex-teacher said about him, but I've promised to keep the other information confidential.' Nash grinned. 'However, I don't recall Clara making any such promise.'

Once Binns had joined them, and they had their drinks, Nash began his explanation.

'I said this wasn't the first solid clue as to the owners of the cottage. That claim belongs to the expensive piece of jewellery found at the crime scene by Robert Pickles. Strangely, it was due to Robert that I stumbled across what might be the second clue. Jonas Turner was at our house on Saturday, doing the gardening. Alondra made him a cheese and pickle sandwich. Jonas said the pickle was "nearly as good as Barty's", which baffled us until he explained.'

Nash took a sip of his coffee. 'There was a local pickle manufacturer back in the day called Roland Bartholomew, who made Barty's Pickles. This made me think of Robert Pickles and the mystery surrounding his father. According to Robert's birth certificate, his father's name was Bartholomew Pickles, but research didn't throw up anyone of that name. At the time, it made me wonder if the name was a fabricated one, used to conceal the man's identity. If my theory is correct, the alias chosen might have hidden a clue as to his background.'

He cast a glance at Jack Binns before he continued, 'Today, along with Dusty, we went to talk to Agatha, Roland Bartholomew's younger sister. Although she's in her nineties, her memory is fine, and after some persuasion, she was able to reveal some extremely interesting facts about her brother — and his offspring.'

Nash saw Pearce about to say something and held up his hand. 'I know you were unable to discover anything, Viv, and that's not your fault, because you were researching the wrong name. Let me explain. From what Agatha, and my gardener, told us, it seems her brother was a ladies' man, with a string of girlfriends. His behaviour, and the liaison he formed later, caused a permanent rift with his parents, who were staunch Methodists.'

Nash paused before adding, 'You must remember much of this was what Agatha overheard as a young girl. She said there were a lot of heated arguments. Apparently during one of them, Roland called his parents mean-minded hypocrites.' He smiled. 'Agatha said she had to go look that up in the dictionary, because she'd never heard the word before. Anyway, the woman he eventually fell for, who returned his affection wholeheartedly, was already married. That was the last straw as far as Roland's parents were concerned, so they disowned him, cut him out of their lives completely.

'Agatha told me what she later learned about Roland's true love. The woman's husband was an unpleasant character, not above mental and physical abuse. He refused to give his wife a divorce, even though she had left him and become Roland's mistress. She became pregnant, and after she moved in with Roland, gave birth to a daughter. Unfortunately, there was some doubt at the time as to whether the child was Roland's or her husband's. Apparently, part of the abuse the woman suffered was her husband's habit of forcing himself on her. Today it would be classed as rape, but back then, things were much different. The baby was registered under her mother's maiden name, along with the "father unknown" tag. The mother's name was Sheila Dawson, nee Phillips, so the child was named Christine Phillips.'

'What happened to the daughter?' Jackie asked.

'We know some, but not everything. Agatha lost touch with Roland. However, Jonas Turner, my gardener, was involved with Christine when they were teenagers, and according to him, "she were a reet cracker". But the affair ended when he was called up to serve overseas in Cyprus with the Territorial Army. When he returned, Christine was married, and eventually gave birth to a son.

'Reverting to what Agatha told us, which we found highly significant, was the fact that Roland Bartholomew purchased a house to hide his mistress, and to use as a love nest. I give no prizes for guessing the name of the house.'

'All Alone Cottage?'

'Hold on a minute, Mike. If your gardener knew Christine Phillips, then surely he knew she grew up at the cottage?' Jackie asked.

'That's as may be.'

'Then why didn't you make the connection?'

'Because I didn't ask him. Why would I? There's been nothing in the press about the findings at the site, and any enquires we've made in the area have been related to the ownership.' Nash shrugged. 'And Agatha certainly didn't know what happened to the cottage after Roland's death.' He sat back and took a further drink, although the coffee was by then almost cold.

'Was that all you learned?' Fleming asked.

'There was one other thing, which may or may not be significant. There is evidence that shows a familial trait of twin births. Agatha told us Roland had a twin sister, but unfortunately, she was stillborn. Given that much of this is hearsay and rumour, we're still little further forward. But given all the circumstances, I did wonder if the victims we found at the cottage might be descendants of Roland Bartholomew. Albeit, possibly in a convoluted manner.'

'I'd say you're more than a little further forward, despite much of your info being second- or third-hand,' Fleming commented. 'So where do we go from here?'

'Before we get too excited about this, I think we ought to get Viv to work his magic on the computer, and see what he can unearth from the new names he has at his disposal.'

* * *

Although Jackie Fleming hadn't planned for an extended visit, she decided to remain in Helmsdale in the hope that Pearce's internet research yielded some results. It was late afternoon by the time he reported on what he'd been able to discover. The outcome was a raft of information that added considerably to their knowledge of Roland Bartholomew's descendants, but seemed at the time to have little other value.

'I found a Christine Phillips listed as the daughter of Sheila Dawson, nee Phillips, father unknown. That ties in with what you were told, as does the registry office, which was Netherdale. I think that's fairly convincing, don't you?'

Pearce glanced at his colleagues, and saw they were in complete agreement. 'Christine Phillips was born in 1945, and died two years ago. When she was eighteen years old, she married a man by the name of Gordon Watson, and later the same year, she gave birth to a son, Simon. Less than two years later they had another son, named Philip. Both sons are now dead.'

Pearce turned to a second sheet of paper. 'The sons were married, and both had daughters. Philip's daughter was the older of the two, named Ursula, and married someone called Douglas Taylor. There's no record of them having any children.'

He turned to another page. 'Simon's daughter, Marion, married Sergeant John Edwards, a soldier killed in Afghanistan.' Again he flipped the paper. 'They had two children, a boy and girl, twins born in 2016. That's as far as I've been able to get. I have full details for everything I've told you to back it up.'

'I'd say that's a remarkably good day's work,' Jackie said as she stood up to leave.

'I agree we seem to be making progress, but I reckon we've still a long way to go,' Nash responded. 'We need Viv to keep on trawling and see what else he can fish out. Lisa can help. That seems to me the only way we'll get to the bottom of this convoluted case.'

CHAPTER TWENTY-THREE

When Nash left the office that evening, he was in a far more upbeat frame of mind than he had been for a considerable while. Despite his cautionary words, he felt certain they were making progress. Only one thought troubled him. He felt certain that in the slew of information they had received during the course of the day, there was one item he'd overlooked. Whether it was important or not he couldn't tell, because the harder he tried to think of it, the more elusive it became. Perhaps it would be like solving a crossword puzzle. Sometimes you have to walk away from it, and when you return, the answer that has been plaguing you all along is staring you in the face.

Recognizing his inability to pin down the elusive scrap of information, Nash switched his attention to other facets of the cases he was certain were interconnected.

That didn't meet with any more success, as he was equally flummoxed by the Mitchell and Stevens murders as he was by the cottage killings. He pondered these during his drive to work the next morning, but eventually, frustrated by what he saw as his failure to think them through properly, he decided to abandon speculation in favour of hard facts.

Viv Pearce had left copies of his internet search reports on each of his colleagues' desks, and Nash spent the first portion of his time studying the paperwork. Clara walked into the CID suite and Nash instructed her to bring her copy of the report, and join him in his office.

Clara held up the sheaf of papers she was clutching. 'Is there a problem with all this?'

'The problem is that I'm having a bad morning. I'm trying to remember something I was told, but can't get to grips with it. Added to that, I feel sure there's something important in the details Viv left for us, but I can't for the life of me spot what it is. I thought a fresh pair of eyes might do the trick.'

They had almost finished when Clara glanced at an entry on the last sheet of paper. She stopped, and then turned back to the previous page. She stared at the details for a long time before muttering, 'That's impossible.'

'What's impossible?'

'Someone has made an error when they entered this data — either that, or they were given misleading information.'

Clara leaned across, and pointed to the relevant sections of Pearce's report. Nash peered at it for several seconds before the significance became clear. 'Yes, I see what you mean, but there could be an innocent explanation, even if the facts recorded here are correct. Let's put it to the others and see if they spot what you saw, shall we?'

'Have you started to develop a liking for quiz shows? Or are you simply tormenting them?'

'No, but what you pointed out demonstrates the value of studying evidence closely, which is where you succeeded and I failed.'

They emerged from Nash's office and greeted Viv and Lisa, who were awaiting instructions. 'I'd like you to look at the final two sheets of Viv's report and see if you notice anything out of place. I have to admit I missed it, but eagle-eyed Clara picked up on it.'

The detective constables examined the paperwork, but even with the pointer Nash had given them, they failed to spot anything untoward.

'OK,' Nash told them, 'go to the registration details for Marion and John Edwards' twins and check their date of birth, then compare it with the date of her husband's death.'

There was a short silence, before Lisa Andrews muttered, 'That can't be right. Someone must have made a mistake. According to this, the twins were born eighteen months after their father was killed. One of these dates must be incorrect.'

'That might well be true, but not necessarily. There are two other explanations that would fit, even if those dates are correct, both of them innocent ones.' Nash paused and then corrected that statement. 'Actually, one of the explanations is totally innocent, the other less so. Marion Edwards might have retained a specimen of her husband's sperm, frozen in the event that he was killed.'

'Can you do that in this country, legally speaking?' Pearce asked.

'You can, but in order to do so, you must have your partner's consent. Remember, he was a serving soldier.'

'OK, that's one explanation. What's the other one?' Lisa asked.

'The less innocent version, if the dates are correct, would be that Marion Edwards entered into another relationship after her husband's death, and, for whatever reason, passed the twins off as being his offspring, thereby concealing the real identity of their father.'

'Do you think the bodies at All Alone Cottage are those of Marion Edwards, her twins and her lover?' Lisa asked.

Nash nodded agreement. 'That's the most likely explanation that fits what few facts we know, Lisa. However, there's no point getting ahead of ourselves. I'd like you to contact Netherdale Registry Office, and if necessary, go there and confirm the facts Viv downloaded are accurate, and not a slip of the typist's finger.'

He turned to Clara. 'While Lisa's doing that, would you contact the Ministry of Defence and ask them to confirm that the date shown for Sergeant Edwards' death is correct?'

'What about me, Mike? Do you want me to carry on with my research?'

'I will do, Viv, but before that, I've another job for you. Go to Shires Bank. See what you can find out about Mitchell's visit. We should have done this before now.'

'What will you be doing while everyone else is busy? Sitting drinking coffee as usual, I suppose.'

Nash looked shocked. 'Certainly not, Clara. I'll be updating Jackie Fleming with this development.'

'Hah! That'll take all of two minutes,' Clara retorted.

* * *

Clara was the first to report back, having decided to short-circuit the usual route, which would undoubtedly involve red tape — probably reams of it. She elicited the assistance of a special contact within the military — her husband. David Sutton was a former Special Forces officer, and thus, via his extensive network of former colleagues, was able to get the reply needed far quicker than through official channels. Consequently, she was able to report to Nash less than an hour later.

'I've got the details on Sergeant Edwards.'

'That was quick. I didn't expect the answer today, knowing the MOD.'

'I asked David to help. He spoke to someone in his old unit, who spoke to someone else, who spoke to someone else, and they came back to David a few minutes ago. Sergeant Edwards died almost exactly eighteen months before the twins, shown on the birth certificate as *his* children, were born. That leaves us with either a mistake at the registry office, his widow having obtained his sperm, or your smutty theory.'

Next to report was Lisa Andrews, who returned from her visit to Netherdale Registry Office bearing two sheets of paper that she placed on Nash's desk. Like Clara, she had used a friendly contact to try and circumvent the normal channels.

'I know the deputy registrar, who is a distant relative of Maureen Riley, our civilian support officer. She not only confirmed the twins' date of birth, but also provided me with copies of their birth certificates, which I had to pay for.' She glanced across the office, looking for Viv. 'Don't worry, I'll tell Viv I got a receipt.' She laughed and turned back to Nash. 'All the details are exactly as Viv reported, so if Edwards' death was recorded accurately, that leaves only the other explanations.'

'How do we go about confirming which of them is the correct one, though?' Clara asked.

'Technically, there might be a way, but I think it's a long shot and should only be considered as a last resort,' Nash replied. 'If memory serves me correctly, I believe the MOD now stores DNA of all servicemen deployed in places such as Afghanistan. Whether they would have retained Sergeant Edwards' for such a long period after his death, and whether they would release it for the purpose we need, is very much open to question. Failing that, we need to think up other ways of proving who the victims are. As things stand, we're faced with another wall of silence. The only people readily available to confirm one way or another would be either Marion Edwards, or her doctor or obstetrician. At present we have no clues as to Mrs Edwards' whereabouts. And if she is one of the victims from All Alone Cottage, the only way to speak to her would be via a Ouija board.'

Ignoring Clara's muttered, 'That's sick,' Nash continued. 'As for trying to get information from her doctor — well, if we thought getting a solicitor to reveal facts was difficult, asking a medical practitioner to talk about his patient will be harder than getting blood out of a stone.'

* * *

They had to wait for Viv to return, but his had been the most difficult of all the tasks Nash had set them.

'OK, how did you get on at the bank?'

'Nowhere near as well as I did at the solicitors the other day, I'm afraid, and that's the main reason I've been so long. I was kept waiting for over half an hour before the manager deigned to see me, and when I did get to speak with him, he was less than helpful. He told me the only way we could expect him to reveal information regarding one of their customers would be with a warrant, and as he'd never heard of such a thing happening before, I think he regarded it as game, set, and match.'

Pearce stopped speaking, and although Clara and Lisa thought he'd finished, Nash guessed he had more to say. 'What else is there, Viv?'

'Nothing really, just a crazy idea I had. If I'm right, that bank manager might have been more helpful than he intended to be, simply by keeping me waiting.'

'Tell us,' Clara encouraged him. 'We do crazy ideas very well here.' She gestured to Nash. 'He's forever having crazy ideas.'

Pearce smiled, then continued, 'I was trying to stave off boredom as I waited, so I started to watch customers coming to and fro. I tried to guess whether they were about to make deposits or withdrawals. I was surprised, because quite a few of those I expected to be in need of money were actually paying into their accounts, and vice versa. Anyway, in the midst of all that, one particular guy caught my attention because he wasn't doing either. This middle-aged bloke came into the banking hall and headed straight for the reception desk, without going anywhere near the line of cashiers. That sparked my interest. I was speculating which other services he was going to use, but after he gave his name, he came and sat alongside me, so I guessed he might be meeting one of the managers.'

Viv paused for a second and smiled. 'About five minutes later, a woman came out of one of the offices, shook hands with the customer, and then led him away. The thing is, she didn't take him into any of the offices. Instead, they went to the rear of the building and stopped in front of a heavy security door. She punched in the combination on a keypad, and they went inside. They were gone about ten minutes, and then reappeared. The bank official shook the man by the hand and he walked straight out of the building.'

'Did you manage to get a look at what was on the other side of the door?' Nash beat Clara to the question by a split second.

'Not really, at least not very much. All I did get a glimpse of was a flight of stairs, but that was enough to give me my crazy idea.'

'Were the stairs leading to the first floor or the basement?'

Pearce smiled at Nash's question. 'You've guessed, haven't you?'

Clara and Lisa groaned in unison, their duet a demand. 'Tell us, please.'

'Safety-deposit boxes,' Nash told them.

'That's exactly what I thought, Mike.'

'Well done, Viv. That was an outstanding example of observation allied to deductive thinking.'

'There's only one problem with my crazy idea. If Mitchell went to the bank to use a safety-deposit box, where's the key? We've searched his house from top to bottom, not once but twice, and we didn't find anything remotely like a safety-deposit key. It isn't the sort of thing you would leave around for any Tom, Dick, or Harry to pick up.'

'Perhaps the person who killed Mitchell took the key,' Lisa suggested. 'If the motive was to ensure his silence, it stands to reason they'd want to control anywhere he might have stashed damaging evidence.'

'I admit that's a possibility, Lisa, but if they had been so diligent in searching Mitchell's house, surely they would have found the basement office? Let's be fair, we didn't know that room existed until our second time round. There's every chance that we overlooked something as small as a key — we weren't looking for one. Alternatively, Mitchell might have concealed it so well we missed it. I reckon it's more than likely the key is still in that house. We'll have to search the property again, but I have an idea that might confirm whether Viv's theory is correct or not.'

'Where do we go from here, Mike?'

Nash could tell from Pearce's expression that he was as frustrated as all of them by the obstacles in their path. 'I'd like you to continue trying to find out as much as possible about all of Roland Bartholomew's descendants. I think it's safe to assume the names you found are from his lineage, but at present, although you've identified three generations, all we know are names. What we need is personal details about their lives. Given the number of people involved, there could be a lot we're unaware of. Only when we can assess their histories will we be able to form an opinion.'

'What about us, Mike?' Lisa gestured to Clara as she spoke.

'Will you return to Mitchell's house and begin searching it from top to bottom? This time you'll have the advantage of knowing exactly what you're looking for.'

'The safety-deposit key?'

'Exactly, and bear in mind Mitchell will have secreted it with the objective of concealing it from anyone trying to find it. Meanwhile, I'm going to seek legal advice from a woman with a nice bottom, and after that, I'll join you and Lisa at Bishop's Cross.'

Viv and Lisa look totally baffled by Nash's curious statement, but Clara twigged immediately. 'You're going to speak to that barrister, Lucinda Hartley, aren't you? What sort of legal advice do you need from her?'

Nash smiled sweetly at her. 'That's for me to know and you to wonder about — until such time as I'm ready to tell you.'

CHAPTER TWENTY-FOUR

Almost two hours later, Nash joined Clara and Lisa at Mitchell's house. 'How's the great key hunt going?' he asked, although the answer was obvious by their downcast expressions.

'All we've found so far is dust,' Clara replied, 'and there's plenty of that. We started upstairs with the bedroom Mitchell and Stevens shared. From there we checked the other bedrooms, the bathroom, the WC, and even the shower cubicle. We looked through every item of clothing in the wardrobes, in case Mitchell hid the key in one of the pockets. We also searched every piece of luggage, including his camera case, but without success. We were about to begin work on the ground floor when you arrived. We didn't think to call for food or drinks on our way here, and we're starving — it's way past lunchtime. I don't suppose you brought anything, did you?'

Nash brought his left hand from behind his back and held up a carrier bag. 'As you requested, Madam,' he replied, in the style of a butler.

As they were seated around the dining room table eating their lunch, Clara broached the subject of Nash's puzzling statement before they left Helmsdale. 'Are you going to let us in on the secret of the legal advice you wanted from Lucinda Hartley?'

Nash waited until he'd swallowed the mouthful of sandwich before replying. 'It wasn't so much legal advice I asked her for, more a question of getting her to use her influence within the legal profession. When Viv told us Mitchell had visited Anderson & Holden, the solicitors in Netherdale, I remembered they specialize mostly in criminal law, and several of their clients were represented at trial by Lucinda Hartley QC. I thought she might be willing to ask Anderson & Holden to cooperate more fully, by telling us the reason behind Mitchell's visit. I was in luck, because she's in chambers today, not in court, so I was able to chat with her. I explained the theory behind my request for them to break protocol, parts of which shocked her so much she promised to do all she could to help. I'm waiting for her to get back to me, but that might not happen today, so in the meantime, we'll have to keep searching for the missing item. Who knows, it might be the key to the whole mystery.'

Clara and Lisa groaned. 'Your puns are getting worse. I'm surprised Alondra puts up with them.'

Nash looked surprised by Clara's comment. 'You don't suppose for one minute I inflict them on Alondra, do you? I prefer to dish them out to people I know will react badly.'

Searching the ground floor took up most of the afternoon. Much of that time was spent within the main building, with the exception of the period taken up by their check of the integral double garage, and for good measure, the greenhouse and potting shed.

By five o'clock they had covered every room, even examining the interior of containers in the kitchen, plus the compartments of the fridge-freezer, all the shelves in the larder, and the cupboards in the utility room. All that remained to search was the basement. 'Why don't you call it a day,' Nash suggested. 'You've been at it far longer than me. I'll stay behind and give the cellar a once-over. If I don't meet with any success, we'll have to rethink Viv's theory.'

Although Lisa accepted Nash's offer, Clara volunteered to stay and help him. 'I've no reason to rush home,' she explained. 'David's away for three days, and I forgot to get anything out of the freezer, so I'll have to call for a takeaway. The only snag is I came in Lisa's car, so would you be able to give me a lift back to Helmsdale, Mike?'

'I might be able to do better than that. Wait there a minute.' Nash wandered away, removing his mobile from his pocket. He returned a couple of minutes later. 'That's all settled. I spoke to Alondra and you're coming to our place for dinner, then you can crash in the spare room overnight. I'll drive you to work in the morning. Besides, Daniel will love to see you.'

* * *

For long enough it seemed as if their efforts were going to be in vain. They had searched every drawer of the desk, and all the compartments in the filing cabinet, taking out each file and shaking it to see if a key dropped out, but without finding what they were seeking. From there they had turned their attention to the wine racks, removing every bottle and feeling inside the cavities. This revealed only more dust and one large, startled spider, whose scurry for cover after being disturbed almost made Clara drop the bottle of Château Lafite Rothschild she was holding.

'That would have cost you the thick end of two thousand quid to replace,' Nash told her.

'Really, is that how much this stuff costs? I think I'll stick to Vin Plonk,' she replied.

As they took a final look round, Nash said, 'I thought Viv's crazy idea was a good one, but maybe I'm wrong. We've no actual proof that Mitchell has a safety-deposit box, let alone that it was the purpose of his visit to Shires Bank.'

Clara didn't respond, her attention being on a commonplace object she'd spotted on top of the filing cabinet. She looked round the room, her frown one of puzzlement as she wondered what it had been used for. 'Mike, what do you make of this?' She held up the roll of duct tape she had seen. 'Did you notice anything that had been taped together? Because I didn't.'

'No, there was nothing I saw with duct tape attached. Maybe it was used to hold something in place, where it might be hidden from prying eyes — a safety-deposit key, perhaps?'

The obvious location was the desk. 'Under the drawers,' Clara suggested.

Each drawer was removed in turn, revealing only bare wood. Fortunately, the desk was light enough to be manhandled by two people. When they had upended it, the detectives stared in disappointment at the underside, which was also completely empty. Then they slid the filing cabinet away from the wall and checked the back, with no success.

'Maybe the key isn't in this room after all,' Clara said, despairingly.

She looked across at Nash, who had turned away from her. 'Or maybe we've just been looking in the wrong place.' As he was speaking, Nash took a step back allowing Clara to see the base of the office chair he had inverted. There, concealed by the criss-cross lengths of tape securing it in place, was a small key.

'Bingo,' Clara exclaimed triumphantly. 'I'd never have thought to look under the chair.'

Nash refused to accept all the credit. 'Viv thought of the key first, then you spotted the duct tape, so I reckon this was a team effort in the best sense of the word. Now let's get out of here and go tackle some beef stroganoff.'

'Some what?'

'That's what we're having for dinner. Beef stroganoff is one of Alondra's speciality dishes.'

* * *

Next morning, Nash and Mironova arrived at the CID suite, to find their colleagues already there, keen to discover how the search had ended. It was obvious from their expressions that they were expecting to hear of yet another failure, so they were surprised when Clara brandished the key. Even more so when Nash explained where they had found it.

'All we have to do now is persuade the manager at Shires Bank to allow us access to the safety-deposit box. That way, we'll find out what Gavin Mitchell put inside it, and why it was necessary for him to take such stringent security measures to conceal the key.'

'Unless he went to the bank to remove something from his box,' Pearce commented.

'That's what I like, Viv, unfailing optimism.'

Pearce then updated them on his research from the previous afternoon. 'I decided to take it generation by generation, and it proved far from easy to find out much about Bartholomew's descendants. I began with his supposed daughter Christine and her husband Gordon Watson. Researching him gave me an interesting start, because it seems Gordon became the owner of an ironmongery-cum-hardware shop in Netherdale.'

Pearce looked up from the page he was reading. 'Gordon Watson died very young, leaving the business to his sons. The older son, Simon, became managing director and they made a great success of it, taking advantage of the boom in DIY to expand their range of products. This included items like power tools and building and decorating materials. Another aspect of the diversification led to them opening a garden centre alongside the shop, and they began opening shops in other towns. By the time Simon Watson died in a car crash, the company had branches throughout Yorkshire, under the brand name Home Comforts. That's as far as I got yesterday, so today I'm going to concentrate on the more recent family members.'

'That company, Home Comforts, is a very good outfit,' Nash commented. 'I remember going into their shop before Daniel and I moved into Smelt Mill Cottage. The stuff they sell is both high quality and reasonably priced.'

'May I remind you just *who* did your shopping for your new home?' Clara stared at Nash.

'Yes, sorry, Clara. But I did go in once.'

Viv glanced at Lisa, who was sitting tight-lipped, trying not to laugh. They both knew how much Nash had relied on Clara to help furnish his new home.

Viv continued, 'A lot of people obviously think the same as you, Mike . . . er . . . Clara, because when I looked at the company's results, their profits are climbing rapidly. They now make several million a year, and as for their turnover, I had to count the noughts to makes sure the commas were in the right place.'

Pearce had just returned to his desk when Nash's office phone rang. Clara, who was watching through the window, guessed that the caller was delivering good news. She was still speculating as to what that might be, when he emerged, telling her, 'My gamble appears to have paid off. I'm going to Netherdale for a meeting. Clara, you come with me.'

He turned to the others. 'We will be out of contact for the next two hours, maybe longer. Our mobiles will be turned off, so there's no point anyone ringing us. However, there should be no need, because I'm sure you two can handle anything that crops up.'

Once they were in Nash's car, safe from eavesdropping, Nash explained, 'The reason I said we'll not be contactable is because where we're going, they frown on the use of electronic devices.'

'OK, Mike, will you stop playing the master of suspense, and tell me where we're going exactly, and who this meeting is with?'

'We're going to Netherdale Crown Court. Lucinda Hartley's arranged a meeting for us with Paul Holden, one of the partners of Anderson & Holden, Solicitors. He's appearing on behalf of two clients in consecutive cases this morning, but has promised to talk to us in the short recess between them.'

'That sounds like good news, or at least I hope it is. Why didn't you tell the others where we're going and why?'

'Because Lucinda asked me to keep it under wraps, and stressed anything Paul Holden tells us will be strictly private and confidential — totally off the record. Given that we're getting a measure of cooperation from the legal eagles at last, I think that's only fair, don't you?'

* * *

Paul Holden was in his late thirties, Clara estimated. As the solicitor greeted the detectives, she noticed the wary expression on his face, and guessed Lucinda Hartley might have had to use all her influence in order to get him to flout convention. This feeling was strengthened when Holden suggested they move into one of the side rooms where their conversation could not be overheard. Clara smiled to herself, recognizing the room to be one usually allocated for last-minute discussions between the accused and their legal representatives.

'I understand from Ms Hartley that you have a specific request to make in respect of the late Gavin Mitchell, is that correct?'

Nash knew Lucinda Hartley had explained precisely what they wanted to Holden, so he assumed this was a way of salving the solicitor's conscience regarding the breach of confidentiality.

'That's right. We examined Mitchell's car, and the satnav showed he had made only one journey in the period between Ms Stevens' death, and the time he was murdered. That trip was from his home in Bishop's Cross to your offices, following which he went to Shires Bank before returning home. From the information at our disposal, we believe Mitchell went to the bank to either place something inside his safety-deposit box, or alternatively to remove something from it. But unless we have access to the box, we can't be certain.'

'I'm not in a position to reveal a lot, as I've no doubt Ms Hartley explained. However, I do want to assist if I'm able. I believe Mr Mitchell *did* place something inside his safety-deposit box, because that was his stated intention when our meeting concluded. I also believe that if you are able to gain access to that box, you might find the information within of use, although I can't be certain, as I only have a vague idea what the box contains.'

Holden paused, and Clara guessed he was marshalling his thoughts, still cautious as to how much he could reveal. 'When Gavin Mitchell and Petra Stevens extended their professional relationship into a more personal one, they visited us to make their wills. Mitchell's will became invalid once Ms Stevens predeceased him, so he visited us to make, and sign, a new one. That was part of the motive for his visit. The other reason was to make a deposition under oath, the contents of which I am forbidden by law to reveal. But as I said previously, with luck, you may be able to view a copy of that deposition, if you can access Gavin Mitchell's safe-ty-deposit box.'

Holden stood up. 'That's all I can tell you, so now you must excuse me, as I have to go champion the rights of a man who is the victim of police harassment, amounting almost to a personal vendetta.' Clara caught the glint of humour in Holden's eyes as he continued, 'That's my client's version of the events leading to his arrest, not mine, I hasten to add.'

CHAPTER TWENTY-FIVE

Outside the court building, the detectives paused to switch their mobiles back on. Having ascertained there were no messages for her, Clara said, 'Holden seems a nice chap, for someone who spends his life defending criminals. I thought he was as helpful as could be in the circumstances.'

'I agree, but I think we might have to ask him for more assistance in the near future.'

'How can he provide further help?'

'If we're unable to get the manager at Shires Bank to allow us access to Mitchell's safety-deposit box, I plan to ask Paul Holden to intercede on our behalf. As he's administering Mitchell's estate, I don't think the bank can refuse a request from him. And I've a shrewd suspicion he knows more than he's able to tell us about the contents.'

'That's a good idea. Are we heading back to Helmsdale now?'

Nash didn't reply immediately as he was studying a text he'd received. 'No, not immediately, I've a call to make first.'

'Where's that, HQ?'

'Hardly,' Nash smiled. 'I've been instructed to call at the nearest supermarket.'

'What for?'

'Chorizo.'

'Pardon?'

'Alondra's making cassoulet for dinner this evening, and apparently one of the main ingredients is chorizo.'

'Oh, OK. But I have one question. What is cassoulet?'

Nash smiled and shook his head. 'I'm not sure, but I think it's some kind of stew. Ask me again tomorrow.'

'You're certainly getting a more varied diet these days. Maybe while we're in Good Buys, we should pick up some sandwiches for the troops.'

'Good idea. Got to keep them happy.'

Good Buys supermarket was on the southern section of the ring road, in the opposite direction to the Helmsdale Road. As they were driving along the high street, Nash noticed a shop sign out of the corner of his eye. He took his foot off the accelerator, a reflex action that caused Clara to glance at him.

As the car picked up speed again, Clara asked, 'Is there a problem?'

Nash didn't reply for several seconds, and then said, 'No, actually I think it's more the solution to something that's been bugging me for days. I'll have to wait until we're back in the office to find out if I'm right or not.'

'Would you care to explain that rather obscure statement?'

Nash did so, and Clara grasped the implication of his idea at once. 'I can't say for certain if you're correct, but it's definitely worth checking.'

When they reached CID, both of their colleagues were staring at their computer screens, so Nash and Mironova headed straight into his office rather than disturb their concentration.

Nash picked up his copy of Pearce's preliminary report into Roland Bartholomew's family tree and turned to the final page. He glanced at it, then passed it to Clara.

'So you were right with your memory, but that still doesn't mean there's any sort of direct connection. After all, it's a fairly common surname around here.'

'That's true enough,' Nash smiled. 'I thought for one moment you were going to say it is pure coincidence.'

'Knowing your disbelief in coincidences, I don't think I dare.'

'Let's wait until Viv's finished what he's doing, and get him to investigate further. In the meantime, if you distribute the rations, I'll make coffee.'

* * *

By mid-afternoon, Viv and Lisa had ended their internet searches, but Nash and Mironova had to wait a while longer for the detective constables to present their reports.

Pearce told them, 'Before we finalize what we have for you, Lisa's speaking to a friend of hers in Netherdale, who she thinks might be able to supply us with some useful background information of the sort you can't get online.' He smiled. 'Or, to put it another way, some local scandal and gossip.'

When Lisa came off the phone, she nodded to Pearce, a signal for him to begin. He started by revealing what he knew about Home Comforts Ltd, the company that had been run by Roland Bartholomew's grandsons. 'There's only one member of the family involved in the business nowadays. After both Simon Watson and his brother Philip died, their daughters took over the management, but the only one still there is Ursula Taylor. Her cousin, Marion Edwards, resigned a few years ago, shortly after her husband was killed in the army.'

Pearce looked across at Lisa, who took up the story. 'What Viv's told you might be factually correct, but the gossip I've heard casts a somewhat different light on those events. I must emphasize what I'm about to tell you is totally unverified, and might be wildly inaccurate. The rumour was that Marion Edwards decided England held far too many unhappy memories, and decided to emigrate, to start a new life somewhere along with her children, who were only babies

210

back then. My informant couldn't tell me any more than that, not even where Marion was rumoured to be heading. So I tried someone else, and boy, did that pay off. Again, this is completely unsubstantiated and highly salacious.

'The other rumour going the rounds was that when Marion and her babies left Britain, she took two additional items with her. One of the items was her pet dog, a Borzoi bitch.' Lisa paused for dramatic effect. 'The other item was Doug Taylor, her cousin Ursula's husband.'

All three of her listeners were completely dumbfounded by Lisa's final statement. There was a moment of stunned silence, before Nash gasped aloud. Clara looked at him and saw the familiar, abstracted, faraway expression on his face. She waited, signalling Lisa and Viv to remain silent, confidently expecting Nash to come out with a telling remark. She wasn't disappointed.

Nash turned to Pearce and asked, 'What was the surname of the owner of the pharmacy where Petra Stevens' faulty medication was dispensed?'

Pearce flicked through his notes, before whistling with surprise. 'Taylor, Barry Taylor.'

'What do you bet that Barry Taylor has a brother named Doug?'

A couple of minutes later, Pearce confirmed the accuracy of Nash's guess. 'You're spot on, Mike. Barry Taylor is Doug's younger brother.'

'Now, what's your favourite choice for what went on? Did Ursula's husband console Marion in her bereavement, and that consolation led to the twins being born? Alternatively, did Ursula simply want some fresher meat in her sandwich? Come to think of it, both theories might be correct.'

'What exactly do you mean about fresher meat?' Lisa asked.

'Mike was being vulgar,' Clara said. 'No change there. He was trying to imply, in his usual coarse manner, that Ursula might have decided to hook up with her brother-in-law,

Barry Taylor, and wanted to get rid of the obstacles to her great romance. It's only natural for Mike to think of sex as the motive.'

'It's not only me, Clara,' Nash protested. 'Why do you think there are so many crimes of passion? Then again, there might be another equally compelling reason for what we suspect happened, one far more sordid than sex.'

'What's more sordid than sex?' Lisa asked.

'Does Alan know you think sex is sordid?' Nash asked. He waited for Lisa's blush to subside before continuing, 'Perhaps the overriding motive for Ursula wanting to be rid of her cousin was greed. Home Comforts was making a lot of money, and maybe Ursula wanted it all for herself.'

'See, you're wrong, Clara,' Viv told her. 'Mike doesn't think of sex all the time. Occasionally, he thinks of other things.'

Clara's disbelief was apparent from her disdainful sniff, before she replied, 'Yeah! Once in a blue moon, maybe.'

Ignoring the badinage, Nash told Pearce, 'Will you get in touch with the Passport Office, please? We need to know if there are current passports in the name of Marion Edwards, her maiden name Marion Watson, or for the twins. At the same time, ask about one for Doug Taylor.'

'Anything else at this stage, Mike?' Clara asked.

'Yes, there is. I think we need to put Ursula Taylor, and her brother-in-law the chemist, under surveillance. Let's find out if there is any relationship. That's going to involve all four of us, working in shifts at both addresses. Will you go talk to Steve Meadows, and ask him to make his men aware? If something else crops up, we may need them to take over. But I certainly don't want a squad car pulling alongside, and alerting anyone to our presence.'

Nash paused, struck by a sudden thought. 'Viv, do you know if Barry Taylor is married, or in a relationship?'

'Neither, from what I could find. There's certainly no record of him getting married, and I checked the electoral roll for his address. He's the only occupant listed, which would tend to rule out anything but an informal relationship.'

'That was an unusually polite way of putting it, especially for you, Viv,' Clara remarked, as she left to speak to Sergeant Meadows. Ten minutes later, she reported back. 'That's all sorted, Mike. All we have to decide is who takes what shift.'

'I don't think the surveillance needs to be twenty-four-seven, otherwise we would need Steve's men, and we know how stretched they are. I suggest an early morning shift, with a 7 a.m. start, breaking at 10.30 a.m., when both the Taylors should be at work. Then an evening shift, encompassing the late afternoon as well, resuming at 4 p.m. and going through until 10.30. You and Lisa can take the mornings, and Viv and I'll do the later ones.'

'That's not fair to Viv with the little one at home. I'm sure he covers for Lianne when she's on late shift. Let him do the mornings. I don't mind. David's still away.'

'Fair enough, but in that case, I want an officer with you.'

'OK, I'll sort it. Shall I call the others in, so you can tell them?'

'No, I'll let you have that privilege. I'm girding my loins to do battle with a bank manager.'

Clara paused in the doorway. 'I thought your loins were always girded.'

* * *

Having instructed Lisa and Viv as to the surveillance arrangements, Clara waited in the main office, watching for Nash to come off the phone. It was a good ten minutes before he replaced the receiver, and she went straight through to ask how the call had gone.

'It was a battle, much as I predicted it would be.'

'Who won?'

'I think it's safe to call it a stalemate. The guy was as obstructive as when Viv spoke to him. He made a point of telling me he could only allow Mitchell, or his legal representative, access to the safety-deposit box, which was useful, as it confirmed the existence of one.'

'What was your response?'

'I asked him how the legal representative would gain access, if he wasn't in possession of the key. He seemed to enjoy quoting company policy. Apparently, the only way would be by having a duplicate cut. That would involve their head office, along with written permission from the box holder. I told him that would be tricky, unless he knew of a local medium.'

Clara smiled, but said, 'It sounds like an impasse.'

'Yes and no. What I didn't tell him was that we are in possession of the said key. So now I'm going to phone Paul Holden, and get him onside for our next move. I'll propose he sets up a meeting at the bank, and we'll tag along. That way, we can hopefully get sight of the box contents.'

'You're enjoying this, aren't you?'

'A little bit, maybe. First off, though, I'm going to pop home and tell Alondra I'll be late home tonight — and possibly for the next few nights.'

* * *

The first shift of the surveillance operation yielded results confirming at least part of Nash's theory to be accurate. Clara was seated in her car, along with an officer from uniform branch, clad for the present in plain clothes, as they waited a safe distance from Ursula Taylor's mansion on the outskirts of Netherdale. It was almost dusk when a rakish-looking sports car hurtled past at high speed, before turning ninety degrees, and entering the long drive leading up to the house they were watching. The vehicle, driven with skill and precision, suggested regular practice on this route.

'Damn, that car went by far too fast for me to spot the registration number,' Clara muttered.

'Me too, I'm afraid,' the constable replied. As he was speaking, he spotted another vehicle in the wing mirror.

'What now?' Clara grumbled. 'It's like Piccadilly Circus round here all of a sudden.'

They waited, expecting the vehicle to drive past them, but it pulled to a halt only yards behind. 'What's this guy up to?' the officer said.

There was a short silence, before someone tapped on Clara's window, making her jump with fright, until the man spoke.

'Having fun?'

Clara opened the window. 'Mike! You scared the shit out of me. What are you doing here? You're supposed to be watching Barry Taylor, or have you forgotten? And why are you driving Alondra's car?'

'My car's too distinctive. And watching Taylor is exactly what I am doing. Whose car do you think has just careered past you as if Lewis Hamilton was at the wheel, and driving up to Ursula's pad like he owned the place?'

'Oh, I see,' Clara said. 'We didn't get the plate.'

'What we need to find out now is if this is a purely social visit or something more intimate. As they're both here, I suggest you go home, Clara. And I'm sure the duty sergeant will welcome *you* back,' he said to the officer. 'I'll stay.'

There was no further movement before the shift ended, so Nash relayed this development to Andrews and Pearce as he drove home.

When the morning surveillance shift ended, Pearce returned to Helmsdale, telling Nash and Clara, 'Lisa said she'd stop off to collect sandwiches on her way back. We waited in separate cars at Ursula's for an hour or so. Just after eight o' clock, Barry Taylor's car emerged from the drive, closely followed by the lady herself. Lisa followed Taylor. I followed Ursula. They both went to their respective places of work, and remained there until our shifts ended.'

'You'd think Barry and Ursula would be too tired for a day's work after sitting up all night playing Scrabble or Monopoly,' Nash responded.

* * *

215

Clara was still smiling at Nash's joke, when his phone rang. He went into his office to answer the call, and a few minutes later emerged to ask Clara, 'Are you busy this afternoon?'

'My diary is completely empty. Why, what have you got planned?'

'I thought a visit to Shires Bank in Netherdale, along with Paul Holden, might be fun.'

'You've the weirdest idea of fun of anyone I know, but OK, I'm up for it.'

'Holden's scheduled the meeting for 3 p.m., and we're to meet him there.'

Any further resistance the bank manager might have wanted to put up was thwarted at the outset by Paul Holden. Having introduced his companions, the solicitor produced the documentation giving him authority to examine and remove any, or all, the contents of Mitchell's safety-deposit box.

'There's one snag with that,' the manager said with a smirk. 'You can't open it without a key.'

'I believe this is what you're referring to.' Nash held the key aloft in his gloved hand. 'You can look, but don't touch. This key could be evidence in the murder of six people.'

The bank manager looked horrified at the thought, and led them to the private vault.

Watched carefully by Nash and Clara, Holden opened the box and examined the contents one by one. These comprised several sets of documents, all in folders, each neatly tabulated. Holden separated them into two piles, the larger of which he passed to Nash. 'These are what you need. The others refer only to the disposition of Gavin Mitchell and Petra Stevens' estates.'

Having glanced through the files, Nash thanked Holden. 'With what's in here, we should now be in position to arrest those responsible for some dreadful crimes — and bring a measure of justice for their victims.'

As they drove back to Helmsdale, Clara asked if what he'd seen would be enough to secure murder convictions.

'Not on their own, perhaps. But there was a lot of detailed evidence relating to other crimes among those papers. I feel confident we have enough to put the perpetrators behind bars for a long time — if not for the rest of their lives.'

CHAPTER TWENTY-SIX

Having photocopied the bank documents, Nash and Mironova began studying them. The first part of the comprehensive paperwork took the form of a deposition by Gavin Mitchell, sworn in front of, and attested to, by James Anderson, senior partner at Anderson & Holden, in his role as a notary public. This comprised Mitchell's confession to his part — assisted, he alleged, by Petra Stevens — in a long-term system of fraud and embezzlement.

The original part of the scheme, Mitchell attested, was hatched when Philip Watson approached Mitchell after the death of his brother, Simon. At the time, Home Comforts was struggling financially. Before he died, Simon Watson had set up a trust fund, covertly, to provide for his illegitimate child.

Philip Watson had persuaded Mitchell the child died in infancy, and the trust was no longer valid. The money should revert to the company, thereby providing much-needed capital to finance the bold expansion that was threatened by shortage of funds. The fee for handling this irregular redistribution of the trust would be increased to a suitable figure, sufficient to compensate Mitchell for his unorthodox activities.

'Unorthodox activities,' Clara exclaimed as she read the document. 'That's a euphemism for swindle if ever I heard one.'

'Tut-tut, Clara, such cynicism.'

'Guess who I learned it from.'

The second part of the scheme came years later, when, as Mitchell freely admitted, he was desperate for money to pay off debts incurred by his gambling addiction.

In what he described as a moment of weakness, he accepted a suggestion put to him by Philip's daughter Ursula. Petra Stevens was persuaded to go along with the scheme, which involved outright fraud and embezzlement.

'*A moment of weakness.* I like that,' Clara muttered. 'A moment that lasted several years.'

Nash couldn't resist teasing her. 'Have I mentioned before that you're becoming rather cynical?'

'Yes, about two minutes ago.'

Ursula's scheme involved diversion of further large sums of money, this time at the expense of her cousin Marion. Ursula had produced a letter purporting to have been written by Marion, which was enclosed with the deposition.

In this, Marion allegedly claimed she had been conducting a long-term affair with Ursula's husband, Doug Taylor, and they were leaving to begin a new life in Australia. Marion stated the purpose of the letter was a formal renunciation of her claim to her shares in Home Comforts Ltd, and her resignation as a director of the company. It also gave Ursula power of attorney to sell her house.

'Luckily for us, Mitchell took the precaution of keeping this letter,' Nash remarked. 'Because I'll bet the arsonist thought it went up in flames during the attack on Mitchell & Co. offices. In fact, I guess the existence of the letter was one of the prime reasons for setting the fire.'

Nash looked at the sheet of paper and told Clara, 'We need to obtain some of Ursula Taylor's correspondence, because I bet a handwriting expert will be able to prove she forged this.'

'It states here, Ursula even had all Marion's correspondence redirected to Mitchell & Co., who had been appointed by her, or so this other document alleges, as her legal representatives. The nerve of the woman!'

Reading on, they noted that the money from the sale of Marion's house was paid to Mitchell & Co., where Petra Stevens handled the sale. After deduction of standard legal fees, plus their agreed percentage with Ursula, settlement of the outstanding mortgage on the property, almost £200,000 was transferred to a spoof bank account in the name of Marion Edwards, opened after Marion allegedly went abroad. This was followed over the next twelve months by a series of withdrawals totalling an almost identical amount.

'What puzzles me is, why Ursula went to all that trouble? Why not simply pay all the money directly into her own account?'

'I reckon the answer to that is down to tax evasion. Given the growing success of Home Comforts, had she been seen to have received another massive chunk of cash, she would have been faced with a whopping tax bill.'

'If you're right, that suggests the motive for her crimes was greed, not just jealousy over the affair between her husband and her cousin.'

'Maybe it was a combination of the two, with the added advantage of taking her unfaithful husband's younger brother to console her.'

Although they thought the papers they'd seen thus far provided all the surprises they could imagine, there was one further document that outdid all the previous ones.

'I'm not sure why Mitchell kept this one among his secret paperwork,' Clara commented. 'There doesn't seem anything remotely sinister about it.'

Neither did Nash, at that moment. It would be another twenty-four hours before they learned the reason.

After viewing everything Holden had given them, Clara vented her feelings about Ursula Taylor. 'There's no stopping this woman. She's totally ruthless.'

'Yes, but we already knew that, Clara. How else would you categorize someone willing to put to death six people who got in the way of her evil scheme?'

The final section of Mitchell's deposition described Mitchell's horror on learning of the skeleton found inside All Alone Cottage, and his assumption of the victim's identity.

Because Mitchell was aware of the circumstances surrounding the derelict property, the information supplied by civilian support officer Bob Greenwood proved to Mitchell that Ursula had lied to him, again and again.

Bob Greenwood's phone call caused Mitchell to do a little research. From this, he learned that the child of Simon Watson had not died in infancy, as Philip had told him. That led Mitchell to discount the remaining part of the web of lies spun by Philip Watson, and later by his daughter. To top all the fraudulent activities he had been persuaded to take part in, Mitchell now suspected that Ursula had orchestrated her cousin's murder, choosing to conceal the body within the derelict cottage.

The chilling final sentence contained speculation by Mitchell as to the fate of Ursula's husband and the twin babies Marion had given birth to.

Guessing that Gavin Mitchell had gone to his death not knowing the outcome of his misgivings was, to the detectives, the most horrific climax imaginable to the sordid tale.

'Whatever else you think of Gavin Mitchell, and it's patently obvious that he was not a very nice person, he was clearly a scrupulous record keeper.'

Nash agreed with Clara, adding, 'As a result of his attention to detail, I believe we now have a cast-iron case against Ursula Taylor and her brother-in-law for a string of offences. What I'm hoping is that we'll be able to pin the murders on them, although we're not on solid ground yet. I certainly think we've enough evidence against her to gain a conviction, so I think our next step should be to bring the pair of them in for questioning.'

'When do you propose to do that?'

Nash told her and then added, 'Before we do that, I want Viv to do a small job for me.'

Thinking about their conversation as she drove home that evening, Clara reflected that it demonstrated Nash's meticulous eye for detail, coupled with an iron determination to bring the full weight of justice to bear on the guilty parties. These were two of the qualities that made her admire him, although she would never in all the world dream of telling him so.

* * *

Next morning, Pearce reported to the team. 'I had a word with Lianne's mother like you asked, Mike, and she spoke to her friend. He agreed to come in this morning and talk to us. I emphasized the need for discretion, and he's consumed with curiosity, so he's promised not to breathe a word to a soul.'

Clara and Lisa looked baffled, so Nash explained. 'A few days ago, Viv mentioned Home Comforts to Lianne, and she told him her mother had a friend who used to work there. I asked Viv to see if the guy would be able to get us a bit of extra background on the firm and the family.'

When their visitor arrived, he spent over half an hour closeted with Nash and Pearce in Nash's office, but when he left he was none the wiser for the meeting. Not so the detectives, as Nash summarized what they'd learned.

'Everyone at Home Comforts knew Simon Watson's secretary was his mistress. They also knew Simon was about to leave his wife, and set up home with her. But before he could, he was killed in a car crash. Philip saw this as a golden opportunity to seize full control of the company.'

Nash paused and then added, 'The next bit is also intriguing. He told us that although Philip Watson's name appears on Ursula's birth certificate, he wasn't her biological father. Philip and Ursula's mother got together soon after Ursula was born. The gossips think the baby was the result of a one-night stand. Despite that, Philip doted on Ursula, spoiled her rotten, and gave her everything she wanted. The result —' Nash glanced down at the notes he'd made — 'is that Ursula became, in our visitor's words, "a right stuck-up bitch who believed the world owed her a living". He also said that if anyone crossed her, or upset her, they lived to regret it.

'There's one part of these revelations I find very interesting. If Ursula wasn't a direct descendant of Roland Bartholomew, Marion wasn't her cousin, and family loyalty wouldn't apply. Neither, if the truth came out, would she be entitled to any part of Roland Bartholomew's legacy, as set out in the Deed of Trust we discovered in Mitchell's safety-deposit box. We wondered why Mitchell kept that document hidden — now we know. I guess the main reason for the arson attack was to destroy that deed, which, if it came to light, would deprive Ursula of everything she had schemed, embezzled, and slaughtered people to achieve.'

* * *

Two mornings later, armed with a search warrant, the detectives assembled outside Ursula's mansion. They were accompanied by a small posse of uniformed officers.

The time chosen by Nash for the raid was 7 a.m., selected, as he'd told Clara, with the principal objective of catching Ursula in the act of cohabitation with Barry. 'Claiming it's a platonic relationship won't be easy when they're both in the same bed.'

When they arrived Clara indicated the two cars parked on the drive. 'So far, so good,' she said.

Nash gave the signal for a burly constable to knock loudly on the heavy oak door. After several attempts the door opened a little to reveal Ursula, dressed in a skimpy dressing gown. 'What on earth?' she exclaimed. 'What do you mean by knocking on my door at this time of the morning?'

Nash identified himself and his colleagues. The woman stared at Nash in disbelief at his words, as the detectives entered the house.

Moments later, a man, wearing only a pair of boxer shorts, appeared at the top of the stairs. 'What's going on?'

Nash ignored him. 'Detective Constable Andrews, would you please escort Mrs Taylor to a bedroom, where she can get dressed into something more suitable? Detective Constable Pearce, would you perform the same service for Mr Taylor? Please select a separate room. While they are doing that, Detective Sergeant Mironova, will you invite the search team to come inside, so they can begin their work?'

Viv headed up the stairs. Barry Taylor was indignant and tried to shrug him off. 'What do you want?'

Ursula Taylor found her voice at last. 'You can't do anything without a search warrant.'

She stared in dismay as Nash held up the relevant piece of paper and asked, 'Would you care to read it?'

The answer was apparently no, as Ursula retired in silence into one of the bedrooms, accompanied by DC Andrews. Moments later, Lisa emerged and handed Pearce a collection of men's garments, before retiring to supervise Ursula.

Both suspects reappeared minutes later, now suitably dressed and wearing matching fashion accessories in the shape of handcuffs.

'I don't think they're necessary,' Nash said, pointing to the handcuffs. Take them into the lounge and make them comfortable — this could take some time. Make them a cup of tea, they could be in shock,' he added, as he and Mironova, along with the officers, commenced their search of the premises.

Having appraised them earlier, he turned to the officers. 'You know what you're looking for. If anyone finds anything that looks the slightest bit interesting, give me a call.'

'Would you prefer the ground floor or upstairs?' Clara asked.

'I'll let you have the upper floor.'

'Really, I thought you'd be more at home in the bedrooms.'

'There are bedrooms and bedrooms — and these are ones I'd rather steer clear of, thank you.'

CHAPTER TWENTY-SEVEN

Ursula Taylor owned a large house, and checking every drawer, shelf, and cupboard for incriminating evidence took time. Almost an hour later, Clara hurried downstairs, having been summoned by a shout from Nash. She entered a study at the rear of the property, where Nash was standing in front of an expensive-looking dresser, clutching two sheets of paper. She told him, 'I can confirm that only one bedroom is in use, so they *are* co-habiting,' she said. 'Have you found something?'

'Look at that photograph on the sideboard, and then read these,' he instructed her.

The photograph was a full-length shot of Ursula Taylor, clearly taken before, or during, a formal event. Clara's gaze was drawn to the neckline of the evening dress Ursula was wearing. 'Oh my goodness,' she exclaimed, 'that brooch looks like the one Robert Pickles found at All Alone Cottage, near where the woman's skeleton was seated.'

'That's because it is the same brooch.' Nash handed her the paperwork.

The first sheet was a receipt bearing the name of a famous Hatton Garden jeweller. It was addressed to Ursula Taylor, c/o Home Comforts Ltd, and described a brooch, along with matching bracelet and earrings. The brooch was listed as being a circle of diamonds with a sapphire centre-piece, mounted in a silver setting. 'Look at the date,' Nash prompted her.

'2014, that's the date stamp on the one Robert Pickles found, and the description is identical.'

'Now look at the other sheet.'

Clara shuffled the papers. The second document was an insurance claim submitted by Ursula via her insurance broker. It was stamped, *Settled in full*. Those, together with the photograph, were, she thought, sufficient to charge Ursula with the cottage murders.

Nash, it seemed, was in complete agreement. 'We've assumed the brooch belonged to the victim. I don't think it occurred to any of us that it might have been the killer's. We need to get that jeweller in Hatton Garden to confirm the brooch was made by them, and I reckon that'll be game, set, and match. In the meantime, see if you can find the matching accessories.'

Minutes later, Clara reported she had found the bracelet and earrings in Ursula's jewellery box. 'At least, I assume they're hers. I don't see Barry as the type to wear that type of jewellery.'

Nash smiled fleetingly. 'Bag them up, along with that photo, and we'll take them to Helmsdale.'

Clara was puzzled as to why he wanted them, until he explained. 'Have you still got that photo of the brooch you took with your mobile?'

'Yes, I wasn't going to delete it until we'd wrapped this case up, which I thought might take forever.'

'OK. Phone the jeweller who made the brooch, and ask him if he can identify it from your photo. Failing which, you might have to go to Hatton Garden with it.'

The result of her phone call was satisfactory, although it delayed their departure considerably.

By the time the detectives and the team had completed their search of the house, it was mid-afternoon. The officers had bagged several files and paperwork, discovered in various parts of the house, but nothing of direct relevance to their investigation. Nash and Mironova were interested in Ursula's complex financial arrangements. 'She's got accounts with every bank and building society I can think of,' Clara commented. 'Why has she got so many?'

'Looking at the sizeable credit balances on all of the latest statements, I'd suggest it was more tax evasion, plus the need to avoid being investigated for potential money laundering.'

'That's interesting, but I don't see it helping us much.'

'Maybe not in the first instance, but if all else fails, it could be used as a last resort.'

'How could we make use of it?'

'Do you know how and where Al Capone died?'

'I haven't the foggiest idea. Was it in Chicago, and was he shot?'

'Wrong, on both counts. Al Capone died of syphilis while he was in prison. Do you know why he was in jail?'

'Murder or racketeering, I suppose.' Clara was clearly puzzled by Nash's train of thought.

'No, he was imprisoned for tax evasion. Because the investigators couldn't get sufficient evidence, or witnesses brave enough, to have him convicted for the many terrible crimes he committed, they got the Internal Revenue Service to come down on him.'

'And you think we could use the same idea with Ursula Taylor?'

'If all fails, I'd definitely threaten her with it. That might just force a confession out of her. I haven't totted all these balances up, but at a rough estimate, I guess there will be in excess of fifteen million pounds. If she's still unwilling to play ball, a phone call to HMRC might pay dividends.'

Nash thought for a moment, and then added, 'In the long run it might not matter, because once we hand Roland Bartholomew's Deed of Trust over, together with the other evidence, Ursula will forfeit the right to all the money she's schemed and worked to acquire. I think it's time to arrest our householder and her overnight guest. I'll let you have the pleasure.'

* * *

At Helmsdale, Detective Superintendent Fleming was waiting for them in the CID suite. 'I thought I'd better come, because Mrs Taylor's lawyer has been jumping up and down, demanding her immediate release. He's also talking about miscarriage of justice, and threatening a punitive damages claim. I hope and pray you've got strong evidence of the fraud and embezzlement offences you've arrested her for.'

'We certainly have. But the financial misdemeanours are going to be the least of Ursula's worries. We've now got sufficient evidence to charge her with at least four murders.'

Jackie Fleming's eyes opened wide with surprise. 'I assume you're talking about the cottage murders. What evidence have you got?'

Having told Jackie what they had discovered, she was in complete agreement they should proceed, so Nash asked Sergeant Meadows to invite Ursula's legal representative to join them in the CID suite. 'Tell him we're prepared to begin disclosure, but whatever you do, don't mention the word *full*, OK?'

'No problem, Mike.'

Nash put the phone down and said, 'Now the fun really begins.'

'I've said it before, Mike — you've got a really weird idea of fun.'

Jackie smiled at Clara's comment, and felt comforted that it showed the level of confidence they had in the strength of their case.

* * *

The solicitor was shocked by the detailed records kept by Gavin Mitchell of Ursula's involvement in each and every transaction that had diverted funds from the Home Comforts account, and from the Simon Watson trust. His surprise turned to horror when Nash told him further charges might be faced, as enquiries were still ongoing.

The subsequent interviews yielded no response from either Ursula Taylor, or her brother-in-law, who adopted the seemingly standard practice of responding to each and every question with 'No comment'. As a result, they were returned to their cells, the interrogation to recommence the following morning.

As the solicitor was leaving, Nash warned him, 'If I was you, I'd go to bed early and get a good night's sleep, because after you hear what I anticipate asking your clients tomorrow, I reckon you'll have nightmares for weeks.'

He reached the CID suite, where Lisa Andrews was prowling around the outer office. 'Mexican Pete's been on the phone for you — twice. He was quite agitated, and wouldn't leave a message. He demanded you call him the minute you're free.'

'OK, let's see what our worthy pathologist is so excited about, shall we? It's a shame Jackie's returned to HQ. She could have spoken to him.'

Nash's call to Professor Ramirez yielded some good news. Having heard the pathologist's initial revelation, Nash told him, 'That's excellent. It tallies with what we suspected. Sorry, there's more, did you say?'

He listened again, and when he heard the extra news, told Ramirez, 'That's even better. Before you go, I've sent a couple of DNA samples for testing. It's a bit of a rush job, as the suspects are in custody.'

After ending the call, Nash walked into the main office. 'Now I know why Mexican Pete was so excited. He's finally got the DNA results back from the cottage victims. The adults were the mother and father of the children, who were twins. The father's DNA is on record because of an offence he committed some years back. The skeleton found in the well is Doug Taylor, Ursula's husband.'

'She's going to find that difficult to explain away,' Clara commented, 'given that she alleged Doug had eloped with Marion and is now in Australia.'

'Hang on, there's more. Let me explain.'

* * *

Next morning, Nash and Mironova sat across the interview room table from Ursula Taylor and her solicitor, ready to resume questioning her. Clara noticed Ursula appeared composed, and seemingly unfazed by the charges so far levelled at her. Would that relaxed air change, she wondered?

After the opening announcement, Nash leaned forward slightly and asked, 'Where's Doug?'

Ursula blinked with surprise and looked at her solicitor, who shrugged, clearly baffled by this line of questioning. 'You mean the cheating bastard I was stupid enough to marry? I assume he's still in Australia, shagging my bitch of a cousin, Marion.'

'I see.' He presented an evidence bag, which he held up in front of Ursula. 'Recognize these?' he asked.

Ursula looked at the bracelet and earrings. 'They're mine. They were in my bedroom. Why have you got them?'

'I fail to see the relevance,' the solicitor stated.

'You will,' Nash pointed out, and turned back to Ursula. 'What about the other piece from this set — the diamond-and-sapphire brooch?'

'I lost that, years ago.' She was becoming indignant.

'Yes, I saw the insurance claim, pinned to the receipt from the jeweller who made the collection to your specifications. If I remember correctly, you stated you weren't sure where you lost the brooch, correct?'

'Yes,' Ursula still looked baffled.

'Well, I'm happy to tell you the brooch has been found.' Nash held up another evidence bag.

Ursula stared at the brooch, the stones twinkling in the light as Nash told her, 'This brooch has been identified by the manufacturing jeweller. It was found on the floor of the dining room in All Alone Cottage, the room where a skeleton was tied to a chair.'

All colour drained from Ursula's face.

The solicitor's head came up from his paperwork. He stared at Nash, who said, 'We believe the skeleton belonged to your cousin Marion. And if, as you say, your husband is in Australia, then how do you account for the fact that a second skeleton, recovered from a well outside All Alone Cottage, has been identified via DNA as belonging to your husband?'

'Don't answer that,' her solicitor intervened, before rounding on Nash. 'I was given to understand this interview was purely in connection with a trumped-up embezzlement charge.'

'That's because new evidence has come to light. I did warn you it might happen, and believe me, there will be even more.'

'I would like to speak to my client.' The solicitor stood up and began gathering his paperwork, until Nash stopped him.

'I haven't finished yet. I think you would be wise to speak to me first.' Nash left Clara supervising Ursula, who was sitting pale-faced and trembling, and led the solicitor to an adjoining room, where he disclosed the full horror of what they'd found at the cottage. 'Those two innocent little infants were no more than eighteen months old, when the poor mites were walled up and left to die a slow, lingering death in a dark, airless, confined space. The children had done nothing to merit such cruelty — merely been born to Marion and her lover.'

Nash could tell the solicitor's sympathy for his clients was evaporating. He continued, 'I'm going to ask the superintendent to apply for an extension in custody for both your clients, while we collect more evidence. Alternatively, I'll go ahead with the evidence before me, and charge them both with four murders. That will still leave me the right to add further charges later. By then, I hope to have proof that Ursula and her lover committed at least two other murders.'

Nash was interrupted at that point, when Steve Meadows tapped on the door. 'Sorry to interrupt, sir, but there's an urgent call for you.'

Nash knew this must be important, as the sergeant knew better than to disturb him. He stepped into Steve's office to answer the call, while the solicitor went to speak to Ursula.

'That was quick work, Professor. What was the outcome?' He listened, and then said, 'Really? That doesn't surprise me, because we'd been told it might be so. I suppose that's why you were able to get the results so quickly.'

Clara had come looking for him, and she knew Nash well enough to realize something the pathologist had told him had shaken him badly. His tone was subdued. She wondered what Ramirez had said to merit such a reaction, but her query was solved almost immediately as they re-entered the interview room. Ursula seemed to have regained her composure, and was again seated comfortably.

That composure was shattered, blown to smithereens, by Nash's opening remarks. 'I'm glad to see you've recovered, Mrs Taylor, because I've some very interesting news for you. For a while, we believed you murdered your cousin, but now, that doesn't appear to be so.'

'Does that mean you think my client is innocent?' the solicitor asked.

'Certainly not. It means we've discovered that your client is not related to her victim, Marion Edwards. And that also means she is not entitled to her share of the trust set up by Roland Bartholomew to protect the affairs of his grandsons and their descendants.'

Nash saw Ursula look up, startled by the extent of his knowledge. 'Oh yes,' Nash told her, 'we have the Deed of Trust in our possession. Although you must have been confident it was incinerated after you and your lover's arson attack on Netherdale Hall. Unfortunately for you, Gavin Mitchell kept all such documentation at his bank. Those papers include some other interesting items, such as a forged letter purporting to be from Marion. The handwriting is being analysed for a match to yours, as we speak. We also have details of the fraud carried out by you and your adoptive father. Part of the Roland Bartholomew trust is Home Comforts Ltd, the company Roland's grandson Philip helped establish, along with his brother, Simon Watson. The whole of that trust, along with another trust set up by Simon, now devolves on the only family member left alive, a child Philip insisted was dead.'

* * *

It was more than three hours later when Nash and Mironova returned to the CID suite bearing the tapes containing the confessions of Ursula Taylor and her lover to all six murders. Barry Taylor had also been charged with the arson attack on Mitchell & Co.'s offices.

'Viv, I want you to take an independent witness, preferably a pharmacist, and go through the records of Taylor's shop. I appreciate he's already confessed, but that could be retracted, so the circumstantial evidence might be useful as backup.'

Having given these instructions, Nash turned to Lisa, asking her to mind the shop next morning. 'Clara and I will be late in, as we've a job to do first. Anyway, well done everybody, we've achieved a terrific result, which at one time seemed impossible.'

'What job might we be doing tomorrow?' Clara asked, once Viv and Lisa had left.

'Will you pick me up at 8.30 a.m.? We need to go to Simeon House.'

The shocking revelations of the day preyed on Nash's mind as he drove home. As he approached Wintersett village, his line of thought gave rise to another, wilder idea. He wondered whether to share his weird idea with Clara or not. In the end, he decided to keep it to himself, at least for the time being. After pulling up outside Smelt Mill Cottage, he made a quick phone call, explained what he needed, apologized for the minor inconvenience his request would cause, and then rang off.

Alondra noticed that her husband seemed distracted all evening, and demanded to know what was wrong. Mike had told her they'd wrapped the case up, so she knew it was something else that was troubling him. When he explained, she told him, 'I don't think it's a weird idea at all, but how will you know one way or another?'

'There is a way.' Nash told her what he had in mind. 'But, in order to do it, I need the consent of the person concerned, and I don't want to alert them if it might be a false alarm. Apart from causing upset, if the information I've asked for doesn't tally, I'd have been wasting my time.'

* * *

Clara arrived promptly the following morning, and was surprised when Nash waved for her to come inside. After greeting Teal and Daniel, she asked, 'I thought we were going straight out?'

'There's been a slight change of plan. I'm waiting for a phone call before we set off, so why don't you grab a coffee? Alondra's on kitchen duty this morning.'

Nash listened to the girls chatting, and when his mobile rang he moved into his study. 'What news have you got for me?'

As the caller responded, Nash wrote the details down on a notepad, and then asked, 'And the other info I needed?' He scribbled this down and said, 'Thanks for that. I'll explain later, if necessary.'

'Do you want to go in my car or yours?' Clara asked.

'We'd better take both. Then you can head straight off to Helmsdale when we've finished. I've another call to make afterwards.'

'Who are you going to see? Is it about the case? Is there something we need to tie up before we send it to CPS?'

'No, it's not to do with the case, not exactly. Well, it is and it isn't . . . or maybe I'm just being a bit fanciful.'

'Now you've got me totally confused. So if that was your intention, you've succeeded, big time.'

He was about to get into his car, when Clara called across to him. 'Are you planning to tell Robert everything about what happened at the cottage?'

'That's a very good question, one I've been pondering since we found out. Obviously, we'll have to tell him the identity of the female victim. I'm not sure how he'll cope knowing the woman whose body he'd found was his half-sister. But for the time being at least, I'm not sure I want to take it much further. We've managed to keep it all out of the press, so far. Let's keep it as low-key as we can, for now.'

As Nash drove along behind Clara, his thoughts were on Robert Pickles. Perhaps also finding out the true identity of his father, and learning the man had cared sufficiently to have left a small fortune in trust for him, would help. Nash smiled as he remembered the line he'd learned from Homer's *Odyssey*: 'It's a wise child who knows his true father.' In the Bartholomew family, perhaps saying 'a *lucky* child', rather than a wise one, would be more appropriate. Every generation, it seemed, had skeletons in their closet.

CHAPTER TWENTY-EIGHT

Nash had paved the way for the meeting with a phone call to Louise Gough, to determine how Robert was, and if he would be able to cope with the news they had to impart.

The couple were waiting when the detectives arrived. 'You said you had something to tell us concerning the cottage and Bobby. I hope it isn't bad news, because he's had more than enough to contend with, and I don't want him getting upset,' Louise told them, as she let them enter.

'There is an element of bad news, but it doesn't concern Robert. The part that is about him is definitely good, some of it extremely so. There is a grim element to the whole story, but I don't believe it will harm Robert to hear it.'

When they were seated at the kitchen table, Nash began to explain the reason for their visit. 'As you know, we've been investigating the crime committed at the cottage, and we've succeeded in making two arrests. But I'm sorry to tell you that during the course of our inquiries, we discovered three more bodies.'

Robert and Louise both looked horrified. Nash allowed them time to recover from the shock before he continued.

'As so often happens, our research took us into some unusual areas. It hasn't been easy, mainly because to aid identification we needed DNA, and recovery of such is a slow and laborious process. In fact, until very recently, we weren't at all certain it would be achievable. When we succeeded, we were able to trace the woman's identity and a lot of her family history.'

Nash paused to ensure what he was about to reveal was said clearly. 'It's in respect of the family history that you're involved, Robert, albeit indirectly. We discovered that the female victim was called Marion Edwards, nee Watson, and she was the daughter of Simon Watson. She was also the great-granddaughter of Roland Bartholomew, a pickle manufacturer. We were very fortunate, because I heard someone mention the name "Bartholomew" and its connection to pickles, and that rang a bell — a very loud bell.'

'Bartholomew . . . that was my father's Christian name, and Pickles was his surname. Are you saying those names are fictitious?' Robert looked puzzled.

'I am, and what's more, we have definite, incontestable evidence to back it up. I mentioned Simon Watson was the victim's father, but Simon had another child, as a consequence of his long-term relationship with his secretary-cum-personal assistant.' He paused and looked directly at Robert. 'Her name was Iris Cameron.'

'But that's my mother!' Robert stared at Nash, in total confusion.

'Yes, and you told us she lost her job. That was after your father died in a car crash.'

'So you're saying my father's real name was Simon Watson? That's my middle name! Hang on, though, surely that means the woman whose body I found must be my sister, mustn't she?' Robert's eyes were wide with alarm.

'Half-sister, to be precise. I'll explain how we found all this out, and what we've discovered that directly affects you.'

'Could you wait please, Inspector Nash? Let Bobby have a moment.' Louise placed her hand on Robert's arm. 'Are you OK?' she asked.

He nodded. 'I think so.'

'Good. I'll make some coffee before the inspector continues.'

Nash waited until he was sure Robert could absorb the next part and explained, 'In the course of our investigation, we discovered a trust fund set up by your father, the intended beneficiary being his son by Iris Cameron. The Deed of Trust actually names you, along with your mother, ensuring there could be no other claimants and no misunderstanding. We also uncovered a scheme involving fraud and embezzlement on a large scale. Part of that was the diversion of funds. Sadly, owing to the subversion of the solicitor charged with handling the trust, that money never reached you. In fact, the fraudster managed to convince the lawyers you had died in infancy.'

Nash drained his coffee, and then turned to the next part of the tale. 'Fortunately for us, and you, the solicitor involved kept meticulous records. Although it might take a while to sort everything out, we understand from the experts that the whole of the funds from that trust, plus another, set up as part of the Bartholomew estate, can be recovered. They will then go to their rightful recipient. Robert —' Nash paused again, deliberately taking his time — 'that is you.'

Robert shook his head in disbelief and grasped Louise's hand.

Nash glanced at Clara, who nodded, encouraging him to continue.

'When that happens, Robert, you will have access to an amount well into seven figures. You will also become the rightful owner of All Alone Cottage, and finally, you will become the sole owner of a company by the name of Home Comforts Ltd that owns a chain of DIY stores. That shareholding became rightfully yours from the moment your other family members died.'

Robert stared, wide-eyed, at Nash. 'I remember the name *Home Comforts* — it was where my mother worked.' Robert sat for a long time digesting the mass of information he'd been given. As Nash watched, he saw Louise grip his hand tightly, providing all the comfort and encouragement possible. It took a long time for the couple to grasp the full extent of what they'd been told, and Nash had to repeat several parts of the story, in some cases more than once before they absorbed it all.

'Did Marion die because of this? I wouldn't be comfortable accepting blood money. Did she have any children? Shouldn't they be the ones to benefit?'

'The motive for Marion's murder, and that of the other victims had little or nothing to do with you, or the trust fund. The other victims found at the cottage were those of Marion's lover and, I'm sorry to tell you, their two children.'

Nash glanced at Clara, who nodded again.

'Thanks to you, we discovered the children in the boarded over alcove in the bedroom.' Nash was carefully trying not to distress Robert. 'The motive for the murders was primarily one of jealousy, allied to greed. As Marion's children had died, there were no other living relatives who could legally benefit from the estate, so you are entitled to it all. There is no point in blaming yourself for something you were powerless to prevent. By my reckoning, you were in Afghanistan at the time Marion was murdered. I also believe those murders would have happened even if money had not been involved.'

As they walked back to their cars, Clara remarked, 'I think that went as well as we could have wished for.'

'I agree, and I hope my next meeting does the same.'

'Are you going to tell me who you're going to see, and why?'

Nash smiled. 'Nice try, Clara, but you're not getting me to fall for that. I'll tell you when I'm good and ready.'

* * *

When Clara arrived back in Helmsdale, she was surprised to see DC Pearce seated at his desk, nursing a mug of coffee as he scanned the *Netherdale Gazette*. 'What are you doing here, Viv? I thought you were supposed to be in Netherdale, examining the records at Taylor's Pharmacy?'

'I was intending to go, but I got a call from Mike yesterday evening with a change of plan. He asked me to come here first, because he needed some info. After I gave it to him, he wanted me to stay here until he arrives.'

'He might be a while yet, because he was going to visit someone after we left Simeon House. Don't ask me what the meeting's about, he's being very mysterious on the subject.'

Pearce smiled, and told her, 'Mike wanted me to check some dates. I'm not sure why he wanted those especially, because as I understood it, everything regarding the case has been more or less settled now.'

It was almost an hour later when Nash finally arrived. Instead of going straight for the coffee machine, he called Pearce through to his office and closed the door. 'I've an extra task for you before you go to the pharmacy.' Nash handed Pearce an envelope. 'I want you to deliver that to Mexican Pete and ask him to ring me as soon as possible.'

Nash had just bitten into his lunchtime sandwich when his phone rang.

'Professor, thank you for calling me, I need a big favour, if you can.' Nash chose his words carefully, aware that his office door was open, and others might be listening. 'It's in connection with the contents of the envelope DC Pearce brought you. When you get the result, I'd be obliged if you can make a comparison. I scribbled the details on the note in the envelope. How long do you think it will take?' He paused. 'Really? That's quicker than I could have hoped for.'

It was two days later, shortly before Nash was leaving the office to go home, when the call he'd been waiting for came in — and with it, the result he'd half-expected.

When Nash arrived home, he explained to Alondra what he'd learned, what was about to happen, and asked for her assistance.

'I'm happy to help,' she replied.

* * *

Next morning, Nash and Clara, along with two companions, drove to their appointment. On arrival, the detectives got out of the car, and Nash rang the doorbell of Simeon House. Louise opened it.

'I know this is getting to be a regular occurrence, but hopefully this will be our last visit,' Nash told her. 'This time, I hope you and Robert will be even happier with the news I've brought.'

The detectives refused Louise's offer of a drink, and Nash pitched straight into the story he'd come to deliver. 'Robert, I recall you told me at our first meeting that one of the big regrets in your life was you had no other relatives apart from your mother. And your father, you barely knew, who died when you were a child.'

Robert nodded.

Nash smiled as he added, 'And now, I think Louise counts too. However, I'm pleased to say that during our investigation, we discovered you have a great-aunt, Agatha Bartholomew, ninety-two years old, living in St Cecilia's Care Home in Helmsdale. She is your great-grandfather's sister.'

'Really? That's wonderful,' Louise exclaimed. 'Do you think she can tell Bobby anything about his family? Good things, that is,' she added, pointedly.

'I'm sure she will. She has all her faculties, and was extremely helpful to us with our enquiries.'

'That's really good news, Inspector Nash. Thank you for coming to tell me,' Robert said. 'I don't think things could get any better.' He turned to Louise and hugged her.

'I, er, haven't finished,' Nash said. 'There's another relative. One who was as unaware of your existence as you were of theirs. Let me explain, because it's quite complicated. When Roland Bartholomew's daughter was seventeen years old, she fell in love with a boy of the same age, and he with her. They were together for only a short while, and she was desperately sad when her lover died. To make matters worse, she was pregnant. She was grateful to accept another man's offer, and they married. When I became aware of this, and from other things we uncovered in our research, I began to wonder who the father was. So I had a DNA test carried out.'

Nash paused for a moment, glanced at Mironova and nodded. Knowing her cue, Clara got up and walked to the back door, opened it, and waved to the occupants of the Range Rover.

Nash smiled at Robert and Louise, who were paying close attention to every word, as they tried to work out where this was leading.

'This gentleman's life has not been without tragedy, but I am pleased to tell you he is extremely anxious to meet you.' As Nash finished speaking, two people entered the room alongside Clara. 'Robert, Louise, this is my wife Alondra, and the gentleman with her is your grandfather, Mr Jonas Turner.'

Robert looked stunned as he stared at the old man. 'My grandfather?'

'Aye, lad, yer grandmother were Christine Bartholomew, an' ah loved 'er. She saw a report o' a bloke wi' same name, an' thought ah were dead. Ah were sent abroad, an' when ah came back, she were married.'

The onlookers watched with increasing pleasure, as the two men shook hands, then embraced. After a few seconds' silence, Jonas pulled away slightly, staring into Robert's eyes as he addressed everyone. 'Ah reckon ah didn't need that there fancy DNA stuff. One look at ye were enough, Robert, lad. Ah 'ad a son, name o' Steven, who died a long while back, when 'e were younger than ye are now. If Steven were 'ere t'day, you and 'e cud be teken fer twins, yer that alike. I allus thought "spittin' image" were an exaggeration up till now.'

An hour later, Nash, Alondra, and Clara left Jonas getting acquainted with his grandson and Louise. As they drove back to Smelt Mill Cottage, Clara expressed her delight at the outcome. As always, she masked her approval of Nash's actions with a veiled insult, as she told Alondra, 'I thought that went really well, and it was all down to your husband's bright idea. I have to admit he does get some good ideas from time to time. It's just a shame it only happens on very rare occasions.'

Alondra smiled and nodded. 'At least everything turned out well for Robert in the end.'

'Yes, and I just hope I never get to see another skeleton,' Clara stated.

It was not long before this proved to be one of the worst examples of inciting Sod's Law.

THE END

ACKNOWLEDGEMENTS

It isn't often you accost your milkman, or in this case milk-lady, with questions about dairies and deliveries, but on this occasion I have to thank Kay Mason for her insight into the business.

I also have to thank my son-in-law, James, a former police officer, for his assistance with procedures and policy.

As usual I have to thank my reader, Wendy McPhee, for pointing out my errors and anomalies.

And as always, my wife, Val, for her tireless and meticulous work with her in-house editing, ensuring my work is suitable for submission.

Thank you for reading this book.

If you enjoyed it please leave feedback on Amazon or Goodreads, and if there is anything we missed or you have a question about, then please get in touch. We appreciate you choosing our book.

Founded in 2014 in Shoreditch, London, we at Joffe Books pride ourselves on our history of innovative publishing. We were thrilled to be shortlisted for Independent Publisher of the Year at the British Book Awards.

www.joffebooks.com

We're very grateful to eagle-eyed readers who take the time to contact us. Please send any errors you find to corrections@joffebooks.com. We'll get them fixed ASAP.